Who Are We Now?

Beth Anderson

Who Are We Now?

Cover art and design by Humble Nations

Special thanks to Brandon Barrows

ISBN: 979-8-9854725-6-1

Published 2025 by Full Speed Publishing / Full Tilt Romance

Printed in the United States
First Edition
10 9 8 7 6 5 4 3 2 1

Dedicated to the readers—who've made
a dream come true.

Prologue

Skylar – June, Fifteen Years Ago

Skylar sat on the edge of her cot, arms around her knees and staring out of the screened window of her cabin. There was nothing to be seen from this vantage point but dense pine trees, hugging close to the back of the small building, but it was better than the alternative. The cabin housed eight girls, and her bed, the lower bunk of the farthest bed towards the back of the cabin, gave her a view of either the window or the long room, now empty. She couldn't really see anything out of the window, but looking at the empty beds, knowing they'd be filled before too many hours, wasn't any better.

No, it was actually worse, because she already felt lonely, but knowing those beds would be filled with strangers in a few hours made her feel even more isolated. She should've been home, in her own room, with her posters on the walls and her books stacked beside her bed, covered in all the plushies she had cherished since she was little. But that room didn't exist anymore, and while she had a room in her mom's new husband's house, it wasn't

1

really hers. She didn't belong there. Maybe she would have in time, if she'd been given the chance, but she hadn't been, and now she was here, at Camp Timbercrest, a place she certainly didn't belong.

As long as Skylar could remember, it had been her and her mom, Natalie. The Hunt girls, her mom called them when she was small, like they were a team. When had they stopped being a team? Skylar couldn't pinpoint any specific time or event. She just realized one day that her mom preferred to spend her time with friends—mostly a long list of "special friends," as she called the men in her life.

Skylar was old enough now to understand what was going on, had been going on for the last couple years. Their family name was Hunt and it fit Natalie to a T, she thought bitterly. Her mom had been husband-hunting, and when she met Brian, Skylar didn't think much of it. He was just another man who would be around for a few weeks and then disappear, soon to be replaced by another one.

But Brian didn't disappear—in fact, Natalie and Brian had been together for almost six months before they took Skylar aside one day after school and shared the news: they were getting married. It was a shock to the system—Skylar had accepted her mother's ever-changing roster of "special friends," but never thought anything would actually come of it. She understood what her mother was looking for, but somehow, she never really believed Natalie would find it.

But Skylar had no objections—not really. Brian was nice to her, and she understood vaguely that he was some sort of rich businessman. Natalie and Brian impressed upon her that afternoon how much better life would be for the three of them together, as a family. Skylar was nervous, but she wanted to believe them. A better life always sounds good.

So Natalie and Brian got married and Natalie Hunt became Natalie Rose, and the Hunts' apartment was let go and Natalie and Skylar moved into Brian's big townhouse, with its high ceilings and rooftop garden and the maid who came in twice weekly to clean. Skylar had wanted to believe that what her mom and her new stepdad told her would be true, that life would be better. She wasn't losing her mom, she was gaining a dad.

And then Natalie sent her away for the summer. As soon as school ended, she simply told Skylar she was going to spend the school break at Camp Timbercrest. It wasn't a question, it wasn't a conversation—it was simply a statement of what was going to happen. Skylar had never been away from home—her old home—for more than a single night's sleep-over at a friend's house, and not very often. Now she was going to spend two and a half months out in the middle of nowhere, over a hundred miles from the city, with a bunch of strangers? It was too much. She started crying just at the thought.

Natalie became angry with her, calling Skylar selfish. She deserved time alone with Brian, more than just the few hours they snatched when they were dating. Besides, she had added, "Your stepfather's wealthy. You know what that means? Well, maybe you don't—but it means social obligations."

No, Skylar didn't understand what that meant and when Natalie didn't explain, she began to suspect that her mother didn't either. But whatever it meant, having a twelve-year-old daughter around for the summer didn't fit into the plan apparently. So, Skylar had been packed off to camp whether she liked it or not.

In the week between Natalie's pronouncement and when the bus came to pick Skylar up for camp, her hurt and sadness became bitterness towards her mother. Natalie didn't want her around? Fine, she didn't want to be around either then. That didn't mean she was excited about Camp Timbercrest, but at least she didn't have to see her mother, that traitor, for a while. She still hadn't realized exactly what she was in for, but it quickly became apparent: as far as the other kids were concerned, Skylar wasn't just a stranger, she was practically an alien.

Everyone else had been coming to Timbercrest for years. They all knew each other, they had friend groups that were separated during the school year, but came together each summer like no time had passed at all. Those groups had inside jokes, secret traditions, and coded conversations Skylar couldn't decipher. She tried, the first few days, to talk to the other girls in her cabin, but the responses were short and distracted, or worse, antagonistic. She quickly learned that her bunk had belonged to another girl who had been rooming with the others for years and because it was assigned to Skylar, their friend Rianne was assigned to a different cabin across camp. To them, Skylar was very much an intruder.

How was that her fault, she wanted to scream, but what good would it have done? Didn't they understand how hard being the newcomer was? They didn't, or maybe they just didn't care, and eventually, Skylar gave up and stayed quiet when the others were around.

One of Skylar's cabinmates stepped into the cabin, making the screen door creak and then clack shut an instant later. Skylar turned and saw Emily, a petite, doll-like blonde and the queen bee of Cabin Four, leader and trendsetter of the friend group. The blonde girl wore a pink and white, two-piece bathing suit, a towel draped around her shoulders. It was the afternoon free period and most of the kids spent it swimming, trying to fend off some of the day's heat. Emily's eyes narrowed when she spotted Skylar, but otherwise said nothing as she hurried past the rows of bunks to the showers at the rear of the cabin. Skylar wasted no time leaving the cabin. If Emily was returning, it meant the other girls would be soon too.

Skylar wandered down the dirt path that led from this cluster of girls' cabins towards the picnic areas along the lakeshore, far from the area where people swam. This time of day, it wasn't likely that too many people would be down there. With any luck, she could spend the time until dinner free from worrying about dealing with anyone else. Before long, she emerged from the trees and the lake was spread before her, shimmering in the afternoon sunshine. Ripples danced across the water, and a breeze carried the scent of the water and damp sand, tickling Skylar's nose. For a moment, it was so beautiful she forgot everything.

And then the boys noticed her.

"Hey, new girl."

She turned, heart in her throat already, knowing what was coming. Most of the kids at camp simply ignored her, but this group of boys—Tyler, Jake, Connor, and their leader, Zack—were the exception. They were older than her, maybe thirteen or fourteen, but at camp, that was enough to make them untouchable. Because of that though, they were also outcasts in a way, and they took it out on those of lower social status. And who was lower than the girl with no friends?

Skylar turned, intending to simply go back up the path, willing herself to disappear, wishing she could turn invisible or fly or teleport or *something* to get her out of there. It was bad enough when they hassled her in the dining hall or yards, but out here, without even the dubious protection of the counselors' not-so-watchful eyes?

"Didn't you hear Zack?" Tyler said, stepping into her path, almost but quite touching her with an outstretched hand. She'd seen these boys do that to other girls: "accidentally" touch their chests. "He said 'Hey.' That's really rude, you know. Ignoring people when they're just trying to be polite?"

Skylar swallowed hard. "Hey," she muttered and quickly turned her eyes down to her sandaled feet.

"There you go." Zack grinned, tilting his head to the side. "Whatcha doin', new girl?"

Skylar glanced around for an escape, but Tyler blocked her path and now Zack stood next to him.

Connor and Jake pressed in close behind her, hemming her in. There was no one else, no other kids at the picnic area, and of course, no counselors anywhere around. Never when you needed them.

"You don't talk much, do you?" Zack continued. "I guess that checks though. Who'd wanna talk to a weird little girl with hair like a bird's nest?" He reached out and touched her hair, just lightly, but it made Skylar flinch and draw back, trying to pull into herself.

The boys burst out laughing.

The alien, Skylar thought. *I'm the alien, I'm not a person, so this is okay, right?* A little fire sparked inside of her, and she clenched her fists. It had only been a few days, and the summer stretched long and lonely in front of her. If she didn't do something now, she finally realized…

"I don't need to talk to you."

"Ohhh," Connor said from behind her, drawing it out. "Oh, *damn*. Mouse-girl's got some fight in her!"

"Bet she doesn't last the summer," Jake said. Skylar whirled to face them, afraid of what they might do.

"Freaks never do," Jake added, lifting his fists to his eyes and rubbing them around like he was wiping tears. "They cry to the counselors 'til those useless shits can't stand it, then call mommy and daddy to come get you."

Skylar's face burned. It was anger and embarrassment mixed together, twisting in her stomach like a knot she couldn't possibly untie. The only way to release the knot would be to cut it, and she knew there was no way to do that. She stepped to one side, trying to go around the boys, hoping, praying even, that they wouldn't touch her again, that this was enough torment to entertain them for at least a little while.

It wasn't. Zack mirrored her movement, blocking her way. "You know, if you want to fit in, you should try being a little friendlier," he said, smirking.

"Or maybe she should just go home now," Tyler added. "Nobody'd miss her. I heard little miss Queen of

Camp Emily talking shit about her." He sneered. "Even her cabinmates think she's a freak."

Something sharp lodged in Skylar's throat. She could feel the sting of tears threatening, but she refused to cry in front of them. It was obvious to all of them that she was barely holding it together and the boys' laughter was harsh, like fragments of metal rattling around in a can.

"Just leave me alone," Skylar managed to choke out, hating how small and weak she sounded.

Zack grinned, but stiffened when a new voice called out, "Hey!"

Two boys stepped out of the trees and onto the path, each with a bug-catching net in hand, and one with a small, plastic cage attached to his belt. Skylar recognized them: Levi and Barrett. She didn't know their last names and had never spoken to either one of them, but Levi was in her plant-identification class and Barrett was in her tennis class. She didn't really know either boy, but she didn't think she had never been so happy to see anyone. Zack and his minions wouldn't dare do anything with an audience, especially two boys who were popular around camp.

"Is this a new group activity?" Levi asked coolly, stepping forward. His gaze flicked over the four boys. Even though he was younger than any of them, it was clear that he was unimpressed. Skylar guessed he was her own age, twelve, or maybe just a little older, but he was already tall, and his shoulders seemed very broad to her—or maybe that was just the feeling of relief flooding through her. "Bullying?"

"We weren't—" Jake began, but Connor cut in, shouting, "Mind your own business!"

"This is our business," Barrett said easily, smiling as if they were all friends. "We were looking for Skylar. Guess we found her." His dark eyes landed on Skylar, warm and reassuring. "You missed bug-catching. We were all gonna get our badges for finding a Hercules beetle,

7

remember?"

Skylar hesitated, then nodded. She had no idea what they were talking about, but it was obvious they were giving her an out and she was glad to take it. She sidestepped Zack and moved closer to Barrett. She wanted to hide behind the boy, even if they were roughly the same size, but she wouldn't give Zack and his friends the satisfaction.

"Come on, Skylar," Barrett said. "We'll show you where we saw some the other day."

Barrett turned, lightly touching Skylar's arm, as if to say, "Everything's okay now," but Levi seemed unwilling to just walk away. His jaw tightened and he glared at the bullies with an intensity few kids his age could muster. "What was the plan? You corner her, make yourselves feel big for five minutes, and then what?" He gave a slow, mocking look at each of them. "Go back to being the most forgettable losers at camp?"

Jake scowled. "Fuck you."

"I'd rather do your mom," Levi shot back. "Like everybody else."

Jake's eyes flared and he took a step forward, but Tyler grabbed him. Levi was younger than them, but bigger than all of them. Together they could take him, but fighting was one of the few rules they had yet to break— that got you kicked out of camp permanently, and none of them wanted to go home when the summer was just beginning.

"You guys are nobodies," Levi went on. "Messing with people doesn't make you cool. Are you even smart enough to understand how pathetic it makes you?"

Connor's face darkened. He wanted to hit the younger boy badly, but he wasn't stupid. Even if Levi didn't tell the counselors, he was popular enough that he could turn the whole camp against them. Their already miserable social standing would sink even lower, and they were already isolated outside of their little friend group.

Having the other kids actively working against them would be hell.

Zack smirked. "Relax, man. We were just talking."

Barrett raised an eyebrow. "Right. Talking. Okay, cool. And now you're done, so find somewhere else to be." He looked the other boys over. Connor still looked like he wanted to hit someone, but none of his friends seemed eager to push their luck.

"Whatever," Connor finally muttered. He turned, shoving his hands into his pockets as he walked away, back towards the lake. Zack hesitated, then tossed one last smirk towards Skylar before following, Tyler and Jake on his heels.

Silence settled over the path, aside from the whirring sound of cicadas in the trees and the lapping of the lake against the rocky shore.

Skylar let out a breath she hadn't realized she was holding.

"You good?" Levi asked.

Skylar nodded, her throat tight. "Yeah. Thanks."

Barrett adjusted his grip on his net, slinging it across his shoulders. "They're wimps," he said simply. "They only bug you if they think you won't fight back."

Skylar looked down. "Well… they're not wrong."

"You don't have to put up with it," Levi said.

Skylar hesitated, then asked, "Why did you—why did you help me?" She hadn't realized the boys even knew her name. Why would they go out on a limb for her?

Levi shrugged. "Because."

Barrett smiled. "Those guys suck."

Skylar looked between them, unsure what to say. At home, she had friends, but no one had ever stood up for her before. Granted, she had never before been in a situation like the one with Zack and his friends, but she wondered if any of the people she knew back home— some of whom she'd been friends with literally her entire life—would do what these boys had done. These boys who were basically strangers.

Levi jerked his head toward the path. "Come on. You can hang with us for a while."

Skylar hesitated only a moment before nodding.

As she walked away from the picnic area, flanked by Levi and Barrett, something settled in her chest. The summer still stretched long in front of her, but maybe it wouldn't be so bad.

Chapter 1.

Skylar – Now

Skylar adjusted her Bluetooth earpiece as she hurried down the glass-lined corridor of TechnoFirm Global's Manhattan headquarters. Her heels clicked against the polished marble floor, her tight skirt swished against her body. Her tablet PC was balanced in one hand, her phone in the other. She wished she had a third hand for a cup of coffee, but if wishes were horses… Only seven in the morning and she'd already had two cups, but she could really use another caffeine boost. It was going to be that kind of day.

"Nathan, I just sent you the updated numbers for the proposed Singapore expansion," she said briskly into her headset. "The team over there is expecting final approval of the figures by four their time, which means you have—" She glanced at her watch, wincing. "—an hour to look them over before the deadline." An hour would be enough for most people to get something so critical done, especially when TechnoFirm's future in the Asian markets depended on it, but Nathan Dyer was always juggling a thousand things at once—which meant Skylar was juggling a million on his behalf. Nathan was terrible about time management and if it weren't for Skylar, he'd be overwhelmed and most of his important tasks would fall through the cracks.

On the other end of the call, Nathan exhaled sharply. "Why am I just getting these now?"

"There was a delay yesterday."

A delay caused by Nathan's poor time management, but how could she say that? He must have known as well as she did, and what good would pointing it out do?

"And by the time it got to the right people's inboxes, their business day was over in Singapore. I've been chasing them for the report since I woke up today." At 4:30, she didn't add.

"That's not an excuse, Skylar. I need those numbers ahead of time so I'm not making decisions under pressure."

Skylar again bit back the urge to remind him that she had, in fact, been warning him about the delays all week—without mentioning precisely whose fault they were—and that he had ignored her concerns, claiming other priorities. "Understood. Do you want me to schedule a call with the team in Singapore? I can probably get most of them on within a few minutes."

"No. Just summarize the key points for me. Five bullet points, no fluff. I don't have time for a novel."

Skylar mentally restructured her notes, detailed down to the very last decimal point, stripping them down to the bare essentials. "Got it. I'll send it over within ten minutes."

"Make it five. Three is better, if you can manage."

The call was cut before she could respond.

Skylar sighed and shoved her phone into the pocket of her blazer. She stopped outside of the executive suite, giving herself a few seconds to take a deep breath and let it out slowly. She opened the door, stepped through, and the moment she was fully inside the glass-walled office, she was met with Nathan's glare, sharp and critical. He stood behind his massive, dark wood desk, his tablet in hand.

"I don't see my coffee," he said, going back to whatever he had been reading.

Skylar barely resisted gritting her teeth. She only had two hands. "It's coming, it should be here—" The door behind her opened and one of the college kid interns handed her a tall, cardboard carton of coffee, the lid already off and hopefully sugared the way Nathan liked it. There'd be hell to pay if it wasn't. She whispered "thank you" to the boy and turned to set the steaming cup on Nathan's desk. Without a word of thanks to either Skylar or the intern, or even looking up from his tablet, he took a sip of coffee, made a small noise that Skylar knew meant it was at least the way he liked it, and set the cup down. Skylar knew he would probably forget all about it until it had gone cold and then demand a fresh cup.

"Good. Something's going right today at least." He glanced up for the briefest instant. "I need you to move my investors lunch to next Monday."

Skylar's fingers flew across her tablet. "That's not going to be possible, Nathan. You have the shareholder meeting all morning, and the New York flight that night."

Nathan frowned. "Then reschedule the flight."

"I already did once this week, and the airline had to make special accommodations to get it done. They're not going to—"

"Call them and have them do it again. I don't care what you need to tell them, just make it happen."

Skylar took a breath. She had been working for Nathan Dyer long enough to know there was no use arguing. She would have to get it done, one way or another, or find herself another job. She only got this job in the first place because Nathan was the father of her boyfriend, Chet. She knew she had since proven herself, but Nathan didn't tolerate any kind of failure. Once he decided you weren't capable of meeting his needs, you were out. She'd seen it happen to any number of high-level executives at TechnoFirm.

"Fine," she said. "But I need to know if you still want to meet with the development team this afternoon about the security breach."

Nathan sighed. "Do I have to? You know I don't care about any of the details of all that techy stuff."

Nathan's attitude towards the company's infrastructure, and even its products, always astounded Skylar. What kind of attitude was that for a tech company's CEO?

"Yes," she said bluntly. "It's a legal liability, and the media is sniffing around. If they get enough for a story, it'll tank the stock."

He pinched the bridge of his nose. "Great. And the investors are already after my blood." He looked up. "Fine. Block out thirty minutes, no more, and make sure they bring someone who can translate the technobabble into English for me."

"They've already scheduled an hour to accommodate an outside consultant."

"They'll get thirty," Nathan said flatly.

Skylar didn't bother arguing. She made a note to warn the team that their time had just been cut in half. Maybe they could hurry the consultant… or maybe even get someone else. She would have to find out.

"Anything else?" Nathan asked impatiently.

"Yes, actually." Skylar pulled out her phone and scrolled, finding the bullet in her note app. "Your wife's assistant called last night. Apparently, she needs an RSVP for some charity event she's hosting." Why Nathan and his wife didn't just have this kind of conversation face to face was beyond Skylar. Rich people were another breed. She was grateful that Brian, her stepfather, was more like a regular guy with money than a rich man.

Nathan made a noise in his throat. "Tell her I'm busy."

"She said—"

"I don't care what she said," Nathan cut in. "You know the drill, Skylar. I don't do charity galas and Evelyn knows that as well as any of us. That's why she sends her assistants to hound me. Jesus, as if I don't have enough on my plate."

Skylar knew not to press the issue now. She could try again when he was in a better mood—if he ever was. It had been a long time since Nathan Dyer had been in a genuinely good mood, at least that Skylar had seen. "I'll let her know."

Nathan's phone buzzed, and he scrolled through a series of messages. "Also, get my tailor in here before six tonight. The suit they sent over was garbage. The material was all wrong and it pinched under the arms."

Nathan had picked the material out himself, naturally. Besides that—

"Your tailor is in Milan this week."

"Then find another one."

"You have meetings until seven tonight, you won't be able to—"

"Then have them come to the office."

Skylar clenched her jaw. "Fine."

Nathan finally looked up, pausing his work for a moment. "You sound annoyed."

"Not at all," Skylar said smoothly. "Just trying to keep up with the constantly shifting goalposts."

Nathan smirked. "I hired you because Chester,"— Nathan was the only one who ever called Chet by his full name—"insisted, but you keep earning it."

No, you hired me because the last girl quit without notice, Skylar thought, *and I just happened to be around, so Chet suggested me,* but she didn't say it, as much as she wanted to. This was as close as Nathan ever came to a compliment.

Skylar moved on. "Will that be all?"

"I need those bullets on Singapore. Your five minutes were up—" he glanced at his smartwatch, "about four minutes ago."

And whose fault is that? she mentally snapped. "As soon as I'm at my desk, I'll send an email."

Nathan tapped his fingers on his own desk. "It'll

have to do."

Skylar turned to go, but stopped as Nathan said, "One last thing—get me a reservation at *Élan* tonight."

Skylar didn't even blink. "That's impossible. They book out months in advance."

Nathan sat in his heavily padded executive chair and leaned back, tablet held before him, not even bothering to look at her. "Then make it possible."

Skylar mentally prepared herself for the groveling that would take.

"I'll see what I can do," she said.

"That's all then."

Skylar turned to leave, already drafting her Singapore email in her head. It wasn't even 7:30 in the morning. The day was only just beginning.

Chapter 2.

Skylar – Twelve Hours Later

Skylar's entire body ached as she stepped off the elevator and into the softly lit hallway of her apartment building. The thick carpeting of the hallway did little to alleviate the weight of the day that clung to her. It felt as if the day was trying to crush her, pressing her body into the soft carpeting with every step she took toward her door. Her heels pinched her toes, and the strap of her work bag dug into her shoulder, but she barely noticed in comparison to the exhaustion. It had been another relentless day of running circles around Nathan Dyer's impossible expectations, and all she wanted now was a hot shower and maybe five minutes to herself before she had to do it all over again tomorrow. She wondered how long she could keep this up. She was so tired lately that she hadn't been able to keep up with her online classwork and this at rate, who knew when she'd earn her degree?

Skylar unlocked the door and stepped inside. She slipped her bag from her shoulder and lifted it to the coatrack she habitually hung it on—and then froze.

The apartment was a disaster.

Beer bottles, red Solo cups, crumpled napkins and an assortment of crumbs littered the coffee table. A half-eaten pizza sat abandoned on the couch, the grease staining the cushions. *Where the hell is the box?* she thought with astonishment. The faint smell of stale beer and the heavy cloying odor of pot smoke clung to the air, mixing

17

with something sickly sweet—probably a spilled drink left to soak into the carpet.

Skylar closed her eyes, inhaled slowly, and exhaled even slower.

She wasn't even surprised. It wasn't exactly a case of "like father, like son," because Chet was demanding in an entirely different way than Nathan. At least Nathan was productive with some guidance. Chet was ostensibly a full-time grad student, but if he ever went to any of his classes, it was a mystery to Skylar how he managed with all the lazing around and partying he did with his buddies.

From the bedroom, she heard movement, and a moment later, Chet emerged, stretching his arms lazily over his head. His blond hair was tousled in a way that suggested he'd just woken up, despite the fact that it was nearly eight at night. He was wearing a t-shirt that said "What the dog doin'?", a phrase that meant nothing to her, and a pair of sweatpants that hung low on his hips. Despite the amount of junk food and beer he consumed, he was still fit, his body lithely muscular. He didn't work out more than once in a blue moon though and his habits would catch up with him one day.

"Oh, hey, babe," Chet said, rubbing at his eyes. "Didn't hear you come in."

Skylar took another slow breath. "I just got home from work."

Chet glanced at the mess, then shrugged. "Yeah, so, uh… you're probably wondering, huh?" He laughed as he looked around at the disaster zone of the apartment. "Had some of the guys over earlier. Things got a little wild. You know Benjy, he takes his WWE totes serious."

Skylar scanned the wreckage. It was more than a little wild. She wondered what FEMA's number was and what the process of declaring a hazardous zone consisted of. "I can see that."

Chet flopped onto the couch, nudging the pizza away with his foot until it smooshed up against one arm of the couch. "Anyway, I'm starving. Think you could make something?"

Skylar clenched her jaw. She wanted to say no. She wanted to tell him to get up, clean up after himself, and make his own damn food. But the words caught in her throat, tangled with exhaustion and resignation and fear of what might happen if she did.

Chet wasn't violent or abusive in any traditional way—he'd never hit her or even said anything intentionally mean to her, and if anyone suggested he might, he'd be shocked and hurt. He wasn't malicious in any way, just lazy and immature. She hadn't realized that until they moved in together. Before, when they were just dating and she was living at her parents' place, he was fun and goofy and sweet. That side was still in there somewhere, she was sure, but he took her for granted now. They hadn't even had sex for months and she wondered sometimes, when she had a moment to think about her situation, if he might be cheating on her—getting his physical thrills somewhere else because she was too busy cooking and cleaning for him while he did whatever he wanted, leaving her exhausted after doing all of that and working full time.

But what choice did she have? Her own parents were wealthy—at least Brian was wealthy and Natalie had access to his fortune—but they weren't willing to pay all of her bills the way Nathan did for Chet. Natalie insisted that Skylar learn the value of hard work the same way she had when she was Skylar's age—by working. That wasn't unfair and they did pay for her college tuition at least.

But Chet didn't understand any of that. He simply didn't understand how hard Skylar worked, both outside the apartment and in, while he lived off of the exorbitant allowance Nathan provided him, without contributing more than the bare minimum to rent or other bills. Skylar paid those herself with her TechnoFirm salary, and that job was always one misstep, one failure in Nathan's eyes, from evaporating. If she broke up with Chet, there was no guarantee Nathan would even keep her around regardless of how well she did her job, and she knew she wouldn't be able to replace it. She worked her butt off, but she made good money and all without even having her college degree. There simply wasn't another job out there like it, not for her anyway, so she couldn't take the risk.

Besides, she knew that no matter what she said, even if she got down on her hands and knees, Chet wasn't going to clean. He wasn't going to make his own dinner. Arguing with him would just drain whatever little energy she had left.

She sighed, hung her bag on its hook, and made her way to the kitchen.

"Something quick, babe. Whatever's easiest. Just no leftovers."

Of course not.

Skylar pulled open the fridge, trying to ignore the fact that she had restocked it *herself* earlier in the week, with money *she* had earned, while Chet had spent his days skipping class and partying in the apartment she mostly paid for, and that the fridge was already mostly empty. Chet's friends must not eat at all outside of the apartment. She grabbed eggs and cheese, intending to make a simple omelet.

Skylar cracked eggs into a pan as Chet stretched out across the couch, phone in hand, already completely at ease. "How was work?" he asked, sounding distracted. It was just a formality. Skylar no longer even tried to fool herself into thinking he cared.

She forced herself to focus on cooking so she wouldn't snap at him. "Long."

"Yeah? My dad giving you a hard time?"

Skylar let out a short, humorless laugh. "Always and forever."

Chet snorted. "Yeah, guy doesn't know how to relax. He ever tell you about the time he made one of his assistants work through *Christmas* because he didn't like how they formatted an email? I mean, an email—who cares?"

Skylar bit back the urge to tell him that his father had made *her* work through Christmas last year. But what was the point? Chet didn't care. He liked the stories about his father's ruthlessness when they weren't about *him.*

"Sounds about right," she muttered.

Chet didn't respond, already completely engrossed in his phone. He wasn't at all interested in her day, her exhaustion, or the fact that she was cooking him dinner after spending fifteen hours catering to his father's endless demands. She was basically the Dyer family's servant at this point.

She plated the omelet and set it on the coffee table in front of him.

"There," she said. "Eat."

Chet sat up, took a bite, and nodded. "Mmm. Thanks, babe."

Skylar watched him a moment, half-wishing he would say something else—maybe *How was your day, really?* or *You look exhausted, do you need anything?*

But he didn't. Of course he didn't. It would never even occur to him.

Chet turned the TV on, flipping through channels aimlessly as he ate. He settled on *Spongebob* reruns.

Skylar turned away and forced herself to start cleaning.

She gathered up the empty bottles, carefully placing them into a garbage bag for recycling, then tossed the cups and napkins into the trash. Using another garbage bag as a giant glove, she picked up the pizza Chet had pushed to the floor and the random detritus from the carpet. She had no idea what she'd do about the grease stains on the sofa and the carpet, but really—what did it even matter anymore?

Finally finished, her back ached, her head pounded. Chet had stretched out across the couch again, unmindful or uncaring about getting his sweats in the greasy spots. He was flipping through his phone again to a soundtrack of Spongebob Squarepants's high-pitched giggles.

"Man, I'm beat," Chet mumbled. "Gonna crash soon." He knuckled his eyes with his free hand and yawned.

Skylar looked at him, sprawled out, completely at ease, completely comfortable. Not a word, and probably even a thought given to the mess she had just cleaned or the meal she had just cooked him, despite it being the end of a long, hard day that had already drained every ounce of energy from her.

Something inside her twisted.

She couldn't do this much longer.

She knew it. She had known it for a while now.

But until she graduated, until she got a better job, until she had the means to walk away—what choice did she have? Go back home to her mother and stepfather with her tail between her legs and admit that she couldn't cut it? Brian wouldn't mind and her mother wouldn't say anything to her face, but she knew Natalie would be disappointed in her and probably silently resent her, even more than she already did. They had been so close when Skylar was little, but the distance between them grew as she got older, finally resulting in the summer Natalie sent her away to summer camp. That cemented it, the final break of their closeness. At least something good had come of that summer.

She wanted to run away, but she wouldn't. Not now. Not yet. She swallowed the lump in her throat, turned off the kitchen light, and said, "I'm going to bed."

Chet didn't look up from his phone. "Night, babe."

Skylar walked into the bedroom, shut the door behind her, and stood there for a long time, staring at her reflection in the mirror hanging from the back of the door.

She barely recognized herself anymore.

Chapter 3.

Skylar – Next Morning

Skylar's eyes blinked open to darkness, but her body instinctively knew the time before she even turned her head to check the clock. **4:30 AM.** Like always. Even on the rare days when she could sleep in, her body refused. Today was supposed to be one of those days. Nathan was scheduled to the gills as usual, but he'd insisted that there be nothing on his calendar before 8 AM, which meant she could relax a bit in the morning and get to work at a decent time—like 7:30, maybe, still an hour before the office officially opened.

So of course, she was wide awake, staring upwards into the darkness, knowing there was no chance of going back to sleep.

She sighed and turned onto her side, only to be met with the cold, empty expanse of the bed beside her. The sheets were still smooth, unruffled, untouched. Chet had never come to bed.

Her first reaction wasn't surprise or concern. It wasn't even anger.

It was just… nothing.

Or maybe it was more like she felt everything at once—annoyance, relief, exhaustion.

She stared at the unoccupied side of the bed for a what seemed like a long time, trying to figure out what she was supposed to feel. Was she supposed to care? Was she supposed to be mad? Because part of her wasn't.

Part of her was relieved.

Not having Chet in the bed meant not waking up to his weight shifting the mattress, not dealing with the way he stole the covers, or put his ice-cold feet on her in the winter, not feeling the inevitable moment when he threw an arm over her, trapping her in his sleep-heavy grip or feeling his breath, hot and moist, against the back of her neck.

Not having him there meant space. Quiet. Relaxation.

And the fact that she felt relief at all—that was the part that unsettled her.

Skylar rolled onto her back, stretched her arms and legs out as far as she could, reveling in the feeling of space, while still unsure of what was in her heart. She stared upwards, her thoughts tangled. She could try to go back to sleep, force herself to take advantage of the extra hour and a half she'd been granted today. But she was wide awake now and knew it wouldn't happen. There was no point in wasting free time.

She reached for her phone on the nightstand and unlocked it, her thumb hesitating for a split second as her muscle memory kicked in. She almost opened her work email, almost let herself slip straight into work mode, but she caught herself at the last second.

She made a noise deep in her throat, a grumble at herself. Not yet. This was her time.

She swiped over to her personal messages. It had been *so long* since she'd checked them. During the day there was no time and in the evenings she was too tired to do much more than the absolute necessities then fall into bed.

Unread texts from people she hadn't spoken to in weeks—maybe even months—filled the screen.

Mara: *Hey! Miss you. Drinks soon?*
Jessica K: *Where have you been hiding? Hope you're alive.*

Kelsie: *Did you seriously bail on trivia night again? Skylar, come on. It's been a month!*

She swallowed, guilt pricking at her. Her eyes felt hot and faintly damp.

And then, lower down in the list, a familiar chat.

Levi, Barrett, Skylar.

Her best friends.

A soft, bittersweet smile tugged at her lips as she tapped the thread. The messages inside were weeks old, and yet the second she started scrolling through them, it felt like no time had passed at all. The chat group had been around for years after all—God, was it since high school? At least.

Levi: *Saw a new guy at the gym today who looked like Zack from camp. Thought about asking if he still wets the bed.*

Barrett: *If it was him, he definitely does.*

Levi: *Yeah, but this guy was benching 250. I like my face the way it is.*

Barrett: *Wuss.*

Skylar let out a quiet laugh. They were exactly the same. Even after all these years, even after everything all of them had been through. Growing up changes so many things, but maybe it doesn't change who you really are, she thought.

Skylar let herself sink into the memory of that first summer—the way the boys had found her on that path, alone and scared, surrounded by bullies who wanted nothing more than to hurt her, see her cry—maybe worse. She had been miserable at that camp, lonely and desperate to go home, an easy target for the bullies. Then Levi and Barrett came along, like knights in shining cargo shorts, chasing off the villains and effortlessly pulling her into their orbit, making her feel like she belonged.

The rest of that summer had been an adventure, and when camp ended, she was devastated—only to learn that Levi and Barrett *lived in the city too*. Not close, not *next door* close, but close enough.

Close enough that they could still be in each other's lives.

And they had been.

Through high school, through college, through all the changes that life had thrown at them, they were her best friends. Their lives had taken them in different directions, but *they were still there.*

Levi and Barrett changed her world and became such a huge part of her life, but how often had she seen them lately? How often had she even spoken to them?

Her chest tightened. When had things gotten so bad? When had she let herself get so swallowed up by work, by stress, by this life she wasn't even sure she wanted? How can decisions trap you so tightly without your even realizing it?

She typed out a quick message.

Skylar: *what's up guys? Sorry to ghost. Ridic busy lately lol*

She hit send before she could talk herself out of it. It wasn't much of a message, but at least they'd know she was thinking about them. Nothing she could do now but wait and see what happened.

She flickered to another message thread.

Her mother.

A text she had sent a *week ago* still sat there, unanswered. Friends were one thing, but family was another—she felt an obligation to at least reach out occasionally, no matter what else was going on.

Skylar: *Hi, Mom! How are you and Brian?*

Read. A week ago, not long after she sent it, but still there was no response.

Skylar frowned. Her mother wasn't always quick to text back, but she always responded eventually.

Nothing after a week was… odd.

She hesitated, then typed another message.

Skylar: *Everything okay?*

She watched the screen.

The message was read *immediately*. Why was Natalie up at—she glanced at the time—**4:43 AM** and using her phone?

The text was read, but still, nothing. No response, not even dancing little dots indicating her mom was typing something.

Skylar's stomach twisted.

That was *weird*. Weird, weird, weird. Nothing about this made sense.

She waited, thumb hovering over the screen, debating whether to send another follow-up. Maybe even call. But before she could, her phone buzzed with a new message—

Not from her mom.

Levi: *Holy shit, she lives.*

A second later—

Barrett: *It's a miracle. Sound the alarms. Alert the media!*

Skylar let out a breath, some of the tension easing from her shoulders.

At least *someone* still cared, and it wasn't that unusual to see Levi up at this time of day. He worked as a personal trainer, and he was always at the gym by 6 in the morning. In fact, it was the gym Chet used—when he worked out at all. Levi had gotten him a friends and family discount around the time Skylar and Chet moved in together.

Barrett though… Skylar wasn't really sure exactly what he did on a daily basis or why he might be up so early. He was, believe it or not, employed by a private investigator. It wasn't like on TV, Skylar knew—not exactly. A lot of Mr. Whittington's work was actually pretty boring stuff, routine background checks and whatnot, Barrett once told her, but still, both Mr. Whittington and Barrett did "fieldwork" as Barrett called it sometimes. Barrett was even sort of a junior private eye himself, covered by his boss's license in a way Skylar didn't quite get. Either way, it was a very cool job and something Barrett was proud of. She was both happy for and envied her friend that.

Skylar lay still, her phone resting on her chest, the faint glow of the screen illuminating the darkness around her. She wasn't looking at it anymore, though. Her eyes had drifted upward as her mind slipped backwards into the past, to a time when things were simpler, when happiness wasn't something she had to search for.

Like at summer camp.

Yes, she arrived feeling abandoned, unwanted, shipped off because her mother wanted a summer alone with her new husband. The camp was full of kids who had known each other for years, and here came Skylar, the outsider, the girl who didn't belong. But then Levi and Barrett happened and just like that, Skylar belonged too.

Skylar blinked, her gaze refocusing on the ceiling, faintly lit by the gray light seeping through the curtains now as the sun began to rise. The warmth of her memories faded as reality crept back in along with the new day.

Her fingers curled around the phone, the nostalgia leaving a hollow ache in her chest.

This life she was living—it wasn't what she had imagined for herself. Not in a million years. Waking up every morning already exhausted, already dreading the day ahead. She never imagined feeling trapped in a relationship that was more like a weight than a comfort. She never expected to work for a man who made her question whether she had *any* worth beyond what she could do for him—or come home to his son, who treated her almost the same way. How could something like that even happen?

And yet, here she was.

How did I get here?

"Oh, God," she said out loud, the thought hitting her harder than she expected, making her stomach churn.

She had spent so long trying just to survive that she hadn't stopped to realize—she wasn't *living*.

She was just… *existing*.

Her phone buzzed in her hand, pulling her back to the moment.

Barrett: *Are you actually free to hang out soon, or was that just a tease?*

Levi: *We demand proof of life. Respond within five minutes or we send a search party. I've already got the torches ready.*

Skylar let out a breath—a small laugh, despite herself.

Even now, even with all the time that had passed, the boys still made her feel *lighter*.

Her thumbs hovered over the screen, but she hesitated, not sure what to say to them. She was alive, yes, but maybe it was only a technicality because the truth was that she *wasn't* free. Not really. She had work, she had obligations, she had—

She stopped herself before heading too far down that line of thought again.

Skylar: *I miss you guys so bad. Let's fix that, okay? Soon.*

For the first time in a long time, she felt like she had made a choice for *herself*.

Chapter 4.

Skylar – That Night

Skylar stood in the doorway of the apartment, the weight of the day pressing down on her. The apartment was a mess—again—but at least not as catastrophic as yesterday. That was a small win, she supposed.

She sighed heavily and hung her bag on its hook by the door. It was still early, barely six. She hadn't expected to get home this soon. Normally, Chet would be here, sprawled out on the couch, playing video games or watching TV, but tonight, the apartment was silent. No TV. No games. No Chet.

That was weird. Did he actually go to a class for once? She wasn't sure of his schedule this semester. Since it didn't seem to matter to Chet one way or another, she hadn't ever looked at it and he hadn't mentioned it.

"Chet?" she called, already knowing she wouldn't get an answer. The apartment had the feeling of emptiness, the kind where you instantly sense you're alone.

There was nothing, no answer beyond the faint echo of her own voice—and that was probably her imagination.

Skylar's brow furrowed. *Where the hell is he?*

Not that she minded the peace and quiet. If anything, it was a relief to come home to a space that wasn't immediately suffocating. She thought of her feelings that morning. It was like a continuation of the discussion she had with herself, but she still wasn't sure how she felt. It had been a long time since she'd gone an entire day without seeing Chet.

She glanced around at the mess—clothes tossed over the back of the couch, dishes in the sink, a few beer bottles lined up on the counter. He had been here at some point, at least, that was clear. The apartment was clean when she left that morning. She sighed again, debating whether to start cleaning now or wait until she'd had a moment to herself.

I won't be able to relax until it's clean, she admitted. *But also… I just want a break.*

Before she could decide, a soft buzzing cut through the quiet.

She turned her head, frowning, searching for the source of the noise.

Another buzz.

It was coming from the couch.

Skylar stepped forward and pulled up one of the cushions, revealing Chet's smartwatch wedged between the fabric. The screen lit up with another incoming message.

Someone's been texting him. A lot. Like, blowing him up a lot.

Her stomach twisted. She knew she shouldn't invade his privacy, even if he barely deserved that small consideration at this point.

But… was it really an invasion if he left it behind? Besides, her name was *literally* on the phone contract because his credit was too much of a disaster to get a phone on his own. Even with all the money in the world to buy the hardware, the phone companies wouldn't sign you up if they weren't sure you'd pay the monthly bills and Chet had a pretty lousy track record there.

She hesitated for another moment before swiping up on the screen.

The messages flooded in.

Her breath caught in her throat.

The new messages were all in the same thread— one that was months old and labeled only "Side." She didn't have to guess what that meant, but still she scrolled to the top, where the conversation first began. The texts there were playful, flirty. Teasing remarks, inside jokes she didn't understand. Then they turned suggestive—little hints, double meanings. And then, about a month ago, they changed completely.

> **SIDE:** *When are we seeing each other again?*
> **SIDE:** *I miss you. Last time was amazing. You're my stallion.*
> **SIDE:** *You're bad for me, you know that? If people knew.. lol*

Her blood ran cold.

Oh my God.

She clenched the watch so hard it was painful, her pulse hammering in her ears. She had suspected—of course, she had. Chet hadn't touched her in months, and he was never good at covering his tracks when he wanted to hide things from her. He had some late nights out recently, and his excuses had made no sense. He hadn't even bothered last night—he just disappeared after she went to bed. She thought also of the times when he suddenly seemed to pay more attention to his appearance when he had nowhere to be. She was so busy with everything else she hadn't put the pieces together, not exactly, but now, seeing the proof laid out in front of her like this?

It still felt like the floor had been yanked out from beneath her. She felt untethered, and worse—foolish.

Her breath came in short, shallow bursts. She scrolled back, reading the texts again even though she knew it would hurt.

And then something nagged at the back of her mind.

Something familiar.

Her grip tightened further on the watch as she read the texts again, more slowly this time, not just skimming, but digesting the words and their meaning.

The way the other person typed—using only two periods instead of three when trying to make an ellipsis.

The phrases they used.

The way they joked.

Skylar's stomach flipped as realization struck her like a fist in the belly.

No…

But she knew.

She *knew*.

Because she recognized that voice, even in text form.

She recognized the way they wrote, the rhythm of their words.

Because she had read them before.

Because she had seen them before.

Because the person Chet was sleeping with… *was someone she knew.* The last person she would have guessed, and the last person she would have believed it of.

She threw the watch down onto the couch before collapsing onto the cushion next to it. What was she supposed to do?

Skylar's breathing was fast and uneven. This couldn't be happening, but it was. Chet—her boyfriend, the man she had been supporting, cleaning up after, *sacrificing for*—had been cheating on her, betraying her in the most foul and hurtful way she could think of.

But wait—did she know that for certain?

The cheating, yes—there was no denying that, but it takes two to tango and she didn't *know* who the other person was. She suspected, part of her felt very sure, but she didn't *know*. She didn't even know for certain whether or not Chet's "side" was a woman. She laughed bitterly. No, it was a woman. No man ever texted the way Chet's "friend" did.

But what woman? If it was who she suspected…

The possibility made her stomach turn. Her ears were ringing, as if she was trapped in a vacuum, an endless void where there was no past and no future.

She sat there, a million thoughts bouncing off one of another inside her head and slowly, it came over her: *rage*. She wanted to jump up, throw Chet's watch against the wall then grab her phone, call him, scream at him until her throat was raw. She wanted to tear through the apartment and destroy his things, throw all of it out onto the street. It was *her* name on the lease. And when that was done, she would finally, *finally* tell him exactly what she thought of him, of the way he used her, of the way he took and took and *never gave anything back*.

But… then what?

Would he deny it? Would he turn it around on her, say she was crazy for going through his things? Would he lie—*again*—until she doubted her own reality?

Or would he admit it, shrug like it didn't matter, like she should have expected it all along?

Would that be worse?

She didn't know and part of her didn't care. Tears burned in her eyes, threatening to spill down her cheeks while her stomach ate itself and her head ached, but another part of her was still calm, rational, logical. That part told her there was another option. She could simply pretend that she never saw the texts. She would act normally, go about her business, slowly gather her things, all while planning her exit carefully, strategically. She could wait until she had somewhere else to go, somewhere safe, before she made her move.

That was the smart way to do it. She knew that, and she'd spent the last few years playing every move smart—you had to in order to keep working for Nathan Dyer for as long as she had. One of the office girls told Skylar that no other assistant to Mr. Dyer had lasted this long. She was a little proud of that at least, and she knew that if she did anything rash, not only would she lose Chet—no, she corrected herself, he was already lost to her; she realized that now—she would lose her job as well, and she couldn't afford that. Not now. Not yet.

No, she needed to play this smart, work intelligently, and to do that, she needed intelligence—information. Before she did anything else, she had to know for sure, because this wasn't just about her, it wasn't even about her and Chet—there was at least one more person this situation concerned and, if Skylar was right, more than that besides. People were going to be hurt by Chet's actions one way or another, but if it was at all possible, she wanted to minimize the collateral damage.

To do that, she had to know. No matter how much it hurt her, she had to know for certain who it was that Chet had betrayed her with, and there was only one person who could help with that.

She picked up her cellphone, opened her contacts, and hit "call."

The phone rang once, twice—and when Barrett picked up, Skylar said, "Hi! Long time no see! Yeah, fine. Listen, I know it's crappy of me, but I need a favor…"

Chapter 5.

Skylar and Barrett – Later That Night

The air was thick with the smell of rain and asphalt as Skylar and Barrett pulled into the motel parking lot. A neon sign, shaped like a heart with an arrow thrust through it, buzzed faintly in the night, casting a dim red glow over the cracked pavement. On the Jersey side of the river, just past the Lincoln Tunnel, the place was called Cupid's Rest, and it was much nicer than Skylar expected—not some run-down roadside dump, but upscale enough that discretion was part of the service.

That only made her stomach churn harder. Chet couldn't even be bothered to help pay their bills unless she nagged him every month, and he was throwing away money on places like this? With—

No, she didn't know that for sure yet. Chet was here, there wouldn't be any doubt about that, but she didn't know for certain who he was with. Who knew? Maybe it was all just some mistake, and he was here sleeping off a drunken binge. She tried to laugh, but it came out a kind of strangled sob. She knew that wasn't true. She'd seen the texts. There was no other reason for Chet to be out here.

"Are you okay, Sky?" There was genuine concern in Barrett's voice. She turned to him, studying for a moment the man she'd known more than half her life. One of her best friends, she knew his face by heart—but had she ever really looked at him? He was twenty-seven, the same age as her, only a couple of months younger. His brown hair was always tousled, as if he absentmindedly ran his hands through it too often. He was of medium build, reasonably fit, but without putting too much worry or effort into it. He was handsome too, but not strikingly so. His features were regular, but not particularly remarkable. You wouldn't have noticed him in a crowd, but when he was on his own, you could sense the steadiness in him, the kindness, and see in his eyes the dry amusement he found in every day. Barrett Teller was just a guy, but he was one of the best.

"I'm fine," she said finally, but it was a lie and they both knew it. The betrayal sat like a stone in her gut, heavy and unshakable.

Barrett was doing her a huge favor, using his employer's resources to trace Chet's cellphone like this. She was technically the owner of the phone since her name was on the contract, so legally she could give permission for Barrett to run the trace and locate, but using Mr. Whittington's resources without permission, especially for something outside of the scope of paying work, was a big no-no. Skylar knew that when she asked, and she felt a guilty doing so, but she had to know where Chet was and who he was with. When she explained to Barrett, saying only that Chet was "missing" and that she hadn't seen him since the day before, something in her voice must have convinced Barrett how important it was—that and she never asked for anything unless it was truly, genuinely necessary—so he agreed, even though he had his doubts.

Skylar was one of the most important people in Barrett's life, and part of him was secretly pleased that he was the one she turned to when she needed help. He would do anything for her that he could; that he had a special set of skills and access to resources others didn't meant there wasn't anyone else she could ask, but that didn't matter. Skylar needed him and he wanted to be there for her. If it came down to it, he'd find a way to make Mr. Whittington understand. He hoped he wouldn't have to, but he was sure it would be alright—at least on that front.

Skylar looked towards the building. She had spent the entire drive in silence, staring out at the passing lights of the city, feeling like she was hurtling toward a moment she wouldn't be able to come back from. And now, here they were.

Barrett parked his SUV in the farthest corner of the lot, cutting the engine. For a long moment, neither of them spoke. Finally, Barrett sighed and turned to her.

"Sky…" His voice was careful, measured. "Are you *sure* you want to do this? I mean—"

"I have to." Her hands clenched so tightly her knuckles were white, though it was invisible in the shadows of the car. But the tension poured off of her in waves, making it impossible to miss how wound up she was.

Barrett's expression was unreadable, but she saw the hesitation in his eyes. She knew he wanted to go in alone. He wanted to protect her from whatever this was. She told him Chet was "missing," but Barrett wasn't stupid—this kind of place only existed for one purpose, and this was where Chet's cellphone had been for most of the day. It stood to reason where it was, Chet would be.

Skylar knew Barrett wanted to protect her, but she wasn't a kid at summer camp anymore. She had to face this herself. Chet was her boyfriend, after all—and, she was finally realizing these last couple of days, her mistake. She always took responsibility for her mistakes.

Barrett exhaled through his nose, shaking his head wearily. "Alright," he muttered. "Let's get this over with."

Skylar swallowed, took a deep breath, and nodded.

They stepped out of the car, their footsteps rasping against the wet pavement. The motel's exterior was modern and clean, with a sleek front office, sporting a miniature version of the sign that faced the road.

Skylar lingered outside the office while Barrett

went in. The desk wasn't far from the door, and she could hear the low hum of his voice, though not the words. Her thoughts were too loud anyway, racing in circles. Barrett showed the night clerk something—a copy of his private investigator's credentials, she guessed—and it seemed to impress the older man. They spoke for a few more moments and then Barrett came outside. "Room 214," was all he said, his jaw tight. He motioned for her to follow him.

They climbed a metal staircase to the second floor. There was a faint breeze off the river, carrying cool, damp air that left her skin feeling faintly clammy. Her heart hammered and her palms were sweating. She was terrified, but she focused on Barrett's back as he walked a step ahead of her. His presence was solid and steady, just as it had always been.

Before she realized it, they were standing in front of room 214.

Skylar stared at the brass numbers on the door, her pulse thundering so hard she could hear it in her ears. She didn't know what she expected to find—she knew what she *feared* she would find, but a tiny sliver of hope inside of her still wanted this to all be some huge misunderstanding. Maybe Chet's phone had been stolen, or he'd lent it to a friend—any excuse that didn't lead to this.

But deep down, she knew. She read those texts and she knew very well how Chet texted. She knew his digital voice and she was pretty sure she knew the woman's as well…

Maybe she didn't yet know who Chet was with, but when it came to Chet? She had known for a long time, she now realized. The truth was just finally catching up with her.

Barrett turned to her, lowering his voice. "Last chance to walk away."

She shook her head. "I'm not walking away."

Barrett visibly steeled himself, but he nodded.

Skylar raised her hand slowly and forced herself to knock.

For a moment, there was nothing.

Then—a muffled rustling from inside. The creak of a bed as someone rolled off of the edge. Footsteps. The curtain beside the door flicked aside for just a fraction of an instant. It wasn't long enough for Skylar to get a glimpse inside the room, but no sooner had the curtain fallen back than the locks on the door made a mechanical sound and then the door itself opened a couple of inches.

Chet stood there, shirtless, hair disheveled. His expression flickered from confusion to irritation in an instant as his eyes swept from Skylar to Barrett and back.

"Skylar?" His voice was thick, like he had just woken up—but there was no mistaking the underlying annoyance. He had to know he was caught; was he going on the attack, trying to somehow weasel out of this?

Skylar tried to speak, but suddenly she couldn't even breathe.

Behind Chet, the room was dimly lit, a sleek overnight bag visible on the chair. The faint scent of perfume lingered in the air—*not hers. No, no, no,* Skylar thought. She knew someone who wore that scent and only one person. The very last person Chet would be with, unless he was intentionally trying to hurt her.

Chet looked directly at Barrett, his frown deepening. "Oh, so you brought *him?*" His voice was sharp, defensive. "Seriously? What the hell are you doing here?"

Skylar's mouth was bone-dry. She swallowed.

Before she could answer, a voice—*a woman's voice*—came from inside.

"Chet? Who is it?"

Skylar's heart stopped.

No.

No, it *couldn't be.* But it was. That voice was

41

unmistakable; she'd been hearing it her entire life.

The door opened a little wider, and Natalie Rose—Skylar's mother—stood behind Chet, wearing only a lacy black nighty.

Chapter 6.

Skylar, Barrett, Chet—And Natalie

The world was dead silent except for the distant
hum of traffic from the tunnel leading back to Manhattan.
The air had grown thicker and colder and the glow of the
buzzing neon sign reflecting off the damp pavement was a
darker, more sinister shade of red than when they arrived.
Skylar stood, arms rigidly at her sides, her heart pounding
painfully and nausea swirling through her.

She came to this fancy little motel in New Jersey
expecting to catch Chet cheating, and she did exactly
that—but why did it have to be like *this*? She thought she
recognized the woman's style of texting, but she couldn't
be certain, not until she saw it with her own eyes. She
never really believed her own mother would be the one
Chet was betraying her with though. Not truly. No, it had
to be a coincidence, someone who just sort of sounded
like Natalie Rose in text. A lot of young people use similar
language, and Natalie had spent a lot of time over the years
keeping up with trends, making sure she was always
Brian's hip, hot, young wife—even though she was only
four years younger than he was.

She expected to catch Chet cheating, and she had
her fears, but she didn't really expect they'd actually be
realized. It could have been anyone, any single woman on
Earth—so why did it have to be *Skylar's own mother*?

It was a double betrayal—her boyfriend, the man
she'd trusted and loved and taken care of, even *pampered*
for years, and her own mother. Her *fucking mother*! She

wanted to scream, she wanted to tear her hair out. She wanted to scratch and claw and kick both of them until there was nothing left but shreds.

The feeling passed as quickly as it came and she was left numb—numb and cold and empty.

"Sky…" Barrett took hold of her arm, steadying her. He was always there to keep her grounded, wasn't he? And at his touch, she returned to herself.

She brushed off Barrett's hand and took a step into the room, saying, "Are you… are you fucking serious?" her voice low and harsh.

Natalie sighed, crossing her arms like she was only mildly inconvenienced by all of this. "Skylar, don't be dramatic."

Behind Skylar, Barrett swore softly.

Skylar's entire body felt like it was about to shatter.

"*Dramatic*?" she repeated, her voice rising. "You—" She swallowed, shaking her head. "You're sleeping with my *boyfriend*!"

Natalie's lips twitched into something that wasn't quite a smirk, but wasn't exactly regret, either. Something strange danced behind her eyes.

Skylar and her mother hadn't been close for a long time, not since before Natalie sent Skylar away to camp all those years ago, but she never imagined her mother could truly be this cruel—this *evil*.

"I don't see what difference it makes, Skylar. You were clearly going to break up with him anyway. Chet's told me all about how you care more about pleasing his father than you do spending time with him."

Off-balance, Skylar actually stumbled backwards, like she had been physically struck. Barrett reached out instinctively, steadying her again, but his gaze was locked on Chet. His posture was stiff and his free hand was clenched into a fist.

Chet, for his part, looked annoyed, like this

confrontation was an irritation, an interruption to a pleasant evening.

"Look, Sky," Chet drawled, running a hand through his messy blond hair. "I mean, let's be real here. We weren't exactly *great*, were we? It was fun, but moving in was a mistake. We both know that, yeah? You were always working, always stressed out. You weren't even around most of the time. What was I supposed to do?"

"We didn't plan this," Natalie put in. "Believe that, at least."

"Yeah," Chet agreed. "We just sort of ran into each other one day and kinda…" He grinned, like a little boy caught with his hand in the cookie jar, and turned to Natalie. "Clicked."

Skylar's entire body shook with rage and hurt. "This isn't happening," she whispered. "This *can't* be happening."

Barrett broke his silence. "You're a real piece of shit, you know that, Chet?"

Chet just shrugged. "Hey, man, don't hate the player."

"You think this is a fucking *game*?" Barrett took a step forward, fist raised, and for a moment, Skylar genuinely thought Barrett was going to hit Chet. Her memory flashed to those bullies in the woods so long ago.

Natalie rolled her eyes. "Oh, grow up, Barrett."

Barrett barked a laugh, a sharp, humorless sound. "Grow up? That's rich coming from the woman sleeping with her daughter's boyfriend."

"Hey, man. You wanna know something? She's not even her real—" Chet began, but Natalie, her expression flickering for an instant, cut him off. "Shut up, Chet.

She focused on Skylar. "You're acting like this is some great betrayal," she said, crossing her arms beneath her breasts, lifting them slightly, as if to remind the others that she was entirely unbothered by being caught *in flagrante.* "Skylar, darling, you and I haven't been close in a long time and we both know your relationship with Chet was over a long time ago. I'm sorry you found out this way, but—"

"What about Brian?" Skylar's fists clenched at her sides, thinking of how it wasn't just her who would be hurt by this—her stepfather was a part of it too. Did he know? No, she told herself, he couldn't. She didn't know the ins and outs of her mother and stepfather's relationship, but she was sure Brian wouldn't tolerate Natalie cheating if he was aware of it. He was a good man, a kind man, but he had dignity and a sense of self that wouldn't allow him to live under the same roof with someone who betrayed him. More than that, Skylar knew he would never want her to be hurt and if he knew her mother was cheating on him with Skylar's own boyfriend, surely Brian would have found a way to tell her.

"What about him?" Natalie countered. "That's entirely between your stepfather and myself, so don't worry about."

"What happened to you?" Skylar snapped. "What is *wrong* with you? You're my *mother*. Do you even understand how *disgusting* this is?"

Even before Natalie married Brian, Skylar realized her mother had grown a selfish streak. She told herself that it was natural—Natalie was young when she had Skylar, and she spent years taking care of Skylar by herself. When her daughter was a little older, it wasn't unexpected that Natalie would want to do something for herself. But it went beyond that once she married Brian. With access to money and social status, Natalie had come to put herself first, always.

But this? *This* was a new low.

And Chet, who had barely even *tried* to pretend he cared, stood there acting like this was some kind of game—

Natalie sighed again, like she was tired of the

conversation. "Skylar, emotions are messy. Life is messy. You're old enough to know that by now. I spent a long time taking care of you, cleaning up after you, holding your hand… I can understand how you'd see me only in a certain light, but you need to understand that I'm a woman too."

Skylar gaped at her. She wanted to scream. Instead, she took a slow, shuddering breath and turned to Barrett.

"We're leaving," she said, her voice hollow.

Barrett hesitated, still watching Chet with barely concealed fury, but he nodded and moved to put himself between Skylar and the others, as if shielding her from further damage.

Skylar took one last look at her mother, her stomach churning with rage and heartbreak.

"I hope he ruins your life," she said softly. "Just like he did mine. I won't tell Brian, not yet, but I expect you to own up to this with him. I'll tell him if you won't."

Natalie blinked. "Skylar—"

But Skylar was already turning away. She didn't need to hear whatever came next. She had heard enough. She had seen enough.

Chet chuckled behind her. "Come on, Sky, don't be—"

Barrett whirled, his voice sharp as a blade.

"Shut the *hell* up, Chet, before I push your teeth down your throat."

And then they were moving slowly but steadily away, down the stairs, back into the night. Skylar's mind was spinning and her heart was cracked wide open. She felt hot all over, like her heart was pumping blood throughout her body, faster and faster, more blood than her veins could hold, like she was going to explode.

But she didn't cry. Not yet. She just kept walking, Barrett—silent, steady Barrett—beside her until they reached his car. Once they were inside, she let herself go.

She collapsed against Barrett's shoulder and began crying harder than she knew it was possible to cry.

Chapter 7.

Skylar and Barrett – Later That Night

Barrett swallowed against a lump, his throat dry as he stared down at Skylar, nestled against his shoulder, his arm draped around her. They sat in the back of his SUV, in the Javits Center's parking garage. When they got back to the city, she didn't want to return to her apartment, even though it was her home, afraid Chet might possibly show up and Barrett wasn't sure where else to take her. The house he and Levi shared in Brooklyn seemed a long ways off. The Javits Center was near the Lincoln Tunnel's Manhattan exit though and they could stay there as long as they liked. It wasn't a good solution, maybe, but it was what they had to work with at nearly midnight.

"Sky…" he murmured, his arm tightening around her. She was no longer sobbing, but crying softly instead now. Almost like a little kid, nursing a wound. It was far worse than that though. Barrett had seen tragedy in the four years he worked for Mr. Whittington, but this was such a personal kind, involving someone he cared for. He couldn't be objective about it and he just didn't know what to do for his friend.

She looked up at him through tear-damp lashes, her face caught in the dim glow of the garage's lights filtering through the SUV's tinted windows. Even in the gloom, Barrett could see that her eyes were red-rimmed, raw with the weight of betrayal, and the burden of her pain, but in this moment—soft and quiet, curled against him in the stillness of the SUV—she was beautiful.

49

And Barrett hated himself for noticing, for feeling anything at all beyond the sheer ache of wanting to protect her, to soothe her hurts and comfort her.

Skylar had been one of his two best friends for years. Since that summer they met at Camp Timbercrest, when she was a lonely outsider and he and Levi had taken her under their wing. Barrett and Levi had already been friends for six or seven years at that point, but adding Skylar to the mix felt natural, felt right. Even though they were just kids back then, Barrett felt a pull towards her, an instinctual understanding that she was important. That she mattered.

She mattered then and she mattered now more than ever after the three of them had shared so many years of friendship, of ups—and downs.

And now, this might be the worst down any of them had experienced. Skylar had been hurt before, all of them had—it was part of being human, of being alive. But now… now she was broken and he didn't know how to fix her.

Skylar blinked up at him. Her mouth opened, lips parting as if to speak, but no words came. She took a shaky breath and shifted closer, pressing herself more fully against his side. Her cheek rested against his chest, and he felt the warmth of her breath through the thin fabric of his shirt.

Barrett exhaled slowly, willing himself to stay still. To be steady for her. That was what she expected of him. Levi was the fun one, Barrett was the steady one—the one she could always rely on.

"You don't have to talk, Sky," he said, his voice soft. "But I'm here. Okay? I'm here. Anything you want to say, anything you want me to do, is okay. If you want me to go back and kick the crap out Chet, I will. I'll give your mom a good smack too, if you think it would help."

She let out a weak, watery laugh. "It wouldn't," she whispered. "But thanks."

Barrett felt himself tense. He was always here for her, but he wondered if she suspected why, that it was beyond just friendship. He was her friend, absolutely and without fail, but there was always something underlying that feeling, something he didn't want to acknowledge even to himself.

He shifted his thoughts away from himself. He wanted so badly to punch Chet back at that motel. More than that—he had wanted to hurt him, to make him feel even a fraction of the pain he was putting Skylar through. Even in that moment, as it was happening, Skylar's pain was as palpable to Barrett as if it was his own. And the smug look on that bastard Chet's face, the way he had dismissed her like she was nothing—Barrett had never felt such fury in his life. And then *Natalie*, Skylar's own *mother*, standing there like it was all perfectly reasonable, like she had no idea in the world why Skylar could possibly be hurt by her sleeping with Skylar's boyfriend.

He didn't understand how someone like Skylar, who was loyal, kind, hardworking, had been stuck with such awful people. He knew Natalie hadn't always been like that, Skylar had told him and Levi many times over the years that she was kind when Skylar was little, but changed as she got older—and got even worse once she married Brian Rose. Brian was a nice guy, too, Barrett thought. Neither Skylar nor Brian deserved having to tolerate that bitch in their lives.

Skylar shifted again, pulling back far enough to look up at him. The movement was slow, hesitant, but when their eyes met, Barrett felt something shift in the air between them.

She had finally stopped crying, and the tears were drying now, leaving faint tracks on her skin that caught the dim light as she moved. Her expression was raw, open, filled with an emotion Barrett couldn't quite name.

Maybe she didn't have a name for it either.

He should look away.

He should.

But he didn't.

Instead, he reached out hesitantly and brushed a stray tear from her cheek with the pad of his thumb. Her skin was warm, soft, and she didn't flinch or pull away.

"Barrett…" Her voice was barely above a whisper.

His heart pounded.

"Yeah?"

She searched his face like she was looking for something—reassurance, maybe. Or understanding. Or something else entirely.

For a second, just a second, Barrett hoped she might—

And then she did—Skylar leaned up, kissing him on the lips, before sighing, closing her eyes again and leaning back against him once more. "I love you, Barr," she said, her voice thick with emotion and exhaustion.

Barrett let out a slow breath, forcing himself to relax again, to push down whatever had just passed between them. *She didn't mean it like that*, he told himself. But what if…?

With his free hand, he slowly, gently tilted Skylar's head up, leaned down and kissed her as she had him— softly and sweetly. He wasn't sure if this was okay, he felt like maybe he was taking advantage of her, but she looked so lovely and she needed the human contact, the reassurance, didn't she? She'd kissed him first after all.

He half-expected her to gasp, to push him away— maybe to scream, ask him what he was doing.

She didn't. She returned the kiss, matching his tone, soft and gentle and sweet. They broke apart, their eyes met. "Barr…" she whispered, and then they were kissing again and it was no longer soft or gentle.

Maybe neither of them meant for it to happen. Skylar's first kiss started as comfort, just warmth and reassurance between friends. She had been hurting, and he had been there, as he always had been, as he always would be. Barrett was her rock. Whether she realized it or not before, she knew now as she leaned into him, and he held her, absorbing her trembling breaths, her sadness, her exhaustion… but something shifted and there was an urgency, a need in both of them. It was like a fire sparked by Skylar's kiss sparked that Barrett's fanned into flames.

Her fingers gripped his shirt, his arms closed around her and something unspoken tipped between them, crossing an invisible line they never even approached before.

Her face lifted toward his, her breath warm and uneven, and for a split second, Barrett hesitated, every rational thought screaming at him to *stop*, to *think*, to be *careful*. Skylar was hurting and this wasn't right—she was emotionally unbalanced, off-center, vulnerable and this was taking advantage, wasn't it? It was—but then Skylar had closed the distance, and he was lost in her, lost in the heat of her body and the scent of her hair. And God, she tasted good. Like mint and something sweet, something uniquely *her*, something that was Skylar and Skylar alone.

Barrett groaned against her lips as she shifted, half-straddling him in the cramped backseat. Her body was warm against his, soft in all the right places, and when she arched just slightly, pressing her breasts flush against him, his breath stuttered and all hesitation, all thoughts of anything but her, evaporated.

He kissed her back, deep and urgent, his hands sliding into her hair, pulling her closer. Skylar melted into him, her fingers curling around the fabric of his jacket's collar, tugging, pressing, desperate for more, wanting this, wanting *him*.

"This—" she murmured between kisses, voice breathless, desperate. "This is probably a bad idea…"

"Yeah," Barrett agreed, but he didn't stop. Couldn't stop. Inside of his jeans, his penis was twitching, growing, responding to the way her weight pressed down against him and how her breasts slid against his chest, soft, but firm. He'd never realized how big they actually were before.

Her nails scraped lightly at the back of his neck, sending shivers down his spine. He responded by deepening the kiss, his hand trailing down the curve of her back, holding her steady, as if grounding himself in her, wanting to feel every moment, every instant, to commit to memory the feelings, the sensations, the sights and sounds and smells of this beautiful woman who had always been so important to him, just in case this was a dream.

Skylar sighed with pleasure, her body pressing closer still, her lips parting just enough for Barrett to taste more of her, to drown in the heat and the want sparking between them. His penis was fully engorged now, uncomfortably tight against his pants. She had to feel it against her crotch—was she responding? Was she—he barely allowed himself to imagine it—getting wet?

He wanted her. Oh, my God, how he wanted her, and it scared the hell out of him. Skylar was his friend, one of his two best friends—could they cross this bridge? Was there any coming back if they did? Would they even want to? This was no longer two people seeking comfort in the aftermath of betrayal. It wasn't even lust. It was *Skylar* and it was *Barrett*. Two people who had a connection already and could find something deeper.

She was his best friend, but she was also the woman he had silently, patiently, hopelessly loved for longer than he cared to admit. And now she was here, in his arms, kissing him like she needed him, like she *wanted* him.

But was it as real for her as it was for him? Or was it just reaction to what had happened?

"Sky," he murmured, voice thick with restraint. Hoarsely, he added, "I want you. *God*, I want you. But not because you're hurting. Not because of *him*." He brushed a thumb lightly over her cheek. "I don't want this to be something you regret."

Skylar pulled back, searching his face. "Barrett…"

Then she kissed him, deeply, fiercely, with even more passion than she had before, as she wriggled out of her jacket. Still kissing him, as if unwilling to break contact for even a moment, she unbuttoned her blouse and pulled her bra down, exposing her breasts, their rosebud tips already stiff with her desire.

"Sky…" Barrett whispered against her mouth, his hands moving to her breasts. Her skin was so soft, and her breasts were yielding but firm as he traced their curve with his thumbs. Lightly, with thumb and forefinger, he teased her nipples, eliciting a sharp breath of pleasure from her. She began grinding her hips against his bulging crotch and he felt the dampness as precum began seeping from his erection.

"Wait. Sky, wait!" he said, pushing her gently back. "Let me get this off…"

She moved back, giving him a fraction of extra space, but her lips traveled down to his chin, his throat. Laughing gently at her eagerness, Barrett slipped out of his jacket, then pulled his shirt over his head without bothering to unbutton it. Skylar collapsed against him, pressing her breasts against his chest, her stiff nipples rubbing against his muscles. God, she'd never realized how broad Barrett's chest was. He wasn't a gym-rat like Levi, it was just natural—he was a solidly built man and for the first time she truly appreciated it.

Barrett crushed her to him, kissing every inch of her face and throat before moving down to her chest. He took first one nipple into his mouth, gently swirling his tongue around the pink bud, and then the other. She gasped in pleasure. It had been so long since she had sex, and even longer since she actually made *love* to someone. She never imagined it would be Barrett, but she was glad this was happening. It felt so right somehow.

She kissed him again, drawing it out so long that they were both gasping for breath before she pulled away.

"Wait, Barr," she whispered against his throat, bucking her hips, trying to find the zipper of her skirt. After a moment's frustration, she gave up and pulled the skirt up to her hips and pushed her panties aside. She brushed a hand over her pussy—God, she was so *wet*.

Barrett couldn't stand it anymore. He lifted his hips, unbuttoned his jeans, and pulled until his pants and jockey shorts were down around his knees, freeing his engorged cock. It stood up straight and long and for an instant, Skylar was surprised again by Barrett's body—it was bigger than any other cock she'd seen in person before. Certainly bigger than Chet's. She stifled a little laugh, afraid Barrett would misunderstand.

His dick pressing against the silk of Skylar's thighs, rubbing gently, spreading his precum across them, he trailed kisses down her throat to her breasts, cupping one lovingly while he gently sucked on the other before switching, all the time gently playing with the lips of her pussy with his free hand, sending bolts of fire throughout her entire body.

Skylar moaned in pleasure, feeling her juices actually dripping out of, mixing with Barrett's to smear both of their thighs. "I want it, Barr," she whispered, leaning down to kiss the top of his head. "I want you inside me."

"Yeah?" he asked, looking up to meet her eyes. He was smiling, but it faded. "I don't have a condom, Sky."

"I don't care," she told him, shifting, positioning her throbbing pussy over his cock, ready to plunge him inside of her. God, he was so big, she thought; what would it feel like? Would it hurt? She almost wanted it to—she knew it would be a delicious kind of pain if it did. "Just let me know when you're gonna cum, okay?"

"I will," he said, almost solemnly, and kissed her deeply, his tongue probing the inside of her mouth, relishing that unique Skylar taste.

She grabbed his cock, guiding his rigid flesh inside of her. Her entire body shuddered as she felt his penis push upwards, probing her pussy, rubbing against her secret places. Barrett was so *big*, and she felt his cock throbbing inside her, reaching parts of her she didn't know a cock could. She began to rock up and down, moving her hips, pushing him as deeply inside of her as she possibly could, before relenting and pulling back, only to do it all over. Each time was as ecstatic as the last, and though it was a little awkward in the back seat of the car, Barrett managed to match her rhythm and soon they were moving together almost as if this wasn't their first time, as if they had been making love for years and knew every word and verse of each other's desires and every inch of each other's bodies.

"Sky…" Barrett moaned. "Oh, God, Sky… I've wanted, for so long—"

"Shhh," she said and pressed her lips against his, flicking her tongue against his teeth. She pulled back. "I know. I can feel it."

His hands found her round buttocks, and gripped tightly as she began moving faster, bringing her hips down as he brought his up to meet her. The rhythm they had built remained the same, but the pace quickened until the fires building inside of them threatened to burst. Skylar felt her pussy tightening and beginning to spasm.

"I'm almost—there," she gasped.

"Me, too," Barrett told her. "I'm really close—I'm gonna—I'm gonna cum! Sky, I'm gonna cum!"

She didn't want to break their connection, to pull away from him. If it was possible, she wanted Barrett to keep fucking her until time ended, but she lifted herself, freeing his cock from her pussy, feeling the delicious wetness seeping from her body and dropped to her knees on the seat next to him. She leaned forward, her breasts against his naked thigh, took his cock in her mouth and began moving her head up and down as quickly as she could, alternately her flicking her tongue against the head of his penis and rubbing it against the back of her throat. *God*, she thought again. *He's so* big*!*

"I'm gonna—Sky, I'm gonna—" the words became a groan as he orgasmed, hot, sticky cum pumping from his cock like a firehose, gushing, filling her mouth until she thought she might drown in it. She kept sucking him though, wanting every drop of his semen, wanting a part of him inside of her even after their lovemaking ended. It took two gulps but she swallowed all of it and then licked his penis until there wasn't a drop left.

"Sky…" Barrett said, breathing heavily. He lifted her and kissed her deeply, then without a word, pressed her back until she was laying on the car-seat, her legs spread, and pressed his face into her still-soaking pussy. He nuzzled his nose against her clit, breathing deeply of her scent before running his tongue up and down her lips, making her shiver deliciously. Without warning, he shoved his tongue inside of her, penetrating her with it as he had with his cock, and lapped at the quivering walls of her vagina until her legs began shaking. It was a different taste than her mouth—salty, instead of sweet—but still uniquely *her*.

"Barr… Barr, I'm almost there. Don't stop!" She grabbed fistfuls of his hair and pushed his face against her pussy as his tongue began moving faster, almost frantically, as if he was desperate for more of her taste, for more of her essence, for more of her love. He brought his arms up, wrapping them around her thighs, pressing his face tightly against her pussy before shifting upwards and sucking directly on the tiny, sensitive sweetness of her clit, sending her over the edge. She orgasmed explosively, harder than she ever had in her life, spraying her wetness all over Barrett's face. It was the first time she had ever squirted, and it left her body a quivering mess. She felt like she was made of wet sponge, and it was the most exquisite feeling.

Barrett rose up on his elbows and kissed his way

up her belly to her breasts, giving each nipple one soft kiss, before finding her lips. Skylar tasted herself on his lips and found herself so aroused she almost wanted to go another round already.

"Sky…" Barrett said softly, looking down at her. "Sky," he said again and kissed her.

She kissed back, the fierceness gone now, leaving a sense of contentment and love in its place. She cupped his cheek in her hand. "Barr…"

"That was…" Barrett began, but wasn't able to finish. Now that it was over, he wasn't sure what came next.

Skylar smiled. "I'm glad you came with me tonight. I'm glad I called you."

"Me, too." Barrett smiled. "But there's still you-know-who to deal with…"

Skylar said, "As far as I'm concerned, right now, there's nobody in the world but you and me." She wrapped her arms around his neck and pulled him down to her, kissing him softly.

Chapter 8.

Skylar – Next Afternoon

"And your calendar is up to date until the 11th. I'm sure there'll be some shuffling, but we should be pretty solid for the next four days at least."

Skylar stood in front of Nathan Dyer's massive desk, looking past him to the huge window that took up most of the wall. The city skyline was breathtaking even after all these years, but that wasn't why she took a steadying breath before continuing. This conversation wouldn't be easy—Nathan thrived on predictability, on control, and especially on having her at his disposal at all times. But she had made up her mind.

"And there's one more thing, Nathan. I need to take a personal day tomorrow. I've already put it into the payroll system, I just need you to sign off on it—or tell human resources to."

Nathan had been rapidly typing on his laptop. He rarely wrote his own emails—mostly that was accomplished by Skylar taking dictation—so it must have been something personal, which would be ironic. Now the typing stopped. His fingers hovered over the keyboard for a fraction of a second before he finally looked at her. His gaze was sharp as it locked with hers; she knew he was scrutinizing every detail of her face like she was a particularly disappointing quarterly report. He didn't like surprises and he absolutely hated them coming from someone he relied on.

"That's… short notice." His voice was calm, but it

contained an unmistakable edge.

"I know," she said evenly, resisting the urge to fidget. She was twenty-seven years old, but authority figures could still make her feel like a naughty kid if she let them. She wouldn't let that stop her though—she needed to get out of the apartment as soon as possible, with minimal fuss. She already contacted the realty company, asking them to transfer the lease to Chet's name, and Levi promised to rent a truck and help her move, but it wouldn't be possible until tomorrow at the very least.

It was only about fourteen hours since she and Barrett had their… moment. She mentally blushed remembering the passion they shared, but kept her face neutral.

Afterwards, they held one another and talked for hours, catching up on the weeks they hadn't been in contact. Finally, around three in the morning, Barrett suggested she spend the night at the house he and Levi had recently purchased together in Bay Ridge, out in Brooklyn. They intended to fix it up in their spare time and flip it, but the mortgage was a bit of a stretch for even their combined resources, so they were living in the house while working on it to save money. There was plenty of room, three bedrooms and two baths, so an overnight guest wouldn't be any hardship.

There wasn't much chance of Chet coming back to their apartment that night, but she hated even the idea of sleeping in the bed they once shared, so she agreed.

When they arrived, they found Levi still awake to both of their surprise. He had somehow gotten himself caught up in a massive monster hunting raid in *Fantasy Tales Online*, the video game he'd been quasi-addicted to for almost a decade. When he saw Skylar though, he dropped his controller and literally leapt for joy before enveloping her in a bearhug and bathing her in the light of his brightest, sunniest smile.

Skylar and Barrett briefly recounted to their friend

what happened with Chet—leaving out what happened between the two of them afterwards—and Levi surprised them both again by saying, "Move in with us, Sky. There's plenty of room and God knows it would help if we could split the mortgage three ways."

The idea hadn't even occurred to Skylar, but it seemed like the perfect solution—at least temporarily. She could get out of the apartment immediately and at the same time, she'd be with the people she cared about most in the world.

Before Skylar even responded, Barrett was urging her to agree. She realized that there might be… complications over what happened with Barrett, but she knew they could work through them. They were both adults and they'd been friends too long to let anything damage that.

"I'd love it," she told the boys.

Now, she just had to clear the final hurdle—and see if she would still have a job to return to.

"I wouldn't ask if it wasn't important, Nathan, and I've already briefed Noreen on anything that might come up and made sure she knows where to find contingency plans if it's necessary."

Nathan leaned back in his chair, expression unreadable. "I see."

"I've also updated your schedule to flag anything urgent, added Noreen as a follower for tomorrow's items, and left notes for anything requiring follow-up. Everything is accounted for, Nathan."

Nathan exhaled through his nose, tapping his fingers against the armrest of his chair. "You rarely surprise me, Skylar," he said, his voice carrying the weight of disapproval. "Especially with something personal. You know how I feel about surprises and personal lives interfering with business."

She kept her expression neutral. "I understand. But this is something I need to do. Like I said, I wouldn't ask if it wasn't important and frankly, it came as a surprise to me as well." She almost added an apology, but stopped herself—she didn't owe anyone any apologies. She had done nothing wrong. She wasn't going to think of herself as a victim, and she wasn't going to defend her need to take care of herself either.

He studied her, searching for cracks in her composure. Finding none, he let out a sharp exhalation and shook his head. "This is a bad time for my right hand to be off galivanting."

Skylar swallowed her irritation. *Galivanting?* The word was so dismissive, as if her life outside of his office was a frivolous afterthought, as if she didn't exist unless Nathan Dyer needed her to. It was true that she'd gotten the job mostly as a favor to his son, but she had worked tirelessly for Nathan, learning the ins and outs of what made the man and then anticipating his needs before he even voiced them—and yet here he was, acting like she was asking for a year's sabbatical instead of a single day.

She forced herself to remain calm and professional. "Everything will be fine," she assured him. "I've made sure every contingency has been covered. You won't even notice I'm gone."

Nathan scoffed. "Doubtful. You know I rely on you." He leaned back in his chair, fingers steepled beneath his chin. "You've spent years making yourself critical to this company and to me," he said slowly. "And now, with barely any notice, you're just… taking off?"

Silence stretched between them. Skylar had expected pushback, but the way he said it—as if she were betraying the company, betraying *him*—stirred an irritation she barely kept in check. She knew this was his way of testing her, trying to make her second-guess herself, to convince her to change her mind. But she wouldn't. She had in the past, but not this time.

"I've made sure everything is covered in my absence," she told him.

Nathan wasn't satisfied. "What's so important that it couldn't wait?"

Skylar hesitated. Her first instinct was to tell him *it's none of your business*, because it wasn't, but he was going to find out one way or another. Chet was Nathan's son after all, and she was already prepared to lose this job when he found out she was leaving Chet. She didn't know if he would be that petty, but she wouldn't put it past him. If she had to leave TechnoFirm a little earlier than she originally planned to get her affairs in order, so be it. *Do it like ripping off a band-aid*, she told herself.

"I'm moving out of my apartment," she said. "It's short notice because something has… come up and it has to be done as quickly as possible."

Nathan's expression didn't change, but his gaze sharpened. "The apartment you share with Chester." It wasn't a question.

Skylar met his eyes, forcing herself not to flinch. "Yes."

There was silence for a long beat.

Nathan studied her, and she could almost *hear* the wheels turning in his head. "I assume this means your relationship is over." Another statement, not a question.

Skylar swallowed. Saying it aloud, admitting it— *really* admitting it—made it more real. She had spent so long stuck in a miserable, unfulfilling loop, making excuses, justifying things to herself. But there was no justifying what Chet had done. It hurt—it hurt *so much*— but she needed to pick up the pieces. Thank God Barrett and Levi were there to help her.

"Yes," she said.

Nathan sat behind his huge desk, watching her like she was some puzzle to be solved, some data point to analyze. "Well. *That's* interesting." With a small, irritated sigh, Nathan waved a hand dismissively. "Fine. Take your personal day. But don't make a habit of this."

She nodded, keeping her relief in check. "I won't.

Thank you. Please don't forget to approve it in the payroll system." She turned to leave, but his voice stopped her just before she reached the door.

"Skylar."

She turned back to find his expression unreadable again, but there was something resembling curiosity behind his eyes. Nathan Dyer almost never took a personal interest in people—partly because he thought it was unprofessional, but primarily it was because he simply didn't care about most people as long as they performed their duties to his satisfaction.

"Please don't make the mistake of believing Chester and I are the same. I know both of you quite well, and if this is something you've decided on, I know you have good reasons. I know you first came to work for me because Chester asked for a favor, but I hope *you* know that you've proven yourself to me a hundred times over."

Nathan's candor caught her off-guard. He was many things—demanding, impatient, a workaholic—but *concerned* was not one of them and concern was what she heard in his voice now. Was Nathan Dyer actually worried about her?

She hesitated for only an instant before offering him the safest answer.

"Yes."

Nathan watched her for another moment, then nodded once. "Good. I'll see you Thursday. We have that call with Denmark at 7:30, so make sure you're here by 7 o'clock at the latest."

Skylar slipped from the office, closing the door behind her. She was all the way back to her own office before her heart began beating normally again.

Chapter 9.

Skylar and Levi – Next Day

"No, Brian—everything's fine here. I just wanted to see how you're doing and make sure you guys have my new address."

Skylar shifted her phone to her other hand, then hit speaker and set it down on one of the cardboard boxes she'd already filled so she could tape up the final box. The roll of tape made a drawn out *scrrrriitch* noise.

"What was that?" Brian asked, his deep voice made somewhat echoey by the speaker phone.

"Just taping up a box. Everything's almost ready to go."

"You sure you want to move all the way out to Brooklyn, Sky? I'd be happy to help you find a place in town—I know a great realtor."

"Of course. I haven't seen much of Barrett or Levi lately, but they offered, and I think it's just what I need right now. I don't know how long I'll be staying at their house, but they're my best friends and it'll be a nice change of pace."

Brian was silent for a moment, and Skylar could feel the tension beginning to build. She was sure he wasn't thrilled with the idea of her living with two guys. He wasn't her father, but he was about as great a stepfather as a girl could ask for, and she knew he cared and worried about her. She was worried about him too—damn Natalie—but she really wanted *that* to come from her mother. She wasn't surprised Natalie hadn't told Brian yet. Skylar suspected her mother didn't believe she would tell Brian if Natalie didn't. She meant it in the moment, but afterwards, she was unsure herself. Was it her place to interfere in their marriage, even if it came from a place of wanting to help?

"This is all pretty sudden, Sky," Brian finally said. "You're sure you're okay?"

Skylar hesitated before responding. "We can talk about it some other time. I just wanted to check in with you and let you know I'm moving."

There was a triple knock on the door—*rap, rap, rap*—followed by two single knocks. Levi's signature.

"I have to go, Brian. Levi's here with the truck."

"All right. I'll give your mother your love when I see her."

Skylar paused, a trickle of ice shooting through her belly before disappearing. "Sure," she said. "Byyyyeee!" she added and cut the connection.

She darted across the apartment, weaving around stacked boxes and the tangle of extension cords she still hadn't coiled after unplugging the electronics she was taking with her. She yanked open the door, and saw Levi standing there. He wore a hoodie and his usual lopsided smile. A flat-billed cap reading GYM LIFE was pulled low over his thick blond hair and he carried a travel coffee mug in one hand.

"Hey," she said, a little breathless. She stepped aside to let him in. "Thanks for coming."

"Naturally," he said as he entered. "It'd be pretty dickish to invite you to stay with us and then tell you to figure it all out on your own." He laughed softly as his eyes swept the apartment's living room, then let out a low whistle. "Wow, this is it? I shouldn't have sprung for the big truck."

Skylar shut the door behind him and followed his gaze across the room. There really wasn't that much, was there? Seven or eight cardboard boxes she picked up on the way home from work the day before were filled with her books, some movies, CDs, toiletries, plus some household stuff, and some small electronics. Besides that, there were her clothes—at least those were easy to transport. Chet had early on claimed the bedroom's closet for his junk and she had purchased a rolling garment rack to serve as her own closet.

While frantically packing, hoping all the while that Chet wouldn't choose that morning to finally come home, it seemed like a lot of stuff, but looking at it from Levi's perspective, it was a pitifully small amount considering it constituted pretty much everything she owned.

All she said though, was "Yep. That's all of it."

Levi looked from the small cluster of boxes to the rolling rack of neatly zipped garment bags and then to the carefully wrapped LCD television leaning against the wall. "I honestly thought you'd have more. You've lived here, what, two years?"

"Two years, three months," she said, voice carefully neutral.

He turned to her, lifting a brow. "Makes your escape easier though, huh?"

"Yep," she said with a small, bitter smile.

She crossed to the rack and began checking the zippers on the bags, mostly just to keep her hands busy. Levi moved toward the TV.

"You sure you want to take this beast? It's light, but it's not exactly easy to maneuver. I'm not sure it'll fit in the bedroom out at the house either.

"I paid for it," she said firmly. "I paid for practically everything in this apartment, even if Chet was the one who mostly used the TV and video games and stuff. It's all mine and I'm taking it."

Levi gave a mock salute. "Aye, aye, cap'n. Fair enough. I respect petty revenge wholeheartedly."

She laughed under her breath. "It's… okay, it's partly that. But also, I need a TV. I might spend the next month doing nothing but binge-watching crappy reality shows to numb myself. Plus—" She whirled towards him. "*Cupcake Wars* gives you step-by-step instructions on how to make the winners' entries and I think I deserve some sugar."

"It is a time-honored and healthful coping mechanism," Levi deadpanned.

Skylar smirked, but it faded fast. She glanced at the boxes and felt that strange mix of shame and relief again. It really wasn't much. It wasn't *everything* she'd accumulated in her adult life, but it was everything she could take with her.

"You're really not taking any furniture?" Levi asked, his brow furrowing as he scanned the room. "You paid for all that too, I assume."

In the light of day—in which Skylar rarely got to see her apartment—the couch looked even worse than she realized. The fresh pizza grease was far from the only stain on it and one of the arms was ripped along the outside. The whole thing seemed to slump like it was exhausted after a long, hard life.

Skylar shook her head. "The couch is ruined. He never took care of anything. And I can't... I can't sleep in the bed again."

Her voice cracked slightly at the end, and Levi immediately softened, stepping closer but not pushing.

"I get it," he said. "New place, new energy. Leave the bad behind."

"Exactly."

"Barrett and I are working on the house here and there when we get the chance—we'll fix your room up any way you want, okay? Your own private queendom."

Skylar smiled at her friend and touched his arm lightly. "Thanks."

She moved away and pointed at the three tall boxes near the kitchen. "I'm taking the kitchen stuff too, by the way. The dishes, pots, utensils. He won't miss them. He never cooked. I'm not sure even he even knows how to use the microwave, honestly."

Levi nodded, already mentally calculating how to stack everything in the back of the truck. He had been worried about fitting everything in on the way over, but now he was concerned about how best to arrange it all so that nothing was damaged.

"Oh," she added. "And I'm taking the floor lamps. I like the warm lighting. It makes a place feel like home."

"You'll be building a whole new one, huh?" he said gently, looking around once more.

Skylar made a soft noise in her throat and nodded. "I have to. This place… it's not mine anymore. I mean, I guess it never really was. I was just kind of Chet's maid, cook, and fuck-toy before he—"

She choked off, her chest tight, feeling the heat growing in her cheeks and behind her eyes as she was suddenly overcome.

She thought she was past the worst of it—being with Barrett helped more than she ever would have imagined, gave her strength, and a kind of closure. At least she thought it had.

But now… now everything came back hard and fast, washing over her like a tidal wave and pulling her down. Everything she'd ignored, compartmentalized, shoved into mental closets to deal with later, later, *later*. And here it was, later, pressing down on her like a weight she could no longer carry. The endless compromises, the empty apologies from Chet, the loneliness, the feeling of being more of a servant than partner, how little of their life together had been hers. And what was she left with? A TV and some lamps.

"Hey, hey. Shh, shh, it's okay." Levi moved quickly to her, putting his hands lightly on her shoulders. When she didn't pull away, he wrapped both arms around her, pulling her in gently but firmly.

"Sky, it's okay, let it out. Leave it all behind. Leave

all the bad shit for that prick. Hell, let's fill this place with bad juju and maybe he'll choke on a burrito if he ever figures out how the microwave works."

Skylar tried to laugh, but it came out as kind of a strangled sob. The tears came hard, hot and silent at first, then louder as her shoulders began to shake. Her body pressed against Levi's, her face against his chest, his hoodie soaking up her tears as the kind of crying that comes from somewhere too deep to truly understand took hold of her.

Gently, Levi guided her to the beat-up couch and together they sank down onto the less-stained end of it. Skylar let herself collapse into Levi, letting him prop her up as she felt herself being drained with the tears that flowed from her. His arms were strong but gentle, and part of her couldn't help comparing them to how Barrett's had felt wrapped around her. Levi was taller than Barrett and more muscular, but one thing was the same: they both made her feel warm and safe and loved.

She didn't know how much time passed—five minutes, ten, maybe more. Eventually her sobs dulled to hiccoughs, and she exhaled a long, trembling breath.

"Sorry," she whispered, her voice hoarse.

"Don't be," he said gently. "You've been through hell, Sky. Anything you need or want to do is fine with me. I'll help you set fire to the place if you think it'll do any good."

She chuckled against his chest, eyes still wet. "I thought I was okay. I really did. But..."

"Look," he said. "I'm not that big into like, psychics and ghosts and stuff, but a house isn't just four walls and a roof. It's got energy, soaked up from the people who lived there, and this place drained the ever-living *fuck* out of you. It wouldn't be natural if it didn't upset you."

Skylar closed her eyes, pressing her cheek into his chest. "I hate that he made me feel like I owed him everything when he never gave me a single thing."

"You don't owe him anything," Levi said firmly. "You never did. You just… cared more than he deserved, I guess. You don't have to forgive Chet, Sky, but you have to forgive yourself, okay?"

Hearing that made her cry again. It was softer this time, quieter, for herself now rather than for what she had lost. Levi held tight, his thumb gently brushing her upper arm in small, steady circles.

Eventually, she shifted slightly, pulling back just enough to look at him. Her eyes were red, cheeks flushed and damp, but there was something clear in her expression. Levi's heart skipped. He'd known this woman more than half of his life, but he was seeing something new. It was a kind of openness, a raw vulnerability, that made her even more beautiful—unguarded, stripped bare of all the armor she had been forced to wear just to get through daily life the last few years.

"Levi," she said softly.

He looked down at her, his brows drawn together. "Yeah?"

She didn't answer with words.

She just looked at him for a long second then tilted her head a fraction.

He kissed her, and it felt as natural as breathing.

But the moment his lips touched hers, he froze. Realization crashed over him, and he pulled back, his hands lifting in panic, disengaging from her.

"Oh—God, Sky—I'm sorry," he stammered. "I shouldn't have done that. I don't know why I did it. I wasn't trying to—"

Skylar cut him off, sealing his lips with another kiss.

This time, she was the one closing the distance, her hand on his cheek, her lips soft but sure against his. Levi froze again, but only for a moment. His hands found her waist, and he kissed her back.

There was no urgency, no desperation—just

warmth and connection and the shared, undeniable knowledge that this wasn't about fixing her. It wasn't about taking advantage of a moment. It was about finally seeing each other—without noise, without Chet between them, without any of their history clouding their view of one another.

The kiss was long and soft and sweet—at first.

Something passed between them, transferred via their lips, and the heat that grew in both of their bodies flowed from one another and back again. Skylar's breath was coming quickly now, and she could feel Levi's heart beating through his sweatshirt. Without a word, she knocked the cap from his head then reached down, grabbed the hem of his hoodie, lifted it up and pulled it off. His shirt came off with it and his bare chest was exposed—she'd forgotten about the full-color Fozzy the Bear tattoo on his chest. He'd gotten it the summer before and she hadn't seen it since. God, she had barely seen anyone this year at all, but it didn't matter now. Levi was here and they were together.

"Oh, God," she moaned as Levi's lips moved down her throat, his tongue flicking lightly against her skin. She leaned back, whipped her t-shirt off, wriggled out of her bra and tossed both aside.

"Sky, Sky," Levi panted, his eyes on her breasts as if mesmerized. As he watched, her nipples hardened until they stood out like pink gumdrops just waiting to be nibbled and sucked. He leaned forward and she pushed his face down to her breasts, kissing the top of his head as he kissed her nipples.

His hands went back to her waist, and she leaned back against the couch, arching her spine to make her breasts thrust forward. His tongue swirled around her right nipple and then her left, and then he was kissing down her chest, down her belly, gently pushing her sideways and down until she was laying on the sofa. She lifted her hips and he yanked her tracksuit pants down to her knees, then off entirely, before pressing his face against her crotch. She felt his nose rubbing against her clit through her panties, and the texture of the fabric combined with the pressure he was exerting made her gasp.

Levi lifted his face, showing her the little kid grin she'd known since they *were* little kids, but there was something else in it now. Skylar had no doubt at all that the boy was gone and Levi was a man.

"You're soaked, Sky," he said, then pulled her panties aside and plunged a finger into her pussy as his tongue went to her clit. She gasped again, louder this time, as a pulsing surge of energy went through her entire body. Levi's tongue worked at counterpoint to his finger, sending her mind skirling away into some far off realm as the heat built inside her body.

Levi might have pleasured her for a minute or an hour she was so lost in sensation. "I'm gonna cum," she gasped finally. "I'm gonna cum!" She tangled her fingers in his hair and pressed his face into her pussy as hard as she dared, not wanting to hurt him, but wanting him closer, deeper, as near to the fires of her body as he could possibly be. His tongue moved more rapidly and he thrust a second finger inside of her, moving them faster and faster until she cried out and orgasmed explosively, her wetness gushing from her body, splattering Levi's face and soaking the broken down couch.

Levi sat back on his haunches, smiling up at her. She saw her own juices on his face and despite just having cummed, she was instantly aroused again. "Fuck me," she told him. "Fuck me, Levi. I want you inside me."

Levi's eyes widened at her bluntness, but then he grinned, stood and dropped his jeans. His cock was literally throbbing, bouncing up and down inside of his boxers as it twitched. He pulled his shorts off and climbed onto the couch as she spread her legs wide, parting her pussy with the fingers of one hand while she gripped his cock with the other and guided him towards her hole.

Levi's penis wasn't as thick as Barrett's, but it was very long and as it slid inside of her, she could feel the very tip pressing against her cervix, making her heart hammer faster in her chest and sending a fresh wellspring of wetness dripping from her pussy.

Skylar groaned as Levi thrust into her again and again, increasing in speed as he found his rhythm. She reached down, clutching his pumping buttocks with both hands. They were so firm, so powerful. She could feel that with her hands, but also in her thighs and in her pussy as he pushed against her, inside of her, over and over.

There were no words between them—they didn't need any. Levi found his pace and Skylar matched him as best she could, bringing her hips up to meet each thrust of his cock, feeling the slippery wetness on her thighs and against her belly as his pubes brushed her with each downward plunging motion. The heat was building up inside of her again and she could feel the heat in Levi, too. Sweat trickled down his chest and his face was red with his exertion.

"Almost," he grunted. "Almost—"

And then he pulled out of her and turned to one side, stroking his cock so quickly his hand seemed blurred. Skylar's own hand went to her pussy and she rubbed her clit, trying to match Levi's rhythm now as she had with her hips, and just as she started to orgasm again, Levi let out a groan and thick, ropey streams of cum gushed from his cock, splattering the sofa cushions again and again until a final, single drop fell from the tip of his head.

For a moment, Levi stood between her thighs, still-hard cock in his hand, and then he collapsed onto the sofa next to her, heedless of the damp spots they had both left on it. He leaned in and kissed Skylar deeply, but gently. When they broke apart, they stayed close, their foreheads resting together in silence.

"I needed that," Skylar whispered.

Levi hesitated. "I wanted it for so long," he finally

admitted. "I just…" He didn't finish the thought.

They both let out soft, half-laughs. They were both exhausted and surprised by this new aspect of their relationship—they were still friends, but now there was something more as well.

Just like with Barrett, Skylar thought.

That was something to consider, but for a few minutes, she could just sit here with Levi, both of them catching their breath, leaning into the quiet and each other.

Chapter 10

Skylar, Barrett, and Levi – That Evening

The scents of basil, lemongrass, and coconut milk filled the house in Bay Ridge's modest living room as Skylar set the last takeout container down on the coffee table. "Okay," she said, eyes sweeping the heavily laden table, "we have pad see ew, green curry, panang with tofu, and way too many spring rolls. Dig in, guys!"

Takeout for dinner was hardly a novelty in her life, but for once, this wasn't a case of a hastily ordered meal, picked up after a too long and too exhausting day at work, only to be gobbled down by a boyfriend who barely remembered to say thank you. It was a celebration of the reunion of three lifelong friends and Barrett and Levi welcoming Skylar into their home.

Barrett was already reaching for a spring roll. "You say 'too many,' but I call it good planning."

Levi, lounging on the far corner of the couch, a glass of wine in hand, grinned. "You know she always over-orders. This is tradition."

"The more you order, the more leftovers, so the more meals you get out of it. It's good financial planning." Skylar grinned and dropped onto the cushion between them. Her hair was up in a messy bun, sweatpants tied loosely around her waist, and she felt, if not entirely *relaxed*, at least not on edge for the first time in a long while. The warmth of the house surrounded all three of them in a kind of safety that she hadn't realized she'd been craving. It was almost—*almost*—like being a little girl again.

They dug into the food, and conversation drifted easily between the three of them: work updates (Levi's newest personal training client was a regular *Law & Order* guest-star), information about the neighborhood (Skylar found the Thai place within an hour of moving in, but Barrett and Levi assured her there were tons of great takeout options), and stories from their childhood (most of which had grown increasingly exaggerated with time).

Barrett, nursing his second glass of wine, leaned back against the plush sofa cushion and chuckled, deep in his throat. "Remember when Levi tried to make s'mores in the toaster?"

Levi groaned. "That was *your* idea!"

"I just said that the part of camp I missed most might have been s'mores," Barrett countered, gesturing with his glass. "You're the one who thought putting marshmallows on full broil was a good plan."

"I still have that scar," Levi said, holding up his arm, showing off the faint pink blotch just above his wrist.

Skylar laughed, genuinely happy, and realized she hadn't heard a genuine laugh of her own in a while. "God, I forgot about that. Your mom was so mad."

Barrett grinned. "She wasn't that mad about the toaster. She was mad about the fire extinguisher foam everywhere—and the melted marshmallow all over everything, and the melted chocolate on the floors, and the smell of sugar-scented smoke on everything in the house for a week."

All three of them laughed, and for a moment, everything felt like it used to—easy, familiar, light. For the first time in ages, they were the three *amigos* again, as Brian used to call them when they were kids.

But it wasn't *quite* the same, because underneath it all, there was something that simmered between them, a vague tension in the air that all three must have been aware of at least on some level.

Skylar could feel it in the way Barrett kept

glancing at Levi when the blond man was talking to her, at least when Barrett thought she wasn't looking. She saw it in Levi's foot tapping rapidly beneath the table every time Barrett moved a little too close to her. And they were both trying not to look at her too much—or maybe they were trying not to look at each other.

She didn't need a sixth sense to know why, but—

They wouldn't have… told each other, right? She wondered. All three of them were best friends, but Levi and Barrett had known each other almost literally their entire lives, and for the past couple of years they'd been more like the Dynamic Duo than the three *amigos* since Skylar wasn't around as much as she would have liked. Even if the guys hadn't told one another about the "moments" they each shared with her, they clearly knew something was different.

Skylar sipped her wine, letting the slight sting of the liquid on her tongue ground her as she stared down at her plate. This was supposed to be a celebration—new beginnings, new place, new chapter in her life and all that—but the unspoken tension was as tangible as the curry-smeared napkins littering the table.

Both of them had slept with her and no matter how much you told yourself it didn't matter, sex changed things. It always did, even if you didn't want it to, even if you swore to yourself and to the heavens above that nothing would change. Being intimate with someone you cared about made the relationship different.

She didn't regret it though. In a weird way, she was actually grateful to both of them.

Barrett had been there that awful night after the motel, when she fell apart in the back of his SUV and found comfort in the warmth and love and security of the closeness they shared. It wasn't planned. It just happened. And in the haze of heartbreak, his presence had been the anchor that she needed to keep herself from drifting away on a sea of pain.

Then, just that morning, Levi had kissed her when she broke down in the middle of her half-packed apartment. That hadn't been planned either, but it also wasn't meaningless. It felt... real. It was like something between the two of them had quietly been waiting its turn, searching for the right time to blossom, and then it did.

And now they were all in the same house and were going to be living together for the foreseeable future. They were sitting on the same couch, sharing Thai takeout, recalling memories of the years they'd already spent together. They were all pretending nothing had changed.

Skylar reached for a second helping of curry and broke the silence. "Who was in charge of dessert?"

"I was given wine duty," Barrett said. "And I bought two bottles, so I feel like I overachieved."

"I was going to get cookies or something," Levi added, "but then I forgot because someone called me six times asking what kind of curry she liked—the green or the red."

Skylar grinned, slightly sheepishly. "Well, I can't remember everything. Curry is curry."

"Except when it isn't, right?"

They all laughed, but the moment felt thinner than before. Skylar leaned back into the couch cushions and let her head fall against the backrest, staring at the ceiling for a moment. She could feel the boys on either side of her. She could feel their warmth, both from their bodies and from their hearts. But there was also the weight of what still hadn't been said.

She closed her eyes.

"I love you guys," she said quietly, not moving. "Both of you. You know that, right?"

Barrett was visibly startled by the softness in her voice. "Yeah," he said. "Of course."

Levi nodded slowly, uncertainly. "Sure." He cast a look at the other man. "We know."

She didn't open her eyes. "Good. Because I don't

know what I'd do without either of you." Still without looking, she reached out, placing one hand on Barrett's thigh and the other on Levi's. "You saved me. Like, for real—I was basically drowning and you guys threw me a lifeline."

They knew, both of them, that she wasn't only talking about the move or the break-up, but about *them*. Their friendship. The history that stretched back more than half of their lives.

Their friendship was more than a lifeline—it was life itself. And if this strange new thing that happened, the overlapping of comfort and friendship and sex and intimacy, threatened that bond, she didn't know what she'd do. Just the thought of losing either of these people felt like being torn apart.

Barrett stood first, stretching. "Okay. I'm gonna do the thing, I guess." He began gathering takeout containers and dirty dishes, piling cartons on top of plates.

"I guess a little adulting won't hurt me," Levi said, standing up a beat later.

Skylar stayed where she was, watching them carry dishes and cardboard containers to the kitchen, then hearing the low murmur of their voices as they figured out what to refrigerate and what to toss.

She loved them. Both of them. And being here, with Barrett and Levi—for the first time in a long time, she didn't feel alone. She felt safe and comfortable and loved.

But she also knew that whatever this new thing was between her and each of the boys couldn't stay undefined forever. If left too long it could become a ticking timebomb, one she desperately didn't want to explode.

Chapter 11.

Skylar and Barrett – Later That Evening

Barrett knocked lightly on the open doorframe
with the back of his knuckles, peeking into the room
where Skylar knelt amid a wreckage of cables, half-
unpacked boxes, and a TV that looked just fine in the old
apartment, but monstrously huge in this smallish bedroom.

"Hey," he said quietly.

Skylar looked up, a strand of hair that had escaped
the messy bun falling into her face. She blew at it and
scowled at the tangle of cords in her hands. "Hi. If you've
come to make fun of me for my questionable interior
design skills, take a number and wait in line. Levi's already
swung by to laugh at my room to TV-size ratio."

The corner of Barrett's mouth quirked in what
might have been a tiny smile as he stepped into the room.
"I never make fun, Sky. I just silently judge." He turned to
the huge TV, giving it a skeptical look. "You really
planning on turning your bedroom into a home theater?"

Skylar huffed. "Look, I told Levi this, but it's one
of the only things I actually own. Chet treated everything
like it was his, but I paid for everything from the TV to his
stupid video game system, and there was no way in hell
was I leaving any of it behind."

Despite herself, she was getting angry at the
thought of everything Chet had taken from her. She knew
neither of the guys meant any harm. Objectively, it was
funny having such a huge TV in a bedroom of this size,
but she explained her reasons and they were important to

her. She wished they would stop harping on the subject.

Barrett crouched next to her. "Look—I'm sorry. I get it, and I didn't mean to upset you."

She paused, head tilted downwards, the anger already fading. "I know. Sorry for flipping out."

"Nothing to be sorry about. I was out of line." He pushed aside a tangle of cables hanging from the input jacks on the side of the huge television. "Let's at least get this thing set up right and situated so it doesn't fall over and crush you in your sleep."

"Ha. Ha," she said, but moved aside to give him room. As he started feeding cords through the slots in the back of the TV stand, she sat back on her heels and watched him.

"Thanks," she said.

Barrett glanced up. "It's nothing."

"It's not nothing," she said quietly. "None of this is. I wasn't just being sappy before—at dinner. I meant what I told you guys."

The weight of that hung for a moment. Everything that had happened over the past few days, the unraveling of her relationship, an unthinkable betrayal by her own *mother* of all people, the move. It all added up to the disarrangement of her entire life.

Barrett didn't answer right away. He plugged in a HDMI cable, then sat back beside her, cross-legged on the floor.

"I've been thinking about something," he said, voice low. "Since that night. At the motel?" He glanced towards her.

Skylar tensed, her breath catching, but she didn't interrupt. She tried not to think about it, but it was impossible. Chet, her boyfriend, and Natalie, her mother— together. The things both of them had said. It was too much, and she wanted to forget it all, but her mind kept picking at it, like a scab. She knew it would only fester if she didn't leave it alone, but it was still too raw.

"When Chet was yammering," Barrett went on, "he said something weird. About your mom. He said something like... she 'wasn't even—' and then Natalie cut him off before he could finish."

Skylar's brows furrowed. "Yeah," she said slowly. "I remember that. I thought he was just... rambling, trying to lash out. Being cruel. He's not really a quick thinker." She laughed bitterly. "Arguments with him were always like that—you'd make some totally valid point and he'd scrunch his face up and call you names or something because he couldn't think of, like, an actual rebuttal."

Barrett nodded. "Yeah, maybe it was just him being a dick—I mean, that's pretty much his default setting. But he wasn't talking to *you*. He was talking to *me*. It wasn't just a taunt or anything. It felt... pointed. Like he was trying to tell me something, like it was something that would excuse it all, make it not as bad as it looked or something." He shook his head. "I don't know. It just seemed out of character and it's been bothering me."

Skylar frowned, searching her memory. "You think he actually meant something by it? Like, he knows something I don't about my mom?"

"I don't know," Barrett admitted. "But I've been working with Mr. Whittington for a while now, and maybe I'm not a real detective or anything, but I've seen enough of how he works to trust a gut feeling when it sticks. And this one has stuck—big time."

Skylar turned the words over in her mind. *She wasn't even...* What? What was Natalie *not*? What was Natalie *not* that would make it okay—at least in Chet's mind—for her to sleep with Skylar's boyfriend? Not a considerate person? Not a decent human being? Not... her mother?

The last one sent a strange chill down her spine.

"I don't know what he meant," Barrett continued, "but Natalie shut him down fast. And I don't think it was just because he was being a jerk."

Skylar felt her stomach twist. "So you think... what? That there's something I don't know but should?"

Barrett hesitated. "I think there might be. At the very least, there's something she doesn't want you to know. Whether you *should* know it..." He lifted his hands in a gesture of helplessness.

Skylar looked down at her own hands. Her fingers were curled loosely in the hem of her oversized sweatshirt, the one she wore when she wanted comfort, not style.

"Natalie's been... hard to read for a long time," she said. "When I was little, she was different. She called us 'the Hunt girls,' like we were more buddies than mom and daughter, and we had a lot of fun. I'm not sure when she changed exactly, but sometime around the end of elementary school or the beginning of middle school— around then, anyway—she started to, like... cool off? Like, she was still my mom, but not my friend? Like I was more of a responsibility than anything else. It got worse when she started dating a lot, and then, after she married Brian, it was like I was just this person who lived in her house. She hardly talked to me unless she wanted something and there wasn't really much she wanted from me."

She paused, staring blankly at the dark, empty face of the huge television set, not even seeing her own reflection in it, but looking back into her memories. "I didn't understand it, but I didn't think too much about it either. I guess I didn't want to. Brian was always good to me—and I had you guys." She reached out and squeezed Barrett's bicep.

Barrett's gaze was fixed on her. "And you've never thought of a reason for any of this? I mean, there's one thing I can think of that would make it all make sense."

The silence that followed was so thick that Skylar almost felt like she couldn't breathe.

"You're not saying what I think you're saying," she whispered.

"I'm not saying anything for sure," Barrett said

quickly, trying to calm the sudden spike of panic in her voice. "It's just a theory. And maybe it's wrong. Maybe it's nothing. But I can't stop thinking about it. If Natalie *isn't* your mom… everything you've told me makes more sense. She cooled off because something happened, something you were too young to understand or maybe even notice, but it was important for Natalie and it changed how she saw you. Or at least her relationship to you."

Skylar stared at the TV, focusing on a soft blue light blinking at its base. Somehow, the enormity of it— the huge black screen, the suggestion, the silence in the room—felt like too much all at once.

"For most of my life," she murmured, "I just thought that Natalie found me hard to love for some reason. Like I was too much for her, or not enough. That's how she made me feel, but I tried not to let it bother me because you guys were there for me and Brian was pretty much my dad when I needed him to be."

Barrett gently reached out and placed a hand over hers. "Sky…"

Skylar looked at him then, her eyes wide and wet. So much had happened and now… this?

"I don't want it to be true," she said, her voice cracking. "But if it *is*—if she really isn't my mother—then everything I've ever known about my life is a lie."

Barrett held her gaze. "If you want, I can look into it. Carefully. Discreetly. Mr. Whittington has access to databases with birth records, and open adoption filings. He wouldn't even necessarily need to know why I'm asking— although if we want to do this the right way, it wouldn't hurt to have his help. He's pretty good at what he does."

Skylar nodded, slowly. "Okay," she said, voice small. "But only if you're sure. I mean, I don't want to take up your time for something that's just—"

"I'm sure, Sky," he said, and meant it. "You want to know, don't you?"

She nodded, then leaned against him, not in

confusion or need like she had that night in his SUV, just—gratefully. Grateful he was there and had been thinking about her this whole time. Grateful that he cared enough to want to help.

They sat like that for several moments, the only sound the low hum of the TV, the mystery of Natalie looming over them, but at the same time, bringing them together.

Chapter 12.

Skylar – Next Afternoon

The humming white noise of the office barely registered in Skylar's mind as she closed her office door behind her. She stood a moment at the window, looking out at the view of the city—not as nice as Nathan's, but not too shabby either—that she rarely got to enjoy. Finally, she settled into her desk chair and let herself relax for a moment. It was the first time all day that she hadn't been scheduled to be in this meeting or that or running around like a chicken sans head, trying to meet some impossible demand of Nathan's.

But the day was going well. The Denmark call was better than she expected. She hadn't expected anything *catastrophic* or anything, but there were challenges to work past. Nikolaj hadn't even mentioned the last-minute change to the export forms though, which she expected to be a sticking point, and Nathan, while predictably erratic, had managed to stay on task with only mild redirection from her. It was a small miracle. Nathan was an excellent CEO, she reflected, but only when he had guardrails. Left to his own designs, he'd never get anything done because his mind was always going in a million different directions until the ideas of streamlining or new products or new markets or new advertising campaigns bogged down into one unworkable morass.

But that's why Skylar was there and that's why she had job security, something she hadn't been sure of until she and Nathan talked the other day. It was a relief to know that he saw her as an asset on her own merits and not just as something that was—what? An extension of Chet? Well, it didn't matter. And she didn't have to categorize it when it didn't matter anymore. Nathan needed her, they both knew it, and he had finally admitted it. Her mind was at ease in that respect at least.

Skylar exhaled, pressing her palms to her cheeks for a moment. Her to-do list was still longer than she would have liked, but the worst of the day was behind her. Maybe she could get through the rest of it without incident.

Her phone buzzed quietly on the desk beside her. She picked it up automatically, expecting a calendar notification or another email, but what she saw instead gave her pause.

Brian (Stepdad): *Hey, Sky. Can you please give me a call when you get a minute?*

The formality of the text made her smile, tight and small. Brian always texted like he was writing from his work email, even to her. She could almost hear his voice in her head, polite and a little unsure of itself when it came to personal matters. *Must be a generational thing*, she thought.

But something about the wording stuck with her. *Can you please give me a call…* Not urgent, but not casual either. They didn't text all that much, but this felt just off enough to make her stomach flutter.

She looked at the time—1:47pm. Nathan had a thirty-minute "media optics strategy sync" at 2:00, which meant she had exactly twelve minutes to make a call if she wanted to avoid being caught in another impromptu TED Talk about the importance of time-management from the CEO himself. The irony of that would be completely lost on Nathan, of course, but he couldn't stand it when other people lost track of time. That was a privilege reserved for the high and mighty.

Skylar hesitated a moment longer, then pulled her phone off the desk and stood, turning to face the window.

She clicked Brian's contact icon and pressed the phone to her ear.

It rang only once before he picked up.

"Skylar," Brian said, a little breathless, as if he was surprised to see who the call was from. "Thanks for calling so quickly."

"Hey, Brian," she said, trying to sound casual even as her nerves spiked. "Everything okay?"

There was a beat of silence.

"Could we talk?" he asked.

Skylar frowned. "We're talking now."

"I mean…" He hesitated. "Could we talk in person?"

She blinked. "Like… today?"

"If possible."

She leaned against the wall, feeling the thud of her heart begin to quicken. "Is something wrong?"

Brian was quiet again, and when he finally answered, his voice was softer than she'd ever heard it and it carried a note she could only describe as fear. "I need to have a conversation about your mother."

Skylar froze.

The buzzing of the fluorescent light overhead suddenly seemed deafening.

"What about her?" she asked, her voice thinner than she intended.

"I'd rather explain it face to face," he said. "I don't really—look, how about this? Please come to dinner tonight. I'll have something brought in, okay? Something nice," he added, as if that wasn't a given. The man was a hedge fund millionaire. He wasn't going to serve Chef Boyardee from the can.

The thought of dinner was a fragment of a second's distraction before a thousand other ideas collided in her mind. What could Brian want to talk about that needed to be said face to face? They had never really had anything like a "serious" conversation before. They had a warm relationship, and Brian had absolutely been there for her more than once when she was a teenager and needed a dad, but they weren't really close. She thought of Barrett's theory, Chet's cut-off sentence, the years of subtle distance from Natalie, of feeling like she was someone next to Natalie's life rather than in it. Was it like that for Brian too? When she lived in Brian's townhouse with him and her mother, they seemed happy, at least from her semi-outsider's perspective, but naturally there would be things they wanted to keep hidden from her… Maybe Natalie's cheating wasn't anything new to him. Maybe she'd been doing it for years and Brian had known all along. Brian didn't deserve that. He was a good guy.

"Okay," she said after a long breath. "I can come after work."

"Thank you," Brian said, sounding relieved.

"Brian?" she added before he could hang up. "Will my mom be there?"

"No," he said after a pregnant pause.

"Oh, well… I'll see you soon then," she said, ending the call.

Skylar stayed where she was for a long moment, staring at her screen, watching the minutes tick closer to two o'clock.

She felt like someone had tilted the floor beneath her. All the clarity she'd been working toward—leaving Chet, starting over, reconnecting with her real friends—was suddenly smudged at the edges by a past she thought she understood.

The conversation with Barrett replayed in her head.

"She wasn't even—"

"Sky, what if that's what he meant?"

And now Brian wanted to talk. About Natalie. Just the two of them.

She took a shaky breath, squared her shoulders, and stepped back towards her desk.

Nathan was in the hallway now, waving her toward his glass office, an iced espresso in one hand and a whiteboard marker in the other, as though the world hadn't just shifted under her feet.

Skylar gave him a quick nod, straightened the hem of her blazer, smoothed her skirt across her hips and then picked up her phone and tablet and followed Nathan.

She could survive another few hours of this. She didn't know if she could survive whatever was waiting for her at Brian's house.

Chapter 13.

Skylar – That Evening

Skylar: *Gonna be home late tonight guys. Gotta stop by Brian's.*

Within seconds, two new messages appeared in the chat group almost simultaneously.

Barrett: *Want company?*

Levi: *Want company?*

Skylar made a small noise in her throat. She appreciated the guys' support, but this might turn into an issue. When all three of them were together, everything was fine, but one on one, it seemed like both of the guys were just a little more eager to be helpful, a little quicker responding when talking to her. She knew why, of course.

"I gotta think about this," she muttered out loud. The woman nearest her on the elevator—a face Skylar recognized from one of the lower floors, but didn't have a name to go with it—glanced at her, but said nothing. Skylar flashed the other woman a quick smile, which she returned before turning silently back to face the elevator doors.

Skylar: *Thanks! I'm good. I'll eat at Brian's so don't wait for me.*

She placed her phone in her purse. The elevator opened and she moved out into the main lobby with the half-dozen other people who rode down with her. It was after six, but the TechnoFirm lobby was still buzzing, people going in every which way, trying to make sure the flow of international business—and cash—stayed flowing.

If Nathan and his wife didn't have a personal dinner engagement, Skylar would probably still be among their masses instead of getting out nearly on time and heading to Brian's.

Dinner... and what else? She wondered.

The glass door closed behind Skylar with a soft hiss, sealing her into the kind of silence that only came from money. It was a silence padded with soft rugs, thick walls, and the gentle hum of climate control that kept everything at exactly the right temperature.

Brian Rose's townhouse on Central Park South was as pristine as she remembered, a marriage of minimalism and luxury, with curated modern art on the walls and furniture that looked like it cost more than a year of her rent at the old apartment. Polished concrete floors reflected the recessed lighting overhead. The place smelled faintly of lemon furniture polish and something expensive and herbal she couldn't name. That was new—she didn't remember that herbal scent from the years she lived here.

In a way, it was hard to believe that she had ever lived here. Brian made her feel welcome after he and Natalie were married, and of course, she had her own bedroom and everything, but she somehow always felt more like she was a guest in a high-end hotel than living in her own home. Natalie was partially responsible for that, the distance she put between them growing wider almost from the instant Skylar returned from that first summer at camp. Mostly though, it was that she could never think of herself as being a rich girl, or even the stepdaughter of a rich man. She wanted to be comfortable, of course—who didn't?—but luxury simply wasn't ever her style, and this house was nothing if not luxurious. There was even an indoor pool in the basement, for God's sake!

"Skylar," Brian said, his smile small but sincere as he stepped toward her, coming from the kitchen. It was open concept, barely divided from the dining room off of the main living space by a narrow breakfast bar. The entire first floor of the house was open, in fact, with minimal barriers placed at strategic locations to give the *idea* of division—living room, kitchen, dining room, library— rather than actually dividing those spaces into separate rooms.

Brian was dressed in a slate blue sweater and dark jeans, his salt-and-pepper hair perfectly combed, like he had just stepped out of a commercial for tasteful wealth. He was about five foot ten, around two hundred pounds. He was heavyset without being fat, with a face that was handsome, but would have been bland without the faint weathering lines that age had given him. She thought that Barrett might look a little like Brian when he was the same age--they weren't built the same way, but there were definite similarities in their faces.

Skylar offered her stepfather a smile as he leaned in to give her a brief, awkward hug. "Hi, Brian. Thanks for having me over."

"Of course. I really appreciate you coming, it's— look, can I get you something? Tea? Coffee? I have beer, or whiskey if you prefer." He was nervous, that much was plain. Skylar couldn't remember ever seeing him like this.

She shook her head. "Not just now, thanks. I'm good."

Brian nodded and motioned toward the sitting area by the floor-to-ceiling windows. Central Park spread out beyond the glass in its early spring palette—pale green buds and lingering winter gray still vying for dominance.

She moved across the room, the pencil-point heels of her shoes echoing in the open space, and sat on one of the low-profile couches that felt more like an art installation than furniture. Brian sat across from her, folding his hands together, elbows resting on his knees.

"I appreciate you coming," he said again. "I know this isn't exactly convenient."

Skylar offered a humorless smile. "I don't even

know what convenient means anymore." She winced at her own tone. "Sorry. I'm just—it's been a lot lately."

Brian nodded slowly. "From what you've told me, I can imagine."

Brian took a deep breath, glanced out of the window, then slapped his thighs and stood. He moved to a small bar in a corner of the sitting area, wedge-shaped, built directly into the corner, selected a glass and a bottle and poured himself a splash of whiskey. Before sampling it, he turned to Skylar, silently lifting the bottle in offer. She shook her head. Her hands were clasped in her lap and her gaze drifted towards the window as Brian drank off the inch of amber liquid in his glass then added another. The ticking of an antique clock somewhere deeper in the townhouse was the only sound between them for a long moment.

"I don't know how to say this, Skylar," Brian finally said, moving back towards the couch where he sat before. His voice was low, as if someone might be listening. "I wouldn't say I'm a proud man, exactly, but I've never liked asking for help. I simply don't know what else to do though."

Skylar blinked and looked at him. "About what?"

"Natalie. She's… gone."

"Gone?" Skylar echoed.

Brian shook his head and sank slowly down onto the couch, careful of his glass. "Disappeared. She's done it before, here and there," he said, swirling the whiskey, looking at it instead of Skylar. "Sometimes for a night, sometimes two. Usually, she's back within a day or, if not, she texts to say she's out of town or staying with a friend. Always vague. Never gives me a chance to ask questions. But she always comes back. This is the first time she's been gone longer than two days and I'm worried. I've tried texting, and calling. The calls go right to voicemail and the texts sit unread."

"How often does she do this?" Skylar asked, her

tone flat.

He hesitated. "Maybe… five or six times a year. Sometimes more."

Skylar leaned back on the sofa. The sting of what she'd seen at the motel had already ripped a canyon through her understanding of her mother. But this… this erratic, unaccounted-for vanishing act was a layer she hadn't even known existed.

"And you never asked where she really goes or what she's doing?" she asked, disbelieving.

Brian smiled faintly, but it didn't reach his eyes. "I did. Once. It didn't go well."

"What happened?"

"She told me it wasn't my business. That I could either trust her or not, but if I ever tried to track her or dig into it, she'd leave for good. That was a long time ago, Sky. Before I realized how… complicated she was." He drained the last of his drink. "I backed off."

Skylar sat with that thought for a moment. The silence between them became heavier, threatened to become smothering. They both loved Natalie, but in different ways. Even after what Natalie had done to her, Skylar still loved her mother. She wasn't sure she could ever forgive Natalie, and she absolutely would never forget, but it didn't mean she didn't love the older woman—and that was part of what made it hurt so much. She understood Brian better with that realization.

"And you love her," she said. It wasn't a question.

Brian looked at her, his brown eyes quietly vulnerable. "I do."

She looked away, staring out the window towards Central Park, where shadows were stretching long and blue-gray across the greenery as the day slipped toward evening.

"But I simply don't know what do with her. She hasn't been home since—"

"Since Tuesday night," Skylar finished for him,

voice barely above a whisper.

Skylar felt a sick twist in her gut. The image of her mother, scantily clad and barely reacting to the volcanic shock she unleashed on her own daughter, resurfaced like acid reflux. Was Natalie still in that motel room—or did she walk out of it and out of her life too?

"She hasn't texted or called?" Skylar asked, already knowing the answer.

Brian shook his head. "Nothing. No credit card charges, either. I checked. She has her own checking account, she could get cash or use a debit card, but I don't know how much she actually has of her own money." He seemed faintly embarrassed. "Mostly, she charges things and I pay the bills when the statements arrive." He composed himself slightly. "Anyway, she didn't take much with her when she left. Just an overnight bag and a purse. Her passport is still in the safe in my den upstairs."

"Have you called the police?" she asked before she could stop herself, knowing the answer to that too. If Brian had called the police, why would they be having this discussion?

"I can't," he said quickly, running a hand through his graying hair. "Sky, you know what she's involved in— those women's leadership groups, all the activism. If the police got involved and this went public... even if they located her, she wouldn't come back after that. She'd never forgive me."

"Over a little embarrassment," Skylar finished coldly.

Brian's jaw tightened. "It would ruin her. She has a very carefully cultivated image, Sky."

"I know," she said carefully, "But she's been hiding things from you for how long? And now she's just gone. Don't you think that matters more than her public image?"

"Of course it matters!" he said, his voice rising before he caught himself. He looked away, ashamed. "I'm sorry. I just… You may not believe it, but I've always loved Natalie. She's not an easy person to love, but I do and have for fifteen years. I won't do anything to endanger our relationship."

Skylar folded her arms. "Do you think she's in danger?"

"I don't know." He exhaled shakily. "But I'm scared. This is different."

"Different how?"

"She's never been gone this long. Never without even a text. Not in all the time we've been married." He leaned forward. "Sky, I don't know where she goes, I told you that, and we've never talked about it—I told you what she said—and I didn't push harder because frankly I was afraid to know. Maybe you can't understand this, but I need Natalie. I need your mother in my life and I'm afraid that if I start prying, that really will be the end of it."

Skylar stared at him, stunned by his honesty, his vulnerability. She felt she was learning more about Brian Rose than she had in the nearly six years she lived beneath his roof.

"You think she's in some kind of trouble?" she asked after a beat.

He nodded. "I don't know. I don't know where she is. I don't even know *who* she is anymore."

Skylar looked down at her hands. Natalie's lies, now this vanishing act, and the strange familiarity of the text messages on Chet's watch… And Brian's desperation, a man who should have had every advantage in the world but was just as lost as Skylar felt. Skylar had started finding her way, but she wasn't sure if she could—or even wanted—to help Brian find his. It wasn't anything against Brian, it was more than she didn't want to help to inflict Natalie on him again.

Skylar turned toward the window, her heart suddenly fluttering in her chest. She had come here unsure of what Brian wanted to talk about, but thinking—maybe more like hoping—that she might get closure to the chaos that had erupted around her over the last few days. On the Uber over, she imagined all sorts of scenarios: Natalie admitting to Brian that she cheated and Brian leaving her; Brian finding out on his own and leaving her. Every scenario, she realized now, ended with Natalie somehow being punished for the pain she had inflicted on both Skylar and Brian. But instead of any of the things she imagined, she had walked into a mystery, one she wasn't sure she was ready to solve or if she even wanted to.

She couldn't answer the questions either she or Brian had about Natalie, but before she even tried, she had to answer one question for herself: if Natalie had vanished into the shadows, did Skylar want to be the one to drag her back out?

Chapter 14.

Skylar and Barrett – That Night

Skylar stepped into the dimly lit foyer of the house in Bay Ridge, shutting the door behind her with a soft click. The scent of the place was already becoming familiar even after just one night in it: something faintly floral and the subtle smell of old hardwood. It should have been comforting, but it only emphasized how the visit with Brian unsettled her. She learned so much about both her mother and Brian, and their relationship, that it was still hard to process.

She kicked off her shoes, her shoulders stiff with the day's exertions and her mind buzzing from the strained evening. Despite the plush setting and chef-prepared meal Brian insisted on having delivered, there had been nothing luxurious about the atmosphere. It was just the two of them at the big dining room table, each of them pretending to be fine, poking at their food and making painfully forced small talk while carefully sidestepping what they were both thinking about.

Where could she be?

Brian had asked the question softly, without accusation, but Skylar still bristled at the implication, as if she knew something and was withholding it. She knew that was her guilt talking, telling her that Natalie was her mother and that she might have been the last person to see Natalie so she *should* know.

But the truth was: "I don't know," she'd said simply. "I haven't heard from her in days."

They hadn't said much after that and when dinner was finished and there was nothing more to even pretend to say, they shared a brief hug and said goodbye and now Skylar was standing in the quiet of the house in Brooklyn.

She was completely drained. She dropped her bag near the hallway table and made her way to her bedroom, unbuttoning her coat, and then undoing the braid in her hair as she moved through the house. Her thoughts were a tangled mess, a whirling jumble of memories and questions, mixed with the realization that even if she wanted to track her mother down... she had no idea where to begin. She realized that night at the motel that she hadn't known the woman very well at all. She was starting to realize that Natalie had always been something of a shapeshifter, always in control of what she revealed. But she was always around, somewhere before and now, for the first time, Natalie was gone in a way that felt like it might truly be final.

And she didn't know how she felt about that. Part of her knew that she and Brian were both better off without Natalie in their lives. Look at all the damage Natalie had done in just a couple of days!

But love isn't logical and Brian clearly still loved and wanted Natalie back. Skylar also had to admit that no matter what Natalie did, she still loved her mother. She wasn't sure how that love would take form now— obviously nothing could be the same between them—but she did still love her.

Skylar sat on the edge of her bed and sighed, rubbing her eyes, wondering if there was anything at all she could do besides calling the police and letting them handle it. She had promised Brian that she wouldn't though—not yet. Not until every other option was exhausted.

There was only one option Skylar could think of though and it wasn't one she liked. Not at all. There was one other person who definitely saw Natalie after Skylar had.

She pulled out her phone, thumbed to Chet's contact, but hesitated. She didn't want to talk to him, didn't want to hear his voice. But he might know something about Natalie. She knew that their little motel rendezvous hadn't been a one-time thing, and Chet wasn't the kind of person to stop doing something just because he was caught. She didn't believe Natalie was either, not after the conversation they had in the doorway of that motel room.

She hit the call button.

The phone rang once. Then a recording played:

"We're sorry. The number you have dialed is not in service. Please check the number and try again."

Skylar blinked slowly then narrowed her eyes. She pulled the phone away, frowned at the screen, then tried again. The same message played after a single ring.

For a moment, she was confused. Then it hit her: *the phone account.* It had been in her name, but after everything that happened, she moved the lease on the apartment and all the utilities into Chet's name, including calling the cell provider and asking them to remove her name from the account and reach out to Chet about putting it in his name. She was sure the cell company would have tried to get in touch with him, but Chet must have blown them off. Typical.

"Guess they shut it off," she muttered, thinking of how quickly companies could move when their bottom line might be at stake.

The funny thing was that it felt final in a weird way. She couldn't reach him. Couldn't yell at him. Couldn't demand answers.

Not that she expected any. Chet had always been a coward. If Natalie was hiding with him, they were probably holed up somewhere Skylar didn't even know existed, feeding off each other's toxicity, reveling in sex and alcohol and whatever else Natalie was into that the people who loved her had never known about.

The thought made Skylar's skin crawl.

She stood abruptly and walked to the bedroom window, cracking it open a sliver. Cold night air rushed in, crisp and bracing, and she leaned against the frame, breathing deeply.

Somewhere out there in the darkness, her mother was either hiding, running, or both. And Skylar had the sinking feeling this wasn't just about Chet. There was more. Something older, deeper. Something that had been kept from her for years.

She turned at the sound of a knock on the door.

"Hey," Barrett said.

"Hey. I thought you guys were out—all the lights were off."

"I was in my room. Levi's got a special session with that 'celebrity' client of his. How was dinner?"

Skylar took a slow breath through her nose, wondering how to even respond to that. Before she could decide, a small bitter laugh erupted from her.

"That good, huh?" Barrett said, a small, wry smile appearing on his lips. "Wanna tell me about it?"

She hesitated, then said, "Give me a second to get out of these clothes and into something more human."

Without a word, Barrett backed out of the room, closing the door as he did. Skylar quickly stripped out of her skirt and blouse and blazer, took off her bra, and put on a pair of pink lounging pajamas. She rarely had time to lounge the last couple of years, but they were warm and comfortable.

"Okay!" she called towards the door and flopped down onto the bed. A moment later it reopened and Barrett asked, "Decent?"

Despite herself, Skylar smiled. "Sure."

Barrett came back into the room, but went no farther than the doorway, where he leaned nonchalantly. "So not good, huh?"

Skylar briefly described the conversation she had with Brian and the situation with Natalie. As she spoke, Barrett's calm demeanor cracked around the edges. She could see the anger simmering inside of him—anger for her and Brian's sake, for the pain Natalie was causing them—but if you didn't know him well, you would see only a quiet, stoic young man whose thoughts were a mystery.

When she was done, Barrett moved closer and sat on the edge of the bed, twisting to face her. "What now?"

"I don't know," Skylar admitted, eyes on her toes, pointed at the ceiling. The robin's egg blue polish on her toenails was cracked and chipped. How long ago had she done her nails? Two weeks? At least that. Just a quick few minutes of luxury she'd given herself on one of the nights she came home late from work and Chet was nowhere to be found. It was almost funny—Chet disappearing occasionally was a relief, but Natalie doing the same thing was causing all this havoc.

Skylar turned, meeting Barrett's eyes. "She's *wrecked* people, Barrett. Me. Brian. Probably others too. Probably Chet by the time she's done with him—not that he has far to go." She laughed again, but without any humor. "Should anyone even *want* to find her?"

"You could call the police and let them worry about it. It's their job and then it'd be out of your hands."

"I suggested that. Brian said he didn't call them because it would be embarrassing for her. *Embarrassing.* Like this is about her image. Like my mother is some socialite princess who can't have scandal attached to her name."

Her face began to flush, with anger or pain or frustration—she didn't even know anymore. "Wall Street wizard Brian, with all his money and power… he could have anything, but he wants *her* and he doesn't even *know* her. He's been living with someone who just disappears for days at a time, and he doesn't even ask where she's been."

Barrett made a small sound of understanding. "Maybe he's scared to ask. And maybe that makes him weak, but… I think he loves her and he doesn't want to call the police because he feels like if someone else gets involved, instead of letting her figure things out herself and come back when she's ready, he'll lose her."

Skylar looked down at her hands in her lap, twisting the fabric of her pajama top. "That's not love. That's just—I don't know what it is."

Barrett gently lay a hand on her thigh. "That's because you're different. You're not Natalie or Brian. You're you, Skylar Hunt, and you don't have to understand them to live your own life."

The room fell quiet, just the hum of the city outside the window and the soft electronic thrum of her too-large TV in rest mode.

She met his eyes. There was always something so steady in Barrett even when they were children. He wasn't flashy or loud or boisterous like Levi. He was dependable. She knew that he could see her at her worst and still wouldn't walk away.

"Barrett?" she said softly.

"Yeah?"

"I don't even understand myself or what I'm doing. With my life. With… you. With Levi." She looked away. "We had that… moment in your car the other night. I don't want there to be any secrets, so I guess I should tell you…"

Like a band-aid, she told herself, not for the first time.

"At my apartment, yesterday—Levi and I, well, we had a 'moment' too."

For an instant, something sharp passed across Barrett's expression.

Quickly, she added, "I just… I want to be honest. With you both. I'm trying to figure it all out, but—"

"I know you're hurting and you're mixed up. You're not the only one."

"I know," she said, looking up, meeting his eyes again. "Everything is just so… *weird.*"

"You're allowed to not have it all figured, Sky. We all are."

Solid. Dependable. Caring. Barrett.

Her throat tightened. "Thanks," she whispered.

He reached over and laced their fingers together gently. She was a little surprised, but didn't resist. "Whatever happens, I'm not going anywhere. We've been through too much for that."

She squeezed his hand gratefully. "Neither am I."

They sat like that for a long moment, surrounded by the chaos of her half-unpacked room, the emotional storm inside her still raging, but soothed by Barrett's presence and by his touch. And as they sat together, close and in contact, a different kind of storm began welling up inside of her. Barrett told her she didn't have to figure everything out, but in that moment, feeling the warmth of Barrett's skin against hers and remembering how she felt the night in his car, she knew one thing very clearly: she wanted him again.

Before she could second-guess herself, Skylar leaned in and kissed Barrett, full on the lips. His eyes widened and then closed as he kissed her back. He didn't have everything figured out either, but he was willing to give the lady what she wanted, if…

He released her, pulled back enough to look into her eyes. "You're sure?"

She kissed him again and pulled her pajama top off, exposing her breasts. Her nipples were already fully erect. "I'm sure."

Barrett's breathing quickened and he hurried to unbutton his own shirt, slipping it off and tossing it aside before he wrapped his arms around Skylar and pulled her close. His lips found hers and their mouths crushed together, causing her to moan deep in her throat. She didn't know what was going to happen in the future, but the next little while was all she cared about at the moment.

Barrett's lips moved from Skylar's to her chin, to her throat, pausing there a few moments before moving down to her chest and then her breasts. He cupped her right breast gently, feeling the curve in the palm of his hand, the swollen nipple against his wrist and took her left nipple in his mouth, gently rolling it across his tongue, making her gasp as delicious little fires raced through her body.

Her hands roamed across his back, marveling at how broad it seemed beneath her touch. She could feel the temperature of her body rising with the fires that Barrett ignited in her and she knew he was feeling the same.

She pushed her pajama bottoms over her hips, murmuring, "Help me," against the side of Barrett's head. With one hand, he gripped the pink fabric and deftly slid it from her legs, leaving her wearing only her pink and blue bunny panties. She might have been embarrassed for anyone to see them another time, but now it didn't matter—they were already sliding down her thighs and then they were off, tossed into a corner of the room.

Barrett kissed down her belly, finding the little patch of pubic hair, rubbing his lips against it, savoring the texture against his skin, and then his tongue lashed out, flicking against her clit. She was already wet and the warmth emanating from her pussy radiated against his face as he tasted her, his tongue traveling the length of her labia from top to bottom and then back up again.

Remembering the night in the SUV—as if he'd stopped thinking about it for more than a few minutes at a time since it happened—he looked up, meeting her eyes and said, "It'll be better this time."

"It was good last time," she told him with a smile and pushed his head back down between her thighs.

Barrett licked and sucked at her sweetness, feeling

her heat against his face and on his tongue, lapping her up as if he could swallow a part of her and keep her with him forever. Skylar moaned and gripped his head, rocking her hips in time with the movement of his tongue for several minutes until she shifted, pushing him away slightly. She said, "I want you inside me."

Eyes never leaving Skylar's, Barrett stood, his erection visibly tenting his chinos. A dark spot of wetness showed where his precum had soaked through his shorts already. He unzipped and slipped from his pants too quickly, nearly losing his balance in his eagerness. Skylar giggled and he grinned back at her. Freed from his chinos, his erection poked out of the slit in his shorts, standing almost straight up.

Barrett climbed back onto the bed and Skylar twisted, shifting onto her belly and then thrusting her ass into the air. Looking over her shoulder at him, she met his gaze and said, "From behind."

He ran a hand over the smooth roundness of one of her buttocks, reveling in the silkiness of her skin, how the flesh felt both soft and supple but firm. Her butt was already slightly spread just by the position she was in, but on impulse, he spread her cheeks wide and, seeing the little pink rosebud of her asshole, he dipped his face down, giving it a quick lick, causing her to gasp in surprise and arch her back.

Grinning, Barrett positioned himself and entered her, his penis disappearing into her vagina. She was warm and wet and it felt like her pussy was trying to grip him, to pull him deeper inside of her. His erection got harder and thicker and longer as he began to push in and out, thrusting as deeply as he could, pushing forcefully enough against her to make his balls slap audibly against her ass and eliciting soft sounds of pleasure from her with each thrust.

He pushed in quickly and hard, pulled back slowly and gently, only to do it again over and over. They were so engrossed in each other and their lovemaking that neither one realized they weren't alone until a third voice cried out, "Jesus Christ!"

Skylar and Barrett's heads whirled in unison. Levi stood in the doorway, gym bag in hand and eyes wide. His gaze moved from Skylar to Barrett and his mouth worked but no more sounds came out.

Panic gripped Barrett, sending icy fingers down his spine and threatening to shrink his scrotum. Skylar said she had slept with both him and Levi—he wondered, the way Levi had been acting the last day or so when it was the three of them—so what would he do now? He and Levi had known each other since their ages were in single-digits and all three of them had been best friends for more than half of their lives. How would Levi react seeing two of his best friends in so intimate a moment?

"Levi…" Skylar said, her voice soft but husky, heavy with the lust and pleasure she and Barrett had been enjoying. Barrett's head turned, his penis still inside of Skylar, and looked down the length of her smooth back. She was reaching out a hand towards Levi and the look in her eyes was an unmistakable invitation.

Levi's face was bright red when Barrett's eyes met his. What seemed like an eternity passed, their eyes locked, questions silently being lobbed back and forth between them. Then he dropped his bag, stripped off his shirt and came into the room.

Hesitantly, Levi approached the bed and when he was within arm's reach, Skylar's left hand shot out, gripped the hem of his workout pants and pulled him closer. She pushed down the nylon waistband of Levi's pants, fished his penis out and began fondling it. Something in Barrett told him to look away. It was ironic that he was nude, that his own cock was inside Skylar, but his mind told him to respect Levi's privacy. But he couldn't look away—he didn't want to. He watched as Skylar fondled Levi's penis, watched as it grew bigger in her hand, and when it stood half-erect, she leaned forward and took the head of his penis in her mouth, making Levi gasp.

Barrett had watched porn plenty of times—the last few years, he rarely dated and porn was all that got him through some of the lonelier nights. He'd seen plenty of guys getting their dicks sucked by beautiful women, but never in person. He couldn't believe how incredibly hot it was and before he realized it, his hips were moving again, thrusting his cock into Skylar, feeling her pussy tighten around him even more, gripping him like a fist as she pleasured his oldest friend.

Soft sounds of pleasure and louder sounds of sucking filled the room, drowning out the noises of the city and all three of their inhibitions.

Levi's breath came in short, quick pants as Skylar's tongue circled the head of his cock, tickling the sensitive little nubs around the base of his head, while she stroked his shaft with her hand. Slowly, he began rocking his hips back and forth, thrusting against the back her throat. She gagged once and he backed off, but then she surprised him by lunging forward, pressing the head of his cock against her tonsils all on her own.

Skylar's entire body was on fire. Barrett's thick cock inside of her pussy, thrusting into her as hard as he could, Barrett rubbing a thumb against her asshole, and Levi's thinner, longer shaft pushing halfway down her throat. She had never imagined herself in his position before—not with her best friends or with any other guys; not *ever*—and now she couldn't imagine any greater pleasure. All thoughts of the chaos in her life were swept away by the heat of her passion for these two men that she cared about so deeply. They had long been the most important people in her life and somehow, though she never even dreamed of it before, this grouping now felt like the most natural thing in the world.

"Barr," Levi gasped, making a little twirling gesture with one hand as he backed up from Skylar, releasing his cock from her gasping mouth. Barrett understood without explanation and pulled slowly out of Skylar's pussy, his penis springing upwards, glistening with her wetness. Gently, he pushed Skylar's butt until she got the message too, and shifted, slipping down from the bed, kneeling between the two men.

Barrett and Levi stood over Skylar, their cocks inches from her face. Mouth open wide, she took a cock in each hand and alternated between them, sucking Levi's long cock while stroking Barrett's thick one, then switching to run her tongue around the head of Barrett's penis while jerking Levi off. After a few moments, she surprised both men by wrapping her arms around their thighs, pulling them in closer until their cocks almost touched, then gripping them both again and wrapping her lips around both of their cockheads simultaneously. Their cocks pressed together inside of Skylar's mouth as her tongue flicked over both of them.

It was too much. It was the most erotic thing any of them had ever experienced—like something out of the wildest dream none of them had ever had. Barrett let out a low groan that slowly rose in timbre as Levi began breathing so quickly it was nearly panting and then both orgasmed, splashing one another's cocks with their cum and filling Skylar's mouth until it overflowed and dripped over her lips to splatter her breasts.

Chapter 15.

Skylar – Late That Night

The spray of hot water beat down on Skylar like a thousand tiny hammers, warm and soothing and rhythmic. It was almost hypnotic, and her body responded, all the muscles in her back and legs and arms relaxing, soaking up the heat and letting out some of the weariness. The steam filled the small bathroom, swirling through the shower stall to wrap around her in a thick, comforting cloud. She leaned against the tiled wall, letting her head rest against the cool surface as water streamed down her neck and back, and over her skin and then down the drain. She imagined the flow of water taking all the trouble, all the complexities, of her life with it, but it was only a pipedream. She chuckled at the pun, wondering what that expression's origin was.

It was only a momentary distraction though. Her body was relaxed now, but her mind wouldn't quiet.

Barrett and Levi.

Their names repeated in her mind, back and forth like a two-tone dance beat, alternating with memories, with sensations, with questions she hadn't been ready to ask until now. They had always been her constants—her boys. Her best friends. Her chosen family. Now her lovers.

Things had changed so rapidly the last few days. No, *she* had changed. Well, more like *yes*, she had changed, but so had everything else.

Chet was gone from her life—her major stressor, her tormentor in a way, though she had to admit she had

113

let him take advantage of her and make her miserable for so long. Part of her, the part that still held the tiniest bit of affection for Chet—a remnant of when they were first dating, she guessed—wanted to give him the benefit of the doubt. Chet couldn't take advantage of her if she hadn't let him. But no, she was done with those kinds of thoughts. Chet was out and she was free of that servitude, regardless of who saddled her with it.

But moving on from Chet meant moving on from the home and routine and life she'd known. She wasn't sorry—not really—but it was still scary to forge any sort of new path for yourself. She was so, so glad and so lucky to have Barrett and Levi by her side when she needed them.

But that was a kind of problem in itself now, wasn't it? She had both of the guys. She had *had* both of the guys—individually and now together. It wasn't anything she'd ever dreamed of. Before a few days ago, she never seriously even thought about either of them sexually, much less romantically. Sure, when she was a teenager, and her hormones were raging, she had some fantasies, but doesn't everyone have those kinds of fantasies about people in their lives?

She never thought they'd actually come true—and more than that, they were beyond the fantasy. Reality was literally wilder than anything she ever dreamt of.

But what was next?

Barrett and Levi.

Her friends. Her boys. Now her men.

She needed them both, but how could she *have* them both? Did she even want to? If it came down to it, could she choose between them? Would she *need* to?

Skylar closed her eyes and let the water stream over her face, mouth slightly open as she tried to breathe through the rising anxiety. These weren't just hookups. Neither the night in Barrett's car or the morning with Levi or what they finished just a few minutes ago—none of it was meaningless. Not to her. And not to them—she was *sure* of that. She had always loved the guys and what they did was an expression of love—but was it *that* kind of love?

But thinking about Barrett's steadiness, his protective arms around her... or Levi's warmth and the quiet understanding in his voice when he told her to let it all go... her chest ached with the knowledge that someone was bound to get hurt. *Maybe all of them were.* What if she ruined the most important friendships in her life by not knowing how to handle this?

Her stomach twisted.

And then, as if that mess wasn't enough, her thoughts shifted, as if someone had changed a channel, sick of this drama and moving on to the next.

Natalie.

Skylar's hands balled into fists at her sides.

Three days. Her mother had been gone for three days. No contact. No word. No answers. She wouldn't have known if Brian hadn't told her. She wanted not to care—Natalie had her own life—but it wasn't that simple. Brian was involved and—she made a noise of disgust in the back of her throat—so was Chet.

Skylar hadn't tried to call her mother. She refused to chase after Natalie—not after what she'd done. But another part... another part still burned with painful curiosity and maybe just plain ordinary pain. No matter what she did, Natalie *was* still her mother.

Where the hell was she? Still with Chet?

The thought made Skylar's lip curl. The memory of the motel room—her mother half-dressed, Chet shameless and smug—it slammed into her like a punch to the chest. She gasped, the heat of the water suddenly not soothing anymore, just suffocating.

How could they?

She suspected Chet was cheating for a while, but never with *her own mother*. That level of betrayal... it felt surreal. Like something from a trashy drama, not her life.

But it *was* her life. That was the worst part.

Still… there was that moment. That *thing* Chet said. Right before Natalie shut him up.

"She's not even—"

Not even *what?*

The sentence had haunted her since. She tried to dismiss it as Chet being cruel, trying to twist the knife as deep as possible. But he hadn't been looking at her when he said it. He'd been looking at Barrett. And Natalie hadn't quite *panicked,* but she definitely didn't want Skylar to hear whatever it was Chet wanted to say.

Skylar's brows furrowed, water cascading down her face as she stood there, motionless.

Was Barrett right? Was Natalie maybe… not her mother? The woman who raised her, at least until marrying Brian… what *if* Natalie wasn't her mother?

She felt a chill across her neck, just below the base of her skull, despite the water's heat. There were so many gaps in her knowledge of her mother's past. She'd never really questioned it growing up. Natalie was just Natalie—chaotic, charming, and later, when Skylar was older, sometimes cruel. As a teenager, Skylar had always tiptoed around Natalie's moods, trying to keep a low profile, biding her time until she could go off on her own. Sometimes she wondered what happened to change Natalie's attitude towards her—they'd been close when Skylar was little.

What changed between them? She was sure she hadn't done anything to Natalie. She was just a kid, for God's sake. But something changed, something affected Natalie in a way that she never got over. Even now, all these years later, it still hung between them somehow.

She reached out and shut off the tap, standing for a moment in the sudden quiet before stepping out of the shower. She wrapped herself in a towel and stared at her own reflection in the fogged-up mirror. A distorted version of herself looked back—wet hair plastered to her head, eyes hollow but burning.

So many threads. So many tangled emotions.

Barrett. Levi. Natalie. Chet. Even Brian was mixed up in it all.

She didn't know which thread to pull on first, but one thing was clear: nothing was going to go back to the way it was, so she had to find a way to move forward by making something new.

Chapter 16.

Skylar, Barrett, and Harry Whittington – Friday

The office buzzed with its usual end-of-week chaos. Voices drifted over cubicle walls, printers churned out last-minute reports, and the sharp *ding* of incoming emails and calendar alerts rang like background music through TechnoFirm's open-plan workspace. It was Friday, and everyone moved like they had somewhere else to be—which they did, home. And nobody wanted to take work home for the weekend if it could be avoided. Skylar especially. This week felt like it had been a year long.

The day was more hectic than usual, even for a Friday. She barely had time to breathe between back-to-back meetings, emergency reschedules, client calls, and Nathan Dyer's constant demands. The man was brilliant, frustrating, and insatiable when it came to wringing the last productive drop out of a Friday. He didn't want to work weekends any more than any of his employees—which was something of a surprise to most people as he was the original workaholic during the week. And as Nathan's indispensable right hand, Skylar needed to be a master of juggling crises with a calm she didn't always feel to ensure that neither of them had to work unpaid overtime after the work week ended.

Skylar was in Nathan's office, halfway through coordinating a rescheduled 2:30 meeting for Nathan with their European partners—the Europeans didn't want to work late on a Friday night any more than Americans did, but there really wasn't a choice in this case—when her phone buzzed. She intended to ignore it, but noticed the text was from Barrett.

She frowned and glanced around to make sure Nathan wasn't watching, then swiped it open.

Barrett: *Hey. I know it's last minute, but can you meet Mr. Whittington and me for lunch today? It's important.*

Skylar's stomach did a little flip-flip. She hadn't expected to hear from Barrett today. In fact, she tried to push her thoughts about him—and Levi, and everything else—into a neat box she could deal with later. Echoes of life with Chet, but not in a negative way—she hoped.

But now he was texting her about lunch with *Mr. Whittington*, his boss. That wasn't usual, but she was sure she knew what it was about. Barrett had offered to look into things for her, hadn't he? Was it possible he and his employer had already learned something? Could it be that… easy?

She tapped back quickly.

Skylar: *I might be able to do 1:15 if I can get Nathan to take a lunch of his own. This is about Natalie?*

The reply came fast.

Barrett: *Yeah. Mr. Whittington wants to talk to you himself. I told him what I heard at the motel and my theory we talked about. He's taken an interest.*

Skylar's heart began to thud dully in her chest.

Mr. Whittington, Barrett's boss at the private investigation firm where he worked as a kind of apprentice, didn't "take an interest" lightly. He wasn't exactly famous, like Sherlock Holmes, but from what Barrett had told her, he was a kind of celebrity in the world of private investigations—he and his staff could find what you needed or fix your problem if anyone could. And if he wanted to meet Skylar, he wasn't just humoring a young investigator in his employ, he must have thought there was something real there.

Skylar leaned back in her chair, suddenly very aware of the pressure building behind her eyes. She wanted to believe that what Chet said—*"She's not even…"*—was just garbage, but somehow, she knew in her heart that it wasn't. Maybe Chet meant it as a final knife twist, and in the moment, it had failed to find its target, but now it was damaging her all the same. If Whittington thought it was worth pursuing, maybe she'd find the answer and be able to put these thoughts to rest once and for all.

She tapped her phone again.

Skylar: *Okay. I'll make it work. Send me the address.*

By 1 o'clock, Skylar had wrangled Nathan into eating his gourmet salad behind his desk while reviewing the draft of a quarterly presentation she knew he would tear apart anyway. She ducked out with a practiced smile, told Noreen at the executive suite's front desk that she would be reachable by phone, and took an Uber downtown to the place Barrett had texted her.

It was one of those older steakhouses that tried to mimic the famous Delmonico's, with small, white-clothed tables centered between two rows of deep, leather-cushioned booths, recessed lighting, and minimal background music. It wanted to feel like an old boys' club, with waiters who made it seem like they knew your order before you even spoke, but everything was just off enough to miss the mark. It was still a nice restaurant, but it lacked the gravitas it tried for.

Barrett was already seated at a table in the back, wearing a collared shirt she hadn't seen before and a sport jacket. He looked neat and clean and very professional. Next to him was a man she recognized only from photos she'd seen on his firm's website: Mr. Harry Whittington.

Older, mid-sixties maybe, the crown of his egg-shaped skull was bald, with a snow-white fringe. His expression was neutral, but he had a presence like gravity. Even sitting down, the man exuded sharpness and intelligence.

"Ms. Hunt," he said, rising politely and extending

a hand as she approached. "Nice to finally meet you. Barrett's told me a lot about you."

"Nice to meet you too, Mr. Whittington," she said, shaking his hand as she slid into the booth next to Barrett.

"I appreciate you taking time to speak with me," the older man said. A waiter approached, but he gestured for the man to give them space. "Barrett brought something to my attention that I think merits a conversation, and I find this kind of thing is best done in person."

Skylar looked at Barrett. His expression was open, serious, maybe just slightly nervous. Skylar wasn't sure about the kind of relationship Barrett had with his boss, but she somehow doubted it was as casual as the one she had with Nathan Dyer. Mr. Whittington didn't seem stern or severe or anything like that, but neither did he seem like the kind of man who would get buddy-buddy with a young employee. It must have taken courage for Barrett to even bring up Natalie with his boss.

She nodded. "You're talking about my mom— Natalie."

"Yes," Mr. Whittington said. "Specifically, what your... ex-boyfriend said, when you confronted him and your mother. 'She's not even...' something. Did I get that right?"

"Yes." Skylar's voice was quiet. "I assumed he was just trying to hurt me, but..."

"Maybe he was," Whittington said. "But Barrett tells me your mother shut him up quickly."

"She did. She practically pounced on him."

"A reaction like that doesn't come from nothing." He paused, steepling his fingers.

Skylar's mouth went dry. "You think Natalie's hiding something."

"Of course, and you do too. We both *know* she's hiding something," he said. "Barrett did a little digging based on what you both overheard, and there are some oddities I think we should pursue. But we won't move forward without your permission—or without giving you a warning."

"A… warning?" Skylar looked from Whittington to Barrett.

Barrett said gently, "Sky, I wouldn't have brought this to Mr. Whittington if I didn't think it could be important. There's only so much I can do on my own." He glanced at his employer. "I don't have the experience yet—but, well, I tried to do what I could and I hit a wall." He looked a little embarrassed now. "I didn't know there were alerts in the system Mr. Whittington uses."

Whittington added, "I'm not a fan of people using my resources without permission—especially without billable hours—but when Barrett explained the situation, I decided to overlook it." He smiled, a small tight thing on his thin lips. "As you can imagine, I enjoy a good mystery."

Skylar looked between the two men.

The memory of Brian's worried face came to mind, and his confession that Natalie disappeared sometimes. She thought of the years her mother had kept her at arm's length. Of the years she spent wondering *why* her mother loved her conditionally—*if* she loved her at all. Sometimes, especially during her teenage years, it felt like Natalie would have been happier if she hadn't been around.

"I've spent my whole life trying not to ask questions," she said finally. "Because Natalie doesn't give answers."

Mr. Whittington nodded. "I understand, but I want to warn you: I've seen a lot of complex family situations over the years, and sometimes it's better to leave well enough alone. I understand your mother is currently—absent, let's say—and you have questions. As often as people have been relieved to find answers, I find they more often wish they hadn't poked the bear, if you understand what I'm saying."

"I do," Skylar said slowly. "But I think it's time I stop avoiding the truth." She looked at Barrett, her pulse beginning to pound. "Whatever that is."

Barrett reached under the table and gave her hand a squeeze. "You're sure?" he asked softly.

Skylar nodded. "I'm sure."

"Alright," Whittington, said, signaling for a passing waiter with his menu. "I'll let Barrett run with this—with my guidance, of course, and as long as his regular workload isn't affected."

Barrett looked relieved. He squeezed Skylar's hand again. "Thanks, Mr. Whittington."

Whittington looked at the younger man. "Keep track of the hours you spend, too. I have a certain number of pro bono hours put aside every year for tax purposes." His gaze shifted to Skylar. "I hope you won't be offended in being my annual charity case." He showed that tight little smile again. "And I hope you won't regret this."

Skylar swallowed. "No, of course not," she said, but she wasn't sure which of Mr. Whittington's points she was answering.

Chapter 17.

Skylar – Later That Afternoon

Skylar's heels clicked softly against the pavement, the sound lost in the mid-afternoon traffic, as she made her way back toward the TechnoFirm building from where she had gotten out of the Uber. The driver would have been happy to bring her to the door of the building, he told her, but she wanted to walk a little bit—and think.

Now the early afternoon sun bounced off the sleek glass facades around her. The city hummed as it always did—darting cabs wove between buses and the low murmur of sidewalk conversations surrounded her. Someone arguing loudly into a Bluetooth headset marched angrily, rapidly past her. The city was alive all around her, but it felt distant, like her thoughts had wrapped her in a thin, invisible bubble of solitude.

She mentally examined the conversation she had with Barrett and Mr. Whittington at lunch. Even now, with the noise and movement of Manhattan pulsing around her, Mr. Whittington's message was the realest thing for her— if they went looking, Skylar might not like whatever it was they found.

She had to know though, no matter how shocking or painful whatever they dug up might be. Barrett's theory that Natalie might not be her biological mother was something she couldn't just laugh off and push aside. She both did and didn't want it to be true.

On the one hand, it might open up avenues she had never imagined—maybe a whole new extended family out there in the world somewhere, something she never had. Until Natalie married Brian, their family had been just the two of them, at least as far as Skylar knew. She'd never been introduced to anyone else and told "this is your relative, so and so," or anything like that. Natalie not being her "real" mother might also explain some of the mysteries of Natalie's behavior towards her. They were close when Skylar was small, but then something changed and she had always wondered what.

The flipside of her feelings were more complicated. If Natalie wasn't her mother, then what was she? Had she adopted Skylar and then decided motherhood wasn't all it was cracked up to be? Or maybe it wasn't her choice—maybe Skylar had been foisted off onto her against Natalie's will. That would certainly explain some things.

It was hard to even put these thoughts into recognizable form. She knew what she was feeling, but she also *didn't*. She was confusing herself, and she tried to imagine the same thoughts being spoken in Mr. Whittington's calm, steady voice as he sat across the table from her and Barrett in an imaginary version of that restaurant.

Mr. Whittington had been so composed, so deliberate. There was a quiet power in the way he spoke, but he didn't talk to her like she was just some girl caught up in family drama—he treated her like a client, even if this was more of a favor he was doing, or rather, letting Barrett do. But still, he treated Skylar like she was someone worth taking seriously.

Barrett had that same quality, in his own way—the steadiness, the quiet dependability. Less polished, maybe, a little rougher around the edges, but Mr. Whittington had probably forty years' experience on Barrett. The younger man would get there. If he stuck with it—if he kept learning—he could be someone like Mr. Whittington someday. Not just competent, but skilled and respected.

The thought made her smile softly to herself.

And then that smile faded.

She remembered the moment they said goodbye. The way Barrett had leaned in a little to kiss her, as if it were natural. As if they were already something more than friends who had some "moments" together and were already in a relationship of sorts. And maybe they *were*— she wasn't even sure—but in public, with Mr. Whittington only a few feet away and waiters bustling nearby, it caught her off guard.

She had turned her head without thinking, and his lips landed on her cheek instead of her mouth. The movement was instinctive, a reflex, but she wondered if it had hurt him. He hadn't said anything, hadn't even acknowledged it, only said that he would be home late that night, that he wanted to put in a few hours working on what they talked about—about finding who Natalie really was to Skylar.

Barrett was doing his part. He was already digging, and not out of any sort of obligation, but because he cared about Skylar and wanted to help. And she was more grateful than she could properly express, but still...

"Sky! Hey, Skylar! Babe!"

The sound of that voice stopped her dead. Her head jerked up—Chet, standing just to one side of the tall, prism-faceted glass entrance of the TechnoFirm building.

It was Chet's voice without any doubt, but looking at him, for just a split second, she didn't recognize him. He looked like the tortured ghost of someone she used to know. His hoodie was stained and hung loosely on his body like he'd been living in it. His jeans were wrinkled, speckled with something dark near the cuffs and streaked white around the pockets, as if he'd used the pants to wipe his hands. His hair, always carefully styled with that irritating precision he thought made him look cool whenever he had to leave the house, was greasy and matted, like it hadn't felt the touch of shampoo in days.

And the smell hit her next—faint, but there. Sour. Sleep-deprived. Unwashed.

"Oh my God," she breathed, taking a step back instinctively.

"I just want to talk," Chet said, moving forward like he didn't notice her recoil—or like he didn't care.

"Chet—what the hell are you doing here?"

"I—Sky, I'm sorry. Okay? About... everything. I fucked up. I know that now. It was just, like... a thing and it's done and I know how messed up it was."

Skylar stared at him, mouth slightly open, blinking slowly like her brain was buffering the moment, as if the connection couldn't quite be made.

"You know that *now*?" she repeated, voice rising.

"Sky, babe—I've been a mess. I haven't slept, I can't eat, I've been going out of my mind without you—"

"Are you seriously trying to spin this?" she snapped, and her voice cracked like a whip, sharp and sudden. "You think you get to roll up here like some tragic ex-boyfriend in a rom-com and beg me to come home, because—what? You learned some life lesson and experienced a tiny fraction of growth? Even if that was true, do you think that erases what you did to me?"

Chet faltered. "I just—"

"You slept with my *mother*, Chet!" she shouted, making heads turn all around them, drawing shocked stares and curiosity. She didn't care.

"You used me, Chet. You treated me like a goddamn maid, a cook, your secretary, your mother—oh wait, no, I guess you already had one of those lined up, didn't you? I think about the only thing you didn't do to me the last few months was *fuck me*. No, you just kept right on fucking me over instead."

Chet flinched, and Skylar took a breath like hot needles, scraping her lungs on the way in.

"You didn't just cheat on me. You *humiliated* me. You made me feel small in my own home for almost as long as we lived together, and then you *defiled* everything just to put the nail in the coffin of, of—" She waved her hands frantically between them. "Whatever *this* was!"

His mouth opened, then closed again, like he'd lost track of the script.

"I was weak," he mumbled. "And stupid, I guess, but—"

"No. You were selfish," she shot back. "You were lazy and entitled and so damn confident that I would never leave you that you didn't even try to hide it. You didn't *care* what you did to me because I didn't matter, not as long as you could do or have whatever you wanted."

"I thought I did," he said, quieter. "Like, I guess you're right. I did all that sh—that stuff. But... I didn't mean it. I really do care about you, and I didn't know how much I need you until you were gone. Like, I don't even know where anything is in the apartment and—"

"Oh, my God," she said again. "No. You don't need *me*. You needed someone to keep your life from falling apart because you never learned how to live like an actual grown-up man. You want a nanny, Chet. You never loved me. You just loved how easy I made your life."

He opened his mouth again, but she cut him off with a sharp shake of her head.

"You know what the worst part is? I still feel sorry for you. Even *now*. And that pisses me off more than anything, because it means you're still taking something from me."

Tears welled in Chet's eyes—from guilt or shame or just desperation, Skylar didn't know and didn't care.

"I can change," he said quietly, his voice barely audible over the traffic. "Just... come home. We can fix this." He tried to smile and it sent worms crawling across her skin. "You and me, babe. Team Unbeatable, right?"

Team Unbeatable, the name of his online gaming group, something she'd never even been a part of. For God's sake...

"'Home'?" she repeated, stunned. "You think that was a home for me? That apartment was like—like a prison where I tiptoed around your moods and begged you for scraps of affection. How is that a fucking *home*?"

He didn't respond. His eyes fell to the sidewalk and his shoulders sagged beneath the weight of everything she was throwing at him. Or maybe beneath the weight of realization, finally dawning.

"You want to change?" she said, her voice low and sharp enough to cut like a blade. "Do it. For yourself. But don't ever—*ever*—ask me to be part of your life again and don't you ever think you're going to be part of mine. I'm done with you. I want to forget you exist."

Chet just stood there, the slump of his body expressing how broken he was better than words could. Skylar was breathing hard, the exertion of getting all of that off of her chest, out of her system and heaping it where it belonged—on Chet's shoulders—took more out of her than she could have guessed. But it was done, it was over, and despite everything else, there was a new sense of lightness in her.

"Please, Sky…" Chet said, his voice so small and weak she barely heard it over the sounds of the city all around them. "I'll do anything you want me to." He looked up. The tears were falling now, leaving shiny streaks beneath his eyes that ended where several days of beard growth began. "Just don't cut me off entirely. *Please*. I couldn't stand that. I'll do *anything*. I mean it."

Skylar's jaw clenched and her body went tense, as if this was a fight or flight moment. She had the upper hand, literally for the first time in all the years she'd known Chet. He was already broken, and her first impulse was to press the attack, to absolutely *destroy* him—but what good would it do? It wouldn't make him a better person. It wouldn't really change anything at all. Chet meant nothing to her now, so why waste the effort?

Besides, a colder, more rational part of her brain

said, there actually *was* one thing that Chet could do for her.

"There *is* something," she said, her voice low and cold, each word measured.

Chet's eyes lit up, hope springing into them. His hands twitched at his sides like he didn't know whether to reach for her or fall to his knees and thank her for even this tiny fragment of a chance.

"Anything," he said eagerly. "Just name it."

"Tell me what happened after I left that motel in Jersey," she said. "Tell me *everything*. From the second Barrett and I walked out that door to the moment you and Natalie... split up, or whatever happened. Leave out any of the gross crap—I don't want details. But I want the truth. All of it."

The shift in his face was instantaneous and painful. His hope twisted into confusion, then something like reluctance, and finally petulance. His eyes flicked away for a beat and his jaw tightened. He was drawing back into himself, despite what he had told her.

Skylar crossed her arms. "You said *anything*, Chet."

He hesitated still, just a moment too long for her liking, but before she could prod him again, he nodded. "Okay," he said. "Yeah. I guess it doesn't matter now anyway."

She gestured to a little concrete and iron bench tucked against the side of the building, not far from the entrance. "Sit." For some reason, her gaze rose to the cluster of security cameras over TechnoFirm's entryway. The stares of strangers on the street didn't bother her, but somehow, the idea of anyone she worked with seeing her with Chet made her feel slightly soiled.

Still, Chet was a link to Natalie—maybe the only one left, as far Skylar knew.

Chet obeyed like a scolded dog, slumping onto the bench. She stood in front of him, arms still crossed. She wasn't going to give him any illusion of closeness or even friendliness.

"So?" she prompted.

He ran a hand through his greasy hair, looked at his hand as if surprised at something he saw there, then began.

"After you left… it got quiet for, like, a few minutes. It was weird. Natalie didn't say anything. She just grabbed her vape and sucked on it, staring at the wall. I didn't even know she vaped 'til then. She was quiet a while and then she laughed. Not like, funny haha, more like… 'haha w-t-f.' She said, 'Well, that went about how I expected.'"

Skylar said nothing, just watched him closely, letting him tell it his own way.

"It made me mad for some reason. Like, I knew we had to sneak around cuz she was married and I—"

He looked up at Skylar, guilt in his face. He flushed and cast his eyes down towards her shoes.

"Uh, anyway. Like, we had to sneak around before, but all of a sudden, I wanted to know where this was going. I asked her what the hell we were doing—like, long term. Were we just having fun? Or did this mean something. She told me I was being dramatic and foolish and to keep my mouth shut for a while, she was thinking. Finally she said that all of this would blow over eventually, that you'd 'come around' once you'd calmed down. I didn't get it."

Skylar's stomach turned. "What did you mean when you said 'she wasn't even,' Chet?"

Chet shook his head, but kept talking as if he hadn't heard her. "I didn't get it," he said again. "Not really. I think I knew, even then, that it was over between you and me. But I wanted to believe something could come out of all this. That maybe Natalie and I could—" He paused, then corrected himself. "—I don't know. Be something."

Skylar's lips curled with disgust, but she kept

quiet. She wanted information.

"I didn't want her to get pissed and take off or anything, so I kept my mouth shut. In the morning, we went to a diner. She was weird. Jumpy. Kept checking her phone and she barely ate. She said Brian was asking where she was. She said she couldn't go back yet because it would look suspicious."

"She told you that?" Skylar asked sharply. "That she was *hiding* from him?"

"Yeah. She said she didn't want to answer any of his questions, that he wouldn't understand."

"Wouldn't understand what?"

Chet rubbed his face with both hands. "I don't know. But I don't think it was even just that, her husband not getting her or whatever. I think she was scared."

Skylar's brow furrowed. "Scared of *what*?"

"I don't know," Chet said again, frustrated. "She wouldn't say. She just kept mumbling that things were 'complicated' and that people wouldn't get it. She wouldn't even let me turn on the TV in the room in case someone tracked the credit card charges or whatever. She paid in cash up front, but they took my card in case we charged anything extra."

Skylar's heart rate picked up. "How long were you together?" Asking the question felt gross, but it was necessary. "And did she tell you where she was going when she left you?"

"No," he said. "She just told me she had to 'take care of something' and she was going out. She took her bag and said she'd call me later. But that was… two nights ago."

"Where was this?"

"Some other motel in Jersey. I wanted to go with her, but wouldn't let me. She said the less I knew, the better."

Skylar's blood ran cold. "Did she say *anything else*? Anything at all?"

Chet looked up at her. "She said she had to deal with something she should've taken care of a long time ago. That was the last thing."

Skylar stared at him, her mind racing.

"Do you think she's in trouble?" he asked, suddenly softer. "I mean… I know it's not really my place to—care or whatever. Not after everything. But she wasn't okay, Sky. She acted like she had control of things, but… it felt like something was catching up to her. And she didn't know how to stop it."

Skylar said nothing for a long moment, staring past him.

"Chet," she said finally.

"Yeah?"

"What did you mean when you said Natalie wasn't even my real—something?"

Chet jolted, as if stung by an electrical shock, and looked up. "Oh, shit, yeah… that, um…"

"What did you mean? What did Natalie tell you?" she pressed, inching closer.

"I was just—" he faltered. "I was being a dick. I don't really think I should be the one—"

"What did you *mean*, Chet?" The hardness in her voice surprised her, but this was important —it was *so* important.

"Oh, Jesus," Chet moaned. "Look, Sky, when we first—when Natalie and me, I mean—when we first started, uh, seeing each other, I felt really guilty about it, and she told me not to worry, you aren't her, uh…" He swallowed hard, making his Adam's apple bob in his throat. Softly, almost a whisper, he finished, "You aren't her real daughter."

Skylar's blood ran cold. *Barrett's investigation just got a whole hell of a lot easier*, she thought bitterly. She didn't know whether to take this at face value. Chet clearly believed it, but it came from Natalie.

Still, it *felt* true. Skylar couldn't deny that.

"Thanks," she said flatly. "That's all I needed."
"Sky—" he began, hopeful again.
But Skylar was already walking away.

Chapter 18.

Skylar and Levi – That Evening

Skylar sat curled up on the end of the couch in the living room, her oversized sweatshirt draped around her like a shield, covering even her knees, pulled up to her chest. The television in front of her—smaller than the one in her room, which normally struck her as funny—flickered with color and movement, but she hadn't processed a single frame or heard a single word of what the figures moving across its screen had said. Not that she wanted to—the volume was low, set just high enough to eliminate the house's silence, but not enough to distract her from the thoughts spinning around in her head.

You aren't her real daughter.

The words echoed, stubbornly refusing to fade. Every time she thought about Chet saying them, her jaw clenched. Not because she necessarily *believed* him—he was hardly a reliable source of information, even in his better days—but because it lined up with the strange things she had been feeling and seeing for a while now—for years even. The weird distance Natalie had kept her at since she was on the cusp of adulthood, not yet a grown-up but no longer a little kid. Not to mention the secrets and inconsistencies she saddled poor Brian with.

And now Natalie had vanished. Brian hadn't heard from her, Chet didn't know where she was and his phone was cut off, so Natalie couldn't contact him even if she wanted to. And Barrett... still hadn't read her texts.

She glanced at her phone again, resting beside her

on the cushion. Nothing. The messages she sent that afternoon, during a momentary break in the chaos of a Friday at TechnoFirm, about what Chet claimed Natalie said, hadn't even been read. Her first message *Need to talk ASAP* was time-stamped 3:14. Five hours was a really long time for Barrett to have not even read a message. Maybe it wouldn't be unusual for someone else, but this was Barrett—always solid and dependable in everything.

Skylar sighed, leaning her head back and staring at the ceiling for a moment before shifting her gaze to the screen. A cooking competition was on now, one of those loud, fast-cut shows with dramatic music and too many slow-motion shots of falling soufflés, where a mixture of amateurs who had no business competing with pros got served over and over to make the pros look even better. She couldn't even remember what channel she landed on. She briefly considered putting *Cupcake Wars* on, but even her favorite reality show wouldn't be enough to distract her—not the way she felt now. She also wasn't sure she wanted to be distracted. After this new twist, forgetting about everything for even a little while would feel wrong somehow.

The front door creaked open, and a gust of spring's fresh-scented evening air followed Levi into the house. A moment later, he appeared in the living room. He kicked off his shoes, sending them flying towards the front hallway with a thump, then padded across the hardwood and dropped onto the couch next to Skylar with the kind of tired flop only someone who had been on their feet all day could manage.

He didn't say anything right away. He just looked at her, then at the TV, then back at her again.

"You look like you lost a game of chicken with the thought train," he said gently.

Skylar let out a soft, humorless laugh. "Yeah. Something like that."

Levi must have been curious, but he didn't push.

She was grateful for that.

For several minutes, they both watched the images dancing across the TV, then she finally said, "Chet said something to me today. After he ambushed me outside the office."

Levi sat up straighter, as if expecting bad news. "You saw *Chet*? At your work?"

"Yeah." She rubbed her face. "I mean—he knows all about TechnoFirm. Remember who his dad is and how I got the job in the first place?" She laughed humorlessly again. "Anyway, he was a wreck. I almost didn't recognize him. He begged me to come back to him, if you can believe that."

Levi made a noise of disdain mixed with surprise. "Yikes."

"Mhm. I told him off, said everything I've wanted to for *so* long—longer than I even realized." She smirked. "I really destroyed him, if I do say so myself." The smile disappeared. "But then I remembered… he's my only link to Natalie right now. So I asked him what happened after Barrett and I left the motel that night."

Levi wanted to ask, but knew she had to tell it at her own pace.

Skylar looked down at her hands, resting on top of her sweatshirt-covered knees. "He said that Natalie told him something. Remember what he tried to tell Barrett? And she shut him up?"

Levi nodded.

"Well, supposedly she told him that she isn't my real mother. That was her excuse—the reason she gave him for why it was okay for them to sleep together."

Levi's eyes widened and then narrowed, as if he was trying to process this information and failing. "Wait—what?"

"Yeah." Skylar's voice was quiet now. "I don't know if it's true. But I don't know that it *isn't* either. It's not like I ever saw my birth certificate or asked questions about where I came from. When I was little, it was just her and me and whatever is normal to a kid if it's all they know, right? But now with Natalie gone again…"

Levi looked at her, his brow furrowed. "That's… that's huge, Sky. Are you okay?"

"I don't know," she admitted. "I'm not sure it even changes anything. It's not like we actually *need* each other, we're barely in each other's lives as it is. But I texted Barrett, tried to tell him since he's investigating. I asked him to call me, but he hasn't read any of the messages. I'm guessing he's working on it right now. He said he'd be home late doing just that."

Levi nodded slowly. "Well… that's good. If anyone can get to the bottom of this, it's Barrett and his boss. The guy is some sort of super sleuth, right? And he's training Barrett."

"Yeah," Skylar agreed, but she sounded uncertain.

They sat in silence for a while, the glow of the TV casting sharply defined shadows on the walls. The occasional sound of distant traffic penetrated the house, competing with the low murmur of the television.

Finally, Levi broke the silence. "So… what do you *want* to do, if it ends up that it's true? If Natalie isn't your actual mom?"

"I don't know," Skylar whispered. "I just want to know who I am, I guess. I never really even thought about it before the last few days, and now—" She broke off, laughing softly, bitterly, her eyes on the ceiling.

Levi reached over and took her hand, squeezing it gently. "We'll figure it out, okay? Whatever comes along, we'll deal with it. You're not alone, Sky. I'm with you all the way—and you know Barr is too."

Her fingers tightened around his. "Thanks, Levi."

Levi leaned closer, lips parted. Skylar saw it and pulled back, but remembering what happened with Barrett outside of the restaurant, she said, "Not tonight, Levi. Okay? Let's just…"

"Okay," he said, resuming his former position. He released her hand. "I'm sorry. I just—"

"It's okay," she told him, the one to take his hand this time. She gave him another squeeze. "It's one more thing to figure out, but—just not right now, okay?"

"Yeah, sure," he said. "Absolutely. Sorry I made it weird."

"You didn't," she assured him, squeezing his hand once more before letting go. "Let's watch a movie or something. Something we can turn off our brains for."

Levi's face lit up. "Oh, yeah. Shit, I got the perfect one—I found it on Yubi after one of my clients mentioned it. He's an awesome guy, loves 80s horror."

"Oh, great," Skylar said, deadpan, then laughed, actually meaning it this time.

"No, really," Levi told her, reaching for the TV remote and switching to the smart TV's streaming menu. "1986's *Meow of the Dead*, zombie cats on an island. Dude swears it's a classic."

"If you say so." Skylar flopped sideways, leaning into Levi. As he started the movie, his arm slipped around her shoulder. She snuggled a little closer against him and let out of a sigh of relaxation and comfort. There was a lot to figure out, but not this. This had been the same between them for a long time and she hoped it always would be—no matter what came next.

Chapter 19.

Skylar and Barrett – Saturday Morning

Skylar stepped through the side door into the kitchen, her hair damp from her morning run, the fresh air and exertion giving her cheeks a healthy flush. She had forgotten how good it felt to just move her body, to enjoy using her muscles. In high school and her one year of on-campus college, she ran almost every morning, but with the craziness of working at TechnoFirm, and everything in her personal life, she'd gotten out of the habit. She was glad she decided to pick it back up.

She tossed her keys onto the kitchen counter then paused when she saw Barrett seated at the kitchen table, hunched over a cup of coffee, his phone resting in one hand. He looked up at the sound of the door and her clattering keys and offered her a tired smile.

It was the first time they had seen each other since the lunch at the restaurant, and she couldn't believe how different he looked. Barrett was usually well-groomed and dressed, but now he looked tired and disheveled. There was a vague chalkiness to his skin and faint bags under his eyes, like sleep had been on offer at some point and he had politely declined. He didn't look like he regretted it though.

"Hey," she said softly.

"Hey," he said, pushing a chair out from beneath the table with his foot. "Sorry I didn't answer your texts. I wasn't ignoring you. I was just… in the zone. Wish I *had* seen them, though. It'd probably give me a better line on things anyway."

Skylar waved it off automatically; he had no real reason to be apologizing. "It's okay," she said as she sank to the chair he'd pushed out, but he was already shifting gears. "Yesterday was kind of... I don't even know."

She told him about Chet, how he ambushed her, looking like a zombie, and what he'd said about Natalie. That chilling statement—*you aren't her real daughter*—had wedged itself into her brain and refused to leave.

Barrett listened closely, nodding, eyes focused. He didn't interrupt or comment until she was finished.

"I spent the afternoon with Mr. Whittington," he said finally, standing to refill his coffee at the single-serve pod-brewer. "He showed me how to use the databases the firm has access to—court filings, public records, genealogy sources, all that. I guess it's a package subscription deal where he gets that stuff and others. Anyway, I figured if I was gonna dig into this thing, I needed more than gut instinct and Google. I didn't want to waste time flailing around aimlessly like when I tried using the databases before."

The corner of Skylar's mouth twitched into a half-smile. "That's smart," she said. "You're really taking this seriously."

Barrett shrugged a little. "Well, yeah—I mean, it's for you. You know I want to help. Honestly, though, I wanted to learn anyway. I've spent almost three years basically being a gofer, talking to people for Mr. Whittington when they're involved in whatever but aren't, like, *important* to it, and running errands related to his clients. If I wanna move up, I have to step up. At any rate, I got really into it once I started learning the ins and outs of everything, and I didn't get home until about midnight. Didn't mean to stay at it that long but... like I said. The zone."

Skylar smiled, watching him move around the kitchen, taking sugar from the cupboard and creamer from the refrigerator. Even as tired as he obviously was, Barrett had a kind of quiet grace in his movements that she'd never really noticed before. "You didn't sleep much, I guess." It wasn't even quite eight.

"Not really," Barrett admitted. "I just kept turning stuff over in my head. The more I dig, the more pieces I see, but I don't have the full picture yet. Let me tell you what I do know—I mean, you already know, but I can add details."

A sensation like cold metal touched her spine, but she nodded slowly, the weight of uncertainty settling in her chest again. At least she wasn't alone in this she reminded herself, looking at Barrett and thinking of what Levi said the night before. "Okay."

Barrett stirred his coffee, sipped it and then took his seat again. His fingers wrapped around the steaming mug, he took a breath, as if bracing himself before he spoke.

"I found it," he said quietly. "It took a while because I didn't know where to look, but I found it."

Skylar's her heart fluttered. "Found what?"

"Your birth certificate," he replied, meeting her eyes. "It wasn't easy. There were a few… inconsistencies in the way it was filed, but I found a certified copy buried in a secondary archive. Part of the problem is that you weren't born in New York."

"I wasn't?" she interrupted, surprised. She'd lived in the city as long as she could remember. She and Natalie had moved a few times during her childhood, but always within Manhattan.

Barrett shook her head. "You were born in Holyoke, Massachusetts. That was part of the problem, like I said: I was looking in New York records, but tried matching your social security number against applications nationwide and finally found it. I double-checked the registry number and matched it against your social security application from when you were born. It's legit."

Skylar's breath caught in her throat. "And?"

He took another sip of coffee, trying to delay the blow, but there was no gentle way to say it.

"Your birthday is what you thought it was. But your parents are listed as Sophia Hunt and Aaron Needham."

Skylar gasped—an audible, involuntary sound that escaped before she could stop it, before she even knew she was making it. She stared at Barrett, trying to process the names, the reality. She thought she was prepared for this—she had *told* herself she was—but hearing it said out loud was something else entirely. A shock to the system. A sudden, seismic shift in her understanding of her entire life.

She realized she was standing, leaning on the table, as if trying to get closer to the source of Barrett's information by proximity to him. Slowly, she sank back down into her chair. "Sophia Hunt…" she murmured.

Barrett nodded gently, letting the moment hang. "Natalie's younger sister," he supplied when she didn't say anything more. "Sophia is close to ten years younger. Natalie is your aunt."

Skylar stared across the table at him, stunned. Her mind was working, but it felt like she was underwater, like a car that flew off a bridge into a swift-moving river, its engine still running but only because the accident hadn't quite caught up with it yet.

Finally, she said, "So Natalie raised me. Pretended I was hers. And never told me anything different. I didn't…" She faltered, unsure of what came next.

Barrett set his coffee down and clasped his hands in front of him. "It looks that way. I'm still working on getting more about Sophia and Aaron. Do the names mean anything to you?"

She shook her head, her gaze dropping to the table. Her fingers traced an invisible line across the surface. "No. I didn't know Sophia existed. I didn't think we had any relatives—Natalie and me, I mean—much less…"

Barrett sipped his coffee before saying, "I haven't turned up much yet, but that could mean the records are sealed or just not digitized. I'm guessing sealed."

"Of course the records are sealed." Skylar gave a dry, bitter laugh, edged with a thin layer of rising hysteria. She wanted to know the truth, but maybe it was coming too fast and too hard. A tiny, miniscule part of her had still hoped this was all some sort of mistake or mean-spirited joke.

"Why wouldn't they be? Turns out everything about my life has been some kind of secret."

"No, Sky..." Barrett said gently. "It's not that simple. Look, once I found your parents' names, I was able to find Sophia's birth certificate. She was only fifteen when you were born, and your grandparents, they died in a boating accident a couple of years before that. Natalie was Sophia's guardian."

Skylar looked up at him, tears welling in her eyes but not yet falling. "And then what? Where are they now? Sophia and this Aaron Needham?"

Barrett reached across the table and laid his hand gently over hers. "I don't know—yet. But I'm working on it. After I shower, I'm going to go back to the office."

Skylar looked at their hands, his thumb gently moving across the back of hers. "You don't have to work on a Saturday for me. I'm not—"

"Shush," he said quietly. "You *need* to know, and I *want* to know too. And even if I just dropped everything, Mr. Whittington is curious now so he would probably pick it up himself and then send you a bill, Ms. Charity Case."

Skylar laughed despite herself.

Gaze gentle, Barret added, "Sky, this is important to you, right?"

Wordlessly, she nodded.

"So it's important to me too."

The tears started to fall now, crawling down her

cheeks as gently as Barrett was holding her hand. "Thanks, Barr."

"We'll figure this out, Sky," he told her, smiling softly. "We'll figure it all out, and put the pieces together, and toss out whatever we don't need, and when it's done, we'll be better than ever. I promise."

Squeezing his hand, she told him, "I'll hold you to that."

Chapter 20.

Skylar and Barrett – Saturday Afternoon

After Barrett left for the office, Skylar was alone
in the house. Levi had left earlier for his gym and his
Saturday morning clients, and the silence throughout the
house was strange, not even the television on as it had
been the evening before. It was strange to be home and
alone on a Saturday, but it wasn't unwelcome. For years,
her weekends had been spent in service to someone else,
whether it was Chet's whims or Nathan's demands that
she hadn't been able to fulfill during the week. Thankfully,
working weekends was rare now, but until very recently,
her Saturdays still weren't her own. Now, though, both the
house and the quiet felt like hers. In fact, it felt like
freedom.

She made herself breakfast—a real one instead of
just something snagged from the fridge or picked up at the
nearest bodega on her way to work. She scrambled eggs,
made toast, and fried strips of bacon until they were dark
and crispy. She ate in the kitchen, listening to music
streamed on her phone, and enjoying the sunlight coming
through the eastern-facing window of the kitchen. After
she was done, she cleaned up the kitchen, started a load of
laundry, and then unpacked the last couple of boxes from
her move. There was no excitement, no drama, no
mysteries to be solved, just the soft hum of the washer
down the hall and the occasional creak of the floorboards
as she moved through the house. It was nicer than she
would have expected.

By mid-morning, every chore she could think of to do was done. Thoughts of what Barrett might be digging into—what he might find—crept into her mind, but she pushed them away, dug her favorite cozy throw out of her closet, and turned her ridiculously giant TV onto *Cupcake Wars*. It had been her favorite show for the last few years, but she was so far behind, she was pretty sure the entire cast of judges and resident pâtissiers had changed since she last watched. She settled back against the pillows on her bed and let herself completely zone out—completely guilt-free—for the first time in months, enjoying the rivalry of bakers whipping up the craziest confections that the judges could imagine, and all under the crushing pressure of time and a live audience. She laughed out loud when one contestant's frosting collapsed in the final seconds, and clapped when one of the amateur bakers nailed a gravity-defying cupcake tower to win the final round of that season.

For a while, she almost forgot about the tangled mess of her life. Natalie, Chet, the truth about herself that, less than a day before, had upended everything she thought she knew about her past.

Knuckles rapped against the frame of her door and Barrett poked his head inside the room. "Hi."

Skylar sat up straighter, the remote falling from her lap. "You're back," she said, trying not to sound too eager—or too nervous. "What time is it?" She hadn't lost track of time in literally years—the time-management training she subtly put Nathan through was ingrained in her now too.

"Almost two," Barrett replied, holding up a brown paper bag with a sandwich chain's logo on it. "I picked up some food. I hope you haven't eaten lunch yet."

Skylar smiled, pleased by Barrett's thoughtfulness. Chet would never in a million years have thought of *her* meal. "As a matter of fact, I haven't."

Barrett grinned and turned away, headed towards

the kitchen. Skylar leapt from her bed and followed and, in the kitchen, hovered near the table as Barrett unpacked sandwiches and drinks.

"Before I say anything else, do you want to eat first and talk after or…?" Barrett left the thought hanging.

Skylar froze, overwhelmed for a fraction of an instant by what the question implied, but recovered quickly. She was committed to this. "We can do both."

"Okay," he said, then turned and took a pair of plates from the cupboard next to the stove. Once the sandwiches were plated and they had settled in, he gave them both a minute or two to dig into their subs.

"I found Sophia," Barrett said.

Skylar nearly choked on a mouthful of bread and ham. Her hand flew to her lips and she coughed once before managing to swallow her food.

"You okay?" Barrett asked, concerned. She nodded and gestured for him to go on. He looked down at his sandwich. "I found Sophia, but not, like, in person. Sorry if that was misleading, I didn't mean—"

"It's fine," Skylar told him, a little sharper than she meant to. She cleared her throat, took a sip of canned iced tea, then said, "Go ahead. Please."

Barrett looked her in the eye, steady and calm. "She's—it's a long story. I read a metric *shit ton* of court documents—family court, then criminal court." He watched for Skylar's reaction, not wanting a repeat of earlier.

He took a deep breath then let it out as a sort of hard, half-sigh. "This might hurt, but—"

"Like a band-aid, Barr," Skylar told him.

Barrett nodded. "Sure. Okay." He took another breath. "So, Sophia is more than nine years younger than Natalie. They grew up in Massachusetts, the western side, near the borders with New York and Vermont. Their parents died in a boating accident when Sophia was thirteen and Natalie was twenty-two. There aren't any other relatives that I can find, unless you want to really stretch the definition of 'relative,' and Natalie was of legal age, so she became Sophia's guardian. She went to Baruch, here in the city, for college and when she graduated she got a job doing secretarial work at an architectural firm. When their folks died, she went back to Mass to take care of Sophia."

Skylar listened, keeping her face carefully neutral. Natalie sacrificing a career that couldn't have been more than a year old at the time for a younger sister... that didn't sound like the Natalie that Skylar knew. But then, Natalie had taken *her* hadn't she, after whatever happened to Sophia? And that didn't sound like Natalie either.

Barrett took a bite of his sandwich. He kept his head half-lowered over his plate, but was watching Skylar surreptitiously, gauging her reaction. This was only the beginning and it was going to get rougher.

He took a swallow from his bottled iced coffee, looked Skylar in the eye and went on. "Sophia was a problem child even before their parents passed—"

"What were their names?" Skylar blurted, surprising herself.

Calmly, as if he hadn't been interrupted, Barrett said, "Ben and Anna Hunt."

"Ben and Anna. Ben and Anna Hunt," Skylar said under her breath, as if testing the sound and feel of the names. She looked up. "Sorry. Go on, please."

"Sophia was a problem child. I don't know why—maybe nobody ever did—but she had trouble in school, got suspended a few times. It's all in notes attached to one of the family court filings. When she was thirteen, about six months after the Hunts were killed, she was in family court on charges of assaulting another girl at her school. There was talk of some drugs too, but she tested clean at the time.

"Sophia's in and out of court and different schools for the next couple years."

"And then I come in?" Skylar asked.

Barrett nodded and made a noise of affirmation. "Yeah. I'm reading between the lines here, which wasn't hard to do, but Sophia had been seeing this Aaron Needham, who was close to six years older than her, for at least a year when she got pregnant. He was a minor dealer, with some breaking and entering and assault charges on his sheet."

"Natalie must have loved that."

Barrett smirked. "She definitely didn't—but she *did* love Sophia, I guess, because she didn't give up on her. I can't find what Natalie was doing for work during these years, but she must have spent a pretty chunk of change on lawyers for Sophia. Anyway, both Aaron and Sophia had already been convicted and sentenced for some drug charges, but the courts in New England are fairly softhearted when it comes to things like pregnant teenagers—at least from what I've seen—and they deferred Sophia's date of surrender until after she gave birth."

"To me," Skylar said with a touch of awe. It was incredible and strange hearing about the life of this stranger who had given birth to her.

"Yes, to you," he agreed. "She went into a reform school—you know, get your high school diploma while serving your time—and Natalie must have agreed to take you."

Skylar shook her head. "I don't remember living in Massachusetts. I've lived in the city my whole life. Until this past week, I'd never lived *anywhere* but Manhattan."

"With Sophia locked up, it looks like Natalie came back to the city—and brought you."

"She must have," Skylar muttered. "So what happened to Sophia then?"

"Well," Barrett said, drawing it out an extra half beat. "That's where things start to get a little wild. I'm not sure how to—"

"Remember what I said, Barr?" Skylar asked. "Like a band-aid."

"Okay," Barrett said, nodding. "Like a band-aid. Let me finish my sandwich and collect my thoughts."

For a few minutes, there was no talk. Barrett ate slowly, gears churning in his head as he ordered his thoughts. Skylar was no longer hungry. She picked at her sandwich, but didn't eat any more of it.

Finally, Barrett pushed his plate aside, sipped from his bottle and said, "Sophia was as rough on the inside as she was in the outside world. She served her time, but as far as I can tell didn't get her diploma. I didn't look into Aaron Needham as deeply, but here's where he comes back into the story: apparently, the day Sophia got out of the reform school, Natalie was supposed to drive up to Mass and meet her. When she got there, Sophia had already been picked up by Aaron."

"How could they allow that?" Skylar asked.

Barrett shrugged. "It wasn't so much 'allow' as it just happened. I don't know. I'm reading reports and court filings and so forth and doing a lot of inferring, but this much I know: after that, Sophia and Aaron fall off the radar for a few years."

"And Natalie's stuck with me."

Barrett leaned across the table, stretching to take her hand. "She was lucky to have you." She smiled, but she didn't quite feel it.

He moved back, clasping his hands together on the table in front of him. "I'm gonna skip the stuff that doesn't matter or we'd be here all afternoon, okay?"

Skylar nodded. "Okay."

"Long story short, about fifteen years ago, Sophia resurfaces in Pennsylvania, charged alongside Aaron Needham with some pretty heavy drug offenses. I don't know why or how, but one way or another, they were granted bail and they actually managed to make bond. They jumped bail and apparently headed home."

Something skittered across the back of Skylar's neck, like an icy finger tracing the contours of her vertebrae. There was something Barrett didn't want to say, but she needed to know and he realized that. He was working up to it in his own way, trying to make it easier on her probably, but part of her wanted to jump across the table and shake him until he just spit out whatever it was.

"Uh, so…" Barrett made a noise in his throat. "So they were headed home and again, to make things short, they tried robbing a convenience store and during the robbery, a clerk was shot and killed."

Skylar's hands flew to her mouth as a gasp escaped her. *Shot and killed* echoed in her ears while her mind reeled. "Did Sophia…?"

Barrett shook his head. "Witnesses say Aaron was the gunman, but Sophia was with him and murder in commission of another crime is automatically murder one… and accessory to murder gets the same penalty as murder."

"Oh, my God," Skylar said, hands still cupped against her mouth.

"Yeah, it's…" Barrett rubbed his cheek. "Sky, your mom—Sophia—is serving twenty-five to life. I'm—I'm sorry," he added, as if any of it were his fault.

Skylar was suddenly dizzy, as if the floor had been yanked out from beneath her and she was spiraling down into a fathomless void. Mr. Whittington had warned her that she might not like what she found—but this? *This?* The woman she thought was her mother betrayed her in the vilest way possible and now she knew that the woman who'd actually given birth to her was a *murderer?* How could she possibly have foreseen *that?*

Skylar pressed her fingers to her eyes. They stung, but she pressed hard, as if to hold back the tears. She refused to cry.

"Sky…" Barrett said from next to her. She opened her eyes and saw him down on one knee beside her. He put a hand on her shoulder, steadying himself with his other on the table. "It gets worse. Aaron Needham isn't in prison. His conviction was overturned on a technicality that I don't really understand. He and Sophia had separate trials, because her lawyer insisted on it, and they were both convicted but he—well, he's out. I don't know where or doing what, but—shit, Sky, I'm sorry. I had no idea I'd find—"

"It's not your fault." She looked at him. Kneeling, Barrett was at a slightly lower level than she was, seated in her chair. She looked down into his eyes. "None of this is your fault or my fault or even Natalie's. It's all so insane and so terrible." She let out a shuddering sigh. "But somehow, just hearing all of this, I think…"

She bit her lower lip. Her mind was suddenly very clear, as if a curtain had been drawn back and the sun was streaming in on dark corners that hadn't seen light in years.

She said, "I think I get Natalie a little better now. Fifteen years ago was when Sophia and this Needham guy—killed the store clerk?"

Barrett nodded.

"That's around when Natalie really started putting distance between us—and when she married Brian, she immediately sent me off to camp, like… like she was pushing away a connection to Sophia, maybe?"

"I don't know." Barrett looked both thoughtful and skeptical. "I'm not a psychiatrist. I'm barely a detective."

Skylar squeezed his shoulder. "You learned more about me in a day than I've known my entire life, Sherlock."

He grinned sheepishly, but it disappeared almost instantly. "So what now?"

"I don't know," she said softly. "I need to think."

"Okay," Barrett said. "That's fair."

Skylar looked down at him. "Thank you, Barr. Really." She leaned down and kissed him, softly, gently, and when she pulled back, she saw something in Barrett's eyes she had never seen before—and wasn't sure she could identify. She wondered what he saw in hers.

Chapter 21.

Skylar, Barrett, and Levi – Sunday Evening

Sunday evening settled over the Bay Ridge house with a hushed kind of stillness, the kind that comes when the weekend is nearly over and the weight of the coming week has started to loom. Monday wasn't what Barrett and Levi were dreading though—they weren't even thinking of it. The heaviness in the house emanated from behind Skylar's bedroom door. Neither of them had seen her since Barrett talked to her Saturday afternoon. He understood she needed time to think and process, and he made sure Levi understood why, but after more than a full day, they were both worried.

Barrett sat on the couch in the living room, flipping absently through channels he wasn't watching, a half-full mug of coffee that had long since gone cold on the side table. Levi walked in from the kitchen with a thoughtful frown, drying his hands on a dishtowel.

"She still hasn't come out." Levi said quietly. It wasn't a question.

Barrett shook his head. "She hasn't even eaten as far as I know. I heard her moving around a little, but when I knocked, she didn't answer."

"She might have her earbuds in," Levi said, but he knew it was a thin straw to grasp at.

He wasn't the greatest thinker on Earth. He was well aware of that, but he'd been wracking his brain all day, trying to come up with something to make Skylar feel better. She was one of his best friends, one of the two people he cared most about in the entire world, and he was pretty sure he knew her better than anyone else, except maybe Barrett. Even then, it wasn't exactly that Levi didn't know Skylar as well as Barrett did, but that they knew one another slightly differently. In either case, Levi knew Skylar well enough that he should have been able to figure something out that would snap her from her funk.

Yes, she had been through a lot, and she had learned some very heavy and deeply distressing things about her family. But—*but*—Levi and Barrett were her family too, weren't they? Best friends for fifteen years, more than half of their lives. That didn't just count for something, that *made* them something. A chosen family, if nothing else.

There were a few moments of silence, save for the disjointed snippets of various TV shows as Barrett channel-surfed, and then Levi spoke again. "Hey, Barr."

"Yeah?" Barrett asked, without turning.

"So this might sound dumb…"

Barrett shifted now, an arm across the back of the couch as he faced Levi. "Those are usually your best ideas."

Levi chuckled once. "You know how, when I was a kid, and I was going through something—bad day, friend drama, failed a test—"

"There were a lot of those tests," Barrett put in.

Levi ignored him. "My mom would throw a 'sundae party,' remember? It would be, like, total chaos. Sprinkles, gummy worms, chocolate chips, like… everything. I'd invite you over and kids from the neighborhood, and my sister would invite friends sometimes. It was dumb and sticky and amazing. And it always worked."

Barrett tilted his head. "You're a pretty simple soul though. I'm not sure a sundae party would work here. Finding out your mom is…" He didn't want to say it, so he didn't. "Finding out what Sky did about her real mom is a bit worse than failing a math test."

"Dude, I know," Levi said, more seriously now. "But, it's like—the dumbest fun and Skylar never got to be part of it, you know? We met her after we were too old for that kind of thing… and she didn't exactly get a warm-and-fuzzy childhood. She could use some of that now."

Barrett considered it. "Fuck, you know what? Let's do it."

Half an hour later, they had turned the kitchen into a candy-colored battlefield, ready for a sugar-hungry army. At the nearest corner store, Levi had bought seven different flavors of ice cream, canned whipped cream, cherries, a jar of chopped nuts, sprinkles, and gummy bears. Barrett had hot fudge warming on the stove, and he'd sliced bananas and strawberries and crumbled Oreos and chocolate chip cookies into bits.

"Guess we're ready as we're ever gonna be," Levi said.

"Go get her," Barrett told him.

Levi knocked gently on Skylar's door. "Hey, Sky? I know you probably want to be left alone, but I've got a surprise and it's mandatory."

He waited and when there was no response, he knocked again, harder. "Sky?"

This time, there was movement behind the door and after a moment, Levi could sense Skylar's presence on the other side. "Levi?"

"Hey, Sky, sorry to bug you but we're throwing a stupid ice cream sundae party and it's a rule that all housemates have to attend. I think it's actually some kind of city ordinance or something."

There was a beat. Then another. Barrett stepped up beside him.

"You don't have to talk," Barrett said. "But you gotta eat, Sky, so just… come eat junk with us, okay? Let's get stupid sugar-high and run around like maniacs."

They heard the soft click of the doorknob turning.

157

Skylar appeared in the doorway. Her eyes were a little puffy, her hair was in a messy topknot, and she was wearing her giant sweatshirt that hung down to her knees, bare legs peeking out beneath it.

"You guys are ridiculous," she muttered. "You're acting like kids and I'm in here, with all this heavy stuff…"

Levi grinned. "That's the point. Pure ridiculousness to ease the, like… whatever you wanna call it."

She looked down the hall towards the living room and the kitchen beyond. It seemed like every light in the house was on, and through the open kitchen doorway, she could see the table piled high with toppings and cartons of ice cream. She didn't want ice cream—but she did want to be with Barrett and Levi. She had plenty of time to think and she had reached a conclusion. She would have come out soon anyway, but why ruin their fun?

Besides, though it had only been a day, she realized that she missed them.

Slowly, Skylar grinned. "All right, you beautiful, wonderful fools. I'm in."

Levi let out a whoop of joy and half-dragged Skylar from her doorway before pushing her down the hallway towards the kitchen, both of them laughing all the way. Barrett, smiling, shook his head and followed.

The kitchen was even more packed with sugary goodness than Skylar imagined: she counted seven kinds of ice cream and every kind of topping she could imagine.

"Wow," she said, genuinely a little awed. It seemed over the top, more than a little ridiculous, but it made her heart sing. The guys had done this for *her*. Because they were worried. She knew it was an echo from Levi's childhood, something she heard the boys talk about before, and she never even considered she would experience something like it herself.

"I've got a special treat too," Levi told them, moving to the kitchen counter where the pitcher from the blender stood, filled with a thick, milky substance. He brandished it like a trophy, grin plastered in place. "Ta-da! I call it the 'Vodka Cake Shake'—vanilla ice cream, sprinkles, and birthday cake-flavored vodka."

He took a sip directly from the pitcher and offered it to Skylar. She made a skeptical face, but accepted it and hesitantly took a sip. "Mm," she said and smacked her lips. "That's actually *really* good!" She took another hefty sip of the sugary drink and passed the pitcher to Barrett, who shook his head and grinned, saying, "I thought he was nuts, but—bottoms up," and drank some himself.

They passed the pitcher around once more, draining it nearly to the bottom and Skylar's doubts began to melt away as all three of them set to work, like kids on a sugar-fueled mission of pure joy.

Skylar rolled up the sleeves of her sweatshirt and opened several cartons, scooping generous piles of vanilla, chocolate, and cookies & cream into her bowl before mixing it all up, adding nuts, sprinkles and cherries, and mixing it all up again.

Barrett, always methodical and deliberate, arranged his ice cream neatly—a scoop each of chocolate, vanilla, and strawberry, all perfectly rounded—in his bowl before covering them in slices of banana, and artfully adding little towers of whipped cream for a classic banana split.

Levi went for sheer chaos, piling a giant mixing bowl high with scoops of all seven kinds of ice cream, creating a mountain of mismatched colors and flavors before putting handfuls of every topping in, including gummy bears, which no one else had touched.

Skylar reached for the can of whipped cream, intending to drown her creation in fluffy sweetness, and accidentally sent a spray flying across the counter, splattering Barrett's sleeve. His mock gasp of betrayal was so theatrical that she burst out laughing. She covered her mouth with sticky fingers, giggling until tears blurred her vision.

Levi was always quick to take things a step too far. He waited for the perfect moment when Barrett was distracted and, with a strange noise—"Hoo-cha!"—flicked a blob of whipped cream at him, hitting him squarely on the cheek.

"Scoundrel!" Barrett shouted and retaliated, grabbing a fistful of rainbow sprinkles and tossing them over Levi's head like confetti at Willy Wonka's birthday party.

Skylar stood at the kitchen table for a moment, bowl in hand, watching the two of them dissolve into childishness, and smiled warmly. She already felt better, having thought her next steps through over the course of the day, but seeing these two guys getting carried away, the tension she had been steeped in cracked and fell apart. The sweetness wasn't just in the ice cream or the sprinkles or the whipped cream. It was in the rare, precious feeling of being surrounded by people who loved her without any expectations. Already her cheeks were starting to ache from smiling so hard. She had missed this feeling *so much*.

"Hey, don't forget about me!" she said, sneaking up behind Levi and dabbing a streak of chocolate sauce across the bridge of his nose before darting away, laughing.

"Ooh, you little devil!" Levi drawled, laughing and wiping at his nose before he leapt around the side of the table and chased her into the living room. He caught up to her near the sofa, wrapped his arms around her waist and carried her back to the kitchen.

"Barr!" he called, motioning with his head.

Barrett, uncharacteristically grinning like a madman, knew exactly what his friend meant. Hands outstretched, fingers wiggling frantically, he leapt from his seat at the table and began tickling Skylar.

Laughter burst out of her rapid fire as she squirmed in Levi's arms. "St-stop!" she cried, through the laughter. "I'll pee!"

Hearing that, Barrett backed off, but Levi didn't release her—not right away. He leaned in and kissed the side of her neck, making her gasp in both surprise and pleasure. "Had some whipped cream there," he said next to her ear. Caught up in the moment, in the fun and silliness and the love that the three of them shared, she twisted her head until her face and Levi's were only an inch apart, then licked the tip of his nose and grinned at him. Levi kissed her again, on the lips this time, and she didn't squirm or resist. It was funny how soft a boy's lips could be, she thought.

Barrett had backed off when Skylar shouted, but he hadn't gone far. Now he stood, watching his friends embracing, looking a little like a deer in a set of headlights. Neither Levi nor Skylar had forgotten him though. Skylar broke the kiss with Levi, turned towards Barrett, her arm outstretched and said, "C'mere, Barr."

"I don't…" he began and looked quickly towards the floor.

Skylar disentangled herself from Levi's arms, moved towards Barrett and, taking hold of his shirt collar, pulled him to her, leaned up and kissed him, as loving and warm and gentle as the kiss she and Levi had shared. It set fire to him, sending heat spreading throughout his body, as if it was passing from Skylar's lips to his and suffusing him. He felt the first stirring in his crotch just as Skylar released him.

She released his lips, but still held onto his arm as she turned and reached for Levi with her other hand. "You too." Levi and Barrett's eyes met and there was uncertainty in both, but the alcohol and the sugar and the atmosphere all combined, breaking down barriers. It had been like this before, hadn't it? They each loved her in their own way, and right at this moment, they both wanted her. Last time it had just sort of happened, and in the moment, there was no time to consider what was happening. But now…?

Levi moved a step closer, then another. Skylar took hold of his arm and pulled him in close, until she was sandwiched between the two men, an arm around each of them. She kissed Levi, long and deeply, her tongue flicking against his teeth, before breaking off with a gasp, leaving a thin tendril of saliva trailing between their lips for an instant before turning to Barrett and kissing him just as deeply and with just as much passion.

Barrett's pulse began to race and he felt the heat inside of him rising to his skin. His penis began to stiffen as Skylar's tongue probed his mouth. *The alcohol*, he told himself. *I shouldn't…*

As if she could sense his thoughts, Skylar broke the kiss and whispered against the side of his mouth, "I want this, Barr. Right now, I think I *need* it," and kissed him again, before turning to Levi, whose hands were roaming over her back, tracing their way down her spine to the hem of her hoodie. His hand found its way under the baggy garment and discovered she wore nothing but panties beneath. His hand cupped her buttock, giving her a little squeeze that make her squeak and then giggle.

Skylar kissed Levi, turned to Barrett, kissed him and, her voice husky, said, "The bedroom."

Levi and Barrett shared another look before Skylar kissed them each in turn again, stripped off her sweatshirt, tossed it towards the sofa in the living room, and began guiding them towards her room. The two men looked at one another again, but this time there was no hesitation.

In her room, Skylar crawled onto the bed as Levi and Barrett shed their clothes. Side by side like this, she couldn't help comparing their bodies—Levi tall and slim, but muscular, while Barrett was a little shorter, his shoulders broader, and fit enough but not cut the way Levi was. Levi was exciting and Barrett was comfortable and she realized how attractive both qualities were. They were unique individuals and for her, they complemented each other perfectly.

When both men were nude—Barrett's cock already standing to attention and Levi at half-mast—Skylar smiled and beckoned the boys with one finger. Levi grinned and leaned over the bed, his penis growing even as she watched. She thought he would climb up, but he surprised her by grabbing her hips, lifting her butt up and stripping her panties off before pulling her to the edge of the bed and burying his face in her pussy.

She gasped in pleasure as his tongue found her clit, probing it, pushing it back and forth as he licked her. One of his fingers made its way inside of her and she arched her back and opened her eyes to find Barrett kneeling on the bed next to her, his cock only inches from her face. She met his eyes, smiled, and took the base of his cock in hand before licking the very tip. She kissed the head of his cock then ran her tongue up and down its length, forcing a small moan out of him.

Barrett gently rocked his hips back and forth, pushing his cock in and out of Skylar's mouth while Levi's tongue traced lines up and down her pussy lips and his fingers stroked her insides. She could feel the energy welling up inside of her, collecting in a small ball in her belly—it was coming, but she didn't want that. Not yet.

She pulled away from Barrett's cock and put a hand on Levi's head. "I want you inside of me," she said, looking from one man to the other.

"Both... of us?" Barrett asked.

"I've always," she said, "wanted to try double-penetration. She rolled over to the side of the bed, reached for the bottom drawer of her dresser and rummaged until she came up with a small tube of lubricant.

She held the lube out, not to either of them in particular, but for whichever one of them would take it. "I've tried with a vibe and it's..." A faint blush rose to Skylar's cheeks. It was silly to be embarrassed now, but... "It's nice," she finished.

Levi looked Barrett in the eye and then both

grinned simultaneously.

Barrett lay down on the center of the bed, on his back, his cock swaying with the momentum so it bounced off of his flat stomach. Gently, hands on Skylar's hips, Levi positioned her so she was straddling Barrett, with her ass in the air. He had never seen her from this angle, her butt slightly spread by the position, her little pink asshole and slick pussy exposed. He felt the urge to let out a low whistle of admiration, but checked the impulse—he didn't want to make this cheap.

Understanding what was needed from her, Skylar reached behind her, gripped the shaft of Barrett's cock and guided him inside of her. Both of them let out little gasps of pleasure as he entered her pussy, and slowly he began thrusting upwards. Levi poured lube from the bottle all over his cock, rubbing it full length until it was shiny with the liquid, then squirted more onto Skylar's asshole, making her jump at the touch of the cold liquid. "Sorry," he muttered and rubbed the lube into her asshole until it was as shiny as his cock.

Barrett kept thrusting up inside of her, the full length of his shaft pressing into her body, as Levi crouched above them and gently, carefully pushed the head of his penis into her ass. It made something inside of her quiver to feel him enter her most secret place—a place no one but herself had ever touched before—and it was delicious. She felt Levi's rigid dick pushing up inside of her ass, like a sexual explorer carving out new territory, while Barrett's rhythmically thrusting penis penetrated her from below. She could feel the walls of her pussy and ass tighten and release, flexing as the two men alternated the cadence of their thrusts so that Barrett was going up while Levi was coming out, but for a split second each time, their cocks pressed on opposite sides of her holes, as if crushing her flesh between them, the way her two boys were crushing her.

Skylar let out a moan, low at first but growing in

volume and timbre. It reached a peak and became quickened breathing as she panted, "More, more, more! Faster! Give it to me!" She looked down into Barrett's flushed face, saw the sweat beaded on his forehead. Their eyes met and she leaned down, kissing him deeply, trying to push herself inside of him the way he was pushing inside of her.

Straightening as much as she could, she looked over her shoulder. Levi's face was as red as Barrett's, and sweat dripped down his muscled, tattooed chest as he pushed his cock into her ass again and again. She wished she could see his penis actually entering her—just the thought of it sent a new trill of excitement through every nerve of her body.

The men fucked her—Barrett her pussy, Levi her ass—and as they did, they perfected the rhythm until all three of them were in almost exact physical harmony. None of them were religious, but Skylar thought this must be what heaven felt like, only all the time. Eyes closed, she tilted her head towards the ceiling and let out another moaning gasp.

"I'm gonna cum!" Levi cried and Skylar twisted, trying to look behind herself as she felt Levi's cock pull entirely out of her ass. He stroked himself rapidly, but it only took three or four strokes before his cock erupted, covering her butt in his hot, sticky semen. She felt a trickle of it run down her crack, over her asshole to where it must have settled on Barrett's balls. The thought gave her a wicked little jolt of excitement and she pressed down hard on Barrett's chest, quickening the motion of her hips, willing him to push inside of her harder, faster. She could feel that tight little ball of energy deep inside of her again and it was going to explode any second.

"Cum for me, Barr," she said, sliding off of him, shifting her hips and turning until she lifted her leg and pressed her pussy down onto his face. She took his cock in her mouth, stroking it up and down while she sucked on his head. His tongue found her pussy and then it was lapping her insides, fucking her almost the way his cock had. She felt the walls of her pussy tighten and her legs began to shake and then she exploded, a rush of heat welling out of her belly to spread throughout her entire body. She let out a squeal of utter pleasure, muffled by Barrett's cock in her mouth and an instant later, he was cumming too. She freed his cock from her mouth, dribbles of cum on her lips, and stroked him as hard and fast she was able until it stopped twitching and only a drop of cum remained, beaded on the tip of his cockhead.

Skylar flopped over onto her back, her head towards the foot of the bed, and threw her arms and legs out, finding Barrett on one side of her and Levi on the other. "You guys," she gasped. "You guys... are amazing."

Her body was sore—especially her butt—but every little ache was delicious. Her entire being was relaxed like she'd never been before, not even after other times she had great sex. This was different. This wasn't just great, it was mind-blowing.

"Hey, it wasn't just us. It takes two—er, three to tango," Levi said, leaning over her, grinning like crazy.

Skylar laughed softly then scrambled up until she was laying on the bed properly, flanked her by best friends—her favorite people in the world. She drew them close to her as she had in the kitchen until it became a sort of three-way cuddle.

"I love you guys," she told them. "I mean it." She kissed Barrett, then Levi, and snuggled down between them, eyes closed.

Some time later—it was impossible to tell how long, the way Skylar felt—Barrett asked, "Feel better?" his hand lightly stroking her thigh.

"Mm," was her only answer. "I'll have to do laundry before I can go to bed though."

Levi chuckled. "Sorry."

"Don't be." She placed a hand on his thigh, as

Barrett had hers. "I needed that. I feel amazing."

"Good," Barrett said, meeting Levi's eyes for an instant before shifting back to Sky. "We were worried about you."

"I know," she admitted. "I didn't mean to worry you guys, I just wanted time to get my thoughts straight."

"And?" Levi asked. "Did you?"

"Mhm," she said, sounding sleepy now. She yawned without bothering to stifle it, then said, "I decided." She opened her eyes and looked from one man to the other. "I need to meet Sophia."

Chapter 22.

Skylar – Monday Morning

Monday morning at TechnoFirm was every bit the whirlwind Skylar had expected, maybe more—but it couldn't bother her. Saturday afternoon, and most of Sunday, had been difficult; she did a lot of wrestling with her thoughts and feelings. Sunday night—every time she thought of it, she felt the heat rising inside of her and hurriedly changed the mental subject, afraid someone would notice—wiped all of that out. She still felt wonderful, both about Levi and Barrett and about the decision she had made. There was a lot to do on a lot of personal fronts, but she knew what she wanted now and that alone made all the difference.

Noon crept closer and the constant clatter of her inbox finally slowed. For the first time all day, Skylar settled at her desk and let herself relax for a few quiet moments. She was checking the status on a vendor payment for one of Nathan's personal projects when the man himself appeared at the door to her office, knocked peremptorily and then entered.

"Skylar," he said, his tone even but unusually grave. "I need to speak with you."

She froze for just a second, her fingers lingering on the keyboard. There was something about the way he said it—not sharp, not impatient like when he was under pressure—but quiet and heavy. Nathan Dyer was rarely less than serious, but this was something else. Her pulse fluttered anxiously. Nathan didn't wear his emotions on his sleeve, but she could tell whatever was on his mind was bothering him and if he was coming to her, it must have somehow involved Skylar.

She stood and smoothed her skirt out of habit, facing her boss across her desk. This was as unlikely a scene as could be imagined in the TechnoFirm offices— generally, it was the other way around. Nathan gestured to her chair and then seated himself at the visitor's chair on his side of the desk. She sat and met his gaze, trying not to fidget.

Nathan leaned back slightly in his chair, his gaze thoughtful, but that aura of discomfort still with him. For a long moment, he didn't speak, and Skylar's mind spun through every possible scenario. Had she missed a deadline? Mishandled something? Was he about to fire her?

No, she thought, *this is personal.* Chet, disheveled, looking almost homeless when he ambushed her outside of the building came to mind. She had felt so good since the night before, he never even entered her mind until that moment.

Nathan spoke, his voice calm but tinged with something unfamiliar. "I wanted to speak to you privately," he began slowly, "and not in my office, because of the implied power imbalance." He paused, as if choosing his next words carefully, then met her eyes across the desk. "The security team alerted me to the incident with Chester on Friday afternoon."

Skylar blinked, her stomach tightening, her fingers twitching slightly in her lap. Nathan had taken her side once against Chet, surprising her, but that was more abstract. Nathan's assistant had been dating his son and then they weren't. It was outside of the office, so it wasn't any concern as long as her work wasn't affected. That was the way Nathan had apparently thought about it. But Chet showing up at the TechnoFirm building, confronting her during business hours, that was something entirely else.

All at once, the thought of Chet, haunting the front of the building like a slumped and dirty ghost, waiting to ambush her, to beg her for forgiveness they both knew he didn't deserve and could never earn… Her stomach flipped, and with it, the nervousness was replaced by anger because now Chet wasn't just wrecking her personal life, he was worming his way into her professional world too. She felt a hot, indignant flush creep up her neck.

Nathan's voice stayed calm, but it was clear this was no small talk. "I understand you've been going through some personal things," he continued, his gaze steady but not without sympathy. "But I want to remind you that those things don't belong anywhere near the workplace."

The words stung, even though they weren't unfair from Nathan's perspective. Skylar still felt she had to defend herself, after all—

"He showed up out of nowhere," she told Nathan. She tried not to sound defensive, but heard the edge in her words. "I didn't ask him to come here. If it were up to me…" The words were out before she could stop them, raw and unfiltered. "If it were up to me, I'd never see Chet again."

There it was. The truth hung in the air between them, almost too personal for a conversation in this sterile glass office. Skylar half-expected Nathan to lecture her, to remind her that Chet was his son—that she had to keep her personal feelings in check. But he was quiet. He studied her for long moments.

When he finally spoke, he surprised her. "I'll have security set a standing order," Nathan said plainly. "If he shows up again, they'll remove him from the premises. You won't have to deal with him."

Skylar blinked, genuinely taken aback—astonished even. Nathan virtually never let his emotions show, he played everything so close to the vest. But this was his own son. She didn't even know how to respond. Nathan's offer—no, it was simply a statement of what he intended doing—was more than professional courtesy. It was like he had thrown up a shield around her, to protect her.

Nathan leaned forward slightly, his hands clasped, his voice a shade softer but still cool. "Business is business, Skylar. The rest is... something else. But all the same, I'm sorry you had to go through that. Chester has a lot of growing up to do, as we both know."

For a flicker of a moment, he looked away, uncomfortable. He had wandered too close to something and now was trying to step back. But the message was clear: Nathan wasn't defending Chet. Whether out of professionalism or some unspoken personal reason, he was taking Skylar's side.

The sense of relief she felt was tinged with something else—triumph, victory. Chet, for all his years of emotional manipulation and control, had finally lost, once and for all. Skylar had defeated him outside of the building Friday, putting him in his place, and now his own father was taking her side. Maybe it was petty, but it was a satisfying win, and Skylar knew that she was no longer powerless.

Chapter 23.

Skylar – That Afternoon

Late in the afternoon, a lull settled over the office as operations began to wind down for the day. For most of TechnoFirm's employees, the last flurry of emails had been sent, and the day's meetings were over and done with. Skylar had just finished shepherding Nathan into his final obligation of the day, a video conference with a potential corporate partner in Seattle, and now that he was safely tucked away in his office, his door closed, his headset on, his focus fully engaged as he went into his CEO-meeting-a-new-person routine, she finally had a few moments to herself.

Skylar let out a heavy breath as she moved down the hallway, headed towards her own office. Her shoulders sagged a little. The office felt oddly still in the late light, most of the staff already gone for the day or simply pretending to work, counting down the minutes until five. But Skylar had one more thing to do, something that had been quietly gnawing at the back of her mind since she came to a decision on Sunday.

She sat down, woke her computer, and stared at the search bar for a long moment before her fingers finally moved.

Western Massachusetts Women's Correctional Facility – phone number

She typed the words carefully, each one more surreal than the last. She had only heard the name once, when Barrett told her a little more about Sophia Saturday afternoon before she holed herself up in her room. Sophia—her birth mother, a woman she had no memories of, just a name wrapped in a cloud of unsettling stories and a childhood shaped by someone else's choices—lived this place with such a cold, institutional name, and seeing it written out felt like something out of someone else's life. There was drama in Skylar's life—a lot more than she'd like lately—but *prison* was something out of movies and TV shows and books, a word she knew but only had a vague concept of its reality.

The search results came up instantly, sterile and bureaucratic, offering nothing of the gravity this moment carried, without any deference to the way she felt. In a way, that seemed appropriate. Skylar clicked on the main website for the Massachusetts Department of Corrections and, poking around, quickly found the number for the women's prison's administrative office. She scribbled it down on a sticky note, knowing there was no reason to— that she was only procrastinating.

Her heart thudded in her chest as she reached for her phone. This wasn't like a business call, or even one of her calls to restaurants or theaters, begging and pleading to procure dinner reservations or show tickets for Nathan when he had one of his last minute whims. This wasn't familiar emotional territory. It was unknown, it was official, a kind of government business in a way, and it was intimidating. It wasn't even just about making the call—it was about a woman who, until three days ago, she hadn't even known existed and who was now her actual, flesh-and-blood mother, serving time in prison for a *murder*. She had never even met anyone who had been to prison as far as she knew, and the first person she did would be her biological mother? She would have laughed if it wasn't so nerve-wracking.

Her finger hovered over the keypad, but she didn't press "call" right away. Instead, she took a deep breath, leaned back in her chair and allowed herself a small, dry smirk. *This is the easy part, Sky,* she told herself. The hard part wasn't dialing the number or speaking to a stranger who worked in a scary place. The hard part was what would come after—meeting Sophia.

And her mind was set. She made the decision, and she wasn't going to second guess herself or back down. She had done far too much of that in her life already. She sat forward, steadied herself, and hit the call button.

The phone pressed to her ear, heart thudding hard enough that she was sure whoever answered on the other end would hear it. Three rings and then line clicked and a tired-sounding male voice answered, "Western Women's, admin."

She swallowed and cleared her throat, trying to sound steadier than she felt. "Hi, my name's Skylar Hunt. I wanted to ask about visiting an inmate."

There was the sound of typing, keys clacking, before the man replied, "Inmate's name?"

"Sophia Hunt," she said, the name feeling sticky on her tongue. It was an ordinary name, but at the same time, foreign and yet weirdly familiar.

"Your name?" the man asked. For him this was routine, impersonal, even boring.

"Skylar Hunt," she answered.

She barely got the words out before she continued, a little too quickly, trying to fill the space. "I assume there's some kind of security clearance or a process for approval, or—"

"You're on the list," he said, interrupting her.

Skylar paused, her mouth open, staring at but not really seeing the other side of the room. "I'm... on the list?"

"Yes, ma'am. Visiting hours are ten to four, Saturday and Sunday. Make sure you call forty-eight hours in advance to schedule any visits."

She blinked, looked down at the desk, trying to make sense of what he was saying. How could she be on the list? She knew enough about prison protocol from media she'd consumed to know inmates had to request people be approved to visit. She only just learned of Sophia's existence, so how could—

The man's voice came again, polite but ready to move on. It was almost five o'clock, after all. "Anything else, ma'am?"

Skylar's voice had gone soft, almost distant. "I'm on the list?"

"Yes, ma'am," he confirmed, patient but flat. "You said your name's Skylar Hunt, right?"

"Yes, that's me."

"You're on the list, ma'am," he repeated, as if that settled the matter. "Anything else I can do for you?"

She shook her head even though he couldn't see her, her voice barely above a whisper. "No. That's... that's all. Thank you."

"Have a good night, ma'am," he said, and the call ended.

Skylar lowered the phone slowly, placing it face-down on her desk. For several minutes, she sat there, staring at the dark screen of her computer as if it might offer some other answer, some hidden piece of the puzzle.

Her thoughts were a jumble. She hadn't even known Sophia existed a few days ago, and now not only was she real, but she had also apparently been expecting Skylar—or at least hoping. Long enough to have put Skylar's name on a visitor's list. The idea was almost too big to wrap her mind around. She never knew Sophia existed, but had Sophia been waiting for her all this time?

She let out a breath that sounded like a tiny, tired laugh of disbelief. And then, in the stillness of her office, she muttered to herself, ordinary words that sounded strange as they left her lips. "I'm on the list."

Chapter 24.

Skylar's Week

After work Monday night, Skylar had a promise to fulfill. She stepped through the door of the house in Bay Ridge, hung her coat, and then moved down the back hallway, greeting Levi, who was doing push-ups in his room, as she hurried to her own bedroom. Closing the door, she kicked off her shoes, then sat on the edge of her bed, and called Brian. As far as Skylar knew, there was still no word from Natalie, but Skylar wanted to let her stepfather know that she was doing something at least. She had a feeling that meeting Sophia would open up the road to finding Natalie, if anything would.

"Skylar—hello," Brian answered after a single ring, his voice tight. "Natalie still hasn't come home," he added before Skylar could even say hello in return. She heard the undercurrent of fear in him, even if he was doing his best to cover it.

The lie came without her even knowing it until it was too late. "I wanted to tell you that I've got someone looking into things, Brian. A private investigator." Maybe it was just a half-lie, only a fib really. Barrett really was an investigator, even if he wasn't a full-fledged one.

Brian exhaled, and she could almost hear some of the weight lift off him. "Good. That's good. I appreciate that and—and send me the bill, whatever it costs. I don't care how much it is and I know those guys aren't cheap. But promise me that you'll call me as soon as you hear anything, Skylar. I mean anything. And I don't care what time it is either, day or night." The words tumbled out of him like a river rushing over a waterfall.

She pictured her stepfather pacing around his big townhouse, alone, worried, feeling helpless. Her heart went out to him, and she almost offered to go over to his place, but caught herself. He would say no, tell her not to worry about him, and she would gently argue and eventually he would give in, but ultimately, what good would it do? She had nothing to tell him yet and they would both be uncomfortable.

Instead, she said, "I will, Brian. I promise. You're taking care of yourself, I hope?" She made it sound like a question, as if she was unsure, when she was actually quite certain—certain that he wasn't.

Brian laughed softly, self-deprecatingly. "If you mean am I drinking too much and sleeping too little, sure, I'm taking care of myself. No," he said quickly. "I'm just kidding." She wasn't sure that he was, but she didn't call him out on it. "I've been eating out a lot and going to the movies. It helps," he added quietly.

"Well, if you need anything…" Skylar told him. Brian said he would let her know and then they said goodbye and the call ended. She sat in the dark for a long time, phone resting on her lap. She was sure Natalie wouldn't have told Brian about Sophia—she hadn't even told Skylar. She wondered what Brian would do when the truth finally surfaced, whatever truth turned out to be.

The rest of the week seemed to slip past almost without Skylar noticing. One day blurred into the next as her time was swallowed up by the relentless pace at TechnoFirm. As much as the job could be frustrating and exhausting, there was something oddly comforting about the sheer normalcy of it, about racing around like crazy while trying to fulfill Nathan Dyer's last-minute demands, his constant shuffling of his schedule. If nothing else, it kept her mind off of the whirlwind of revelations, confrontations, and heartbreaks that had flooded her life over the last week. Ironically, the familiar chaos of Nathan Dyer's world as she acted as his tether to reality and its obligations felt like solid ground beneath her feet.

In the evenings, the house was... peaceful. More peaceful a home than she had experienced in the last couple of years. She, Barrett, and Levi had settled into something soft and warm and unspoken. The air between them had shifted—the tension had lifted, and they were almost like the three kids who spent summers together again, enjoying one another's company, as close as three people could be—closer now, in fact, since they had shared such intimacy. They still hadn't talked about what the three of them were to one another or how the lines had blurred, but it was as if an understanding had quietly and mutually grown between them, and for now, while other things loomed over their heads, they were content— even happy—to leave things as they were.

Skylar snatched minutes here and there for her online classwork, but most nights, all three of them would collapse onto the worn living room couch after dinner. Sometimes they would squabble over what to watch or which takeout place to order from, but even that was fun in a way. They ran through whole seasons of shows on streaming services, trading commentary and making jokes; they played favorite games on Barrett's battered PlayStation 3—something they hadn't done since high school. Skylar had forgotten how easy it was to let her guard down around Barrett and Levi, how happy and safe they made her feel. Being able to sink into the security and warmth of being around people who knew her better than anyone else was as close to paradise as she could imagine.

Thursday night was the highlight of the week. Levi received tickets to a Broadway production from a client who couldn't use them, and it ended up being a funny and light show that was exactly the kind of mindless escape Skylar needed. The three of them had fun dressing up enough to make the outing feel like an occasion without taking it too seriously. Skylar dove into Barrett and Levi's closets and used them like her own personal Ken dolls, mixing and matching outfits until they were the perfect blend of dressy and relaxed.

On the way home, Skylar sat in the front of Barrett's SUV and Levi sat on the middle seat in the rear so he could see either of them at a turn of the head. Levi made Skylar laugh until her sides hurt pretending to be a theater snob, giving overly dramatic critiques of the actors and plot. Barrett's only comment was that the set design seemed like a lot of work, but it looked nice. Skylar found herself caught between genuine joy in these moments with the people closest to her and the bittersweet awareness of how hard they were working, trying to distract her. They knew her well enough to know that this coming weekend—that meeting Sophia—loomed over her like a storm cloud.

Thursday morning, Skylar ducked into her office, closed the door behind her and called the Western Massachusetts Women's Correctional Facility. She was nervous doing so, but it wasn't like the first time—this time it was easy to speak to the man on the other end, to make sure she could visit Sophia on Saturday. They would let Sophia know a visitor was coming, the man said, and Skylar wasn't sure how she felt about that. It seemed wrong for someone in a drab prison uniform to be the bearer of the news that Sophia was going to meet her daughter for the first time.

By Friday, the week had taken on the feel of something suspended in time. Most of the week had been fine, fun even, but now it was like Skylar was holding her breath, waiting for the inevitable. Waiting for Saturday. Waiting to meet her mother. Just those words felt so bizarre, like she had stepped through the looking glass into another world.

But it was real, and it would happen. On Saturday

morning, Barrett would drive her and Levi up to Chicopee, Mass and then Skylar would be sitting across from Sophia Hunt, her birth mother, a complete stranger whose existence she only learned of a week before. "Birth mother." She had turn those words over countless times in her head, repeating them like some kind of mantra.

Friday evening, at home, as the sun began to set, the house was quiet again. Levi was making his monthly visit to his family, and Barrett was still at Mr. Whittington's office, finishing up some background check work, which he'd fallen slightly behind on after Mr. Whittington had allowed him to tackle the mystery of Skylar's birth the week before. Skylar sat on the front porch of the house with a cup of tea, staring up at the fading sky, feeling the weight of her thoughts pressing in around her.

It was funny, she realized, how ordinary the world looked even when she felt so completely mixed up and topsy-turvy. People were walking dogs, cars rolled past, kids' voices floated from somewhere down the block, and she sat there with her tea cooling in her hands, on the edge of a reality she hadn't asked for, but knew she couldn't refuse. It was just *so strange* how quickly things had changed—and it might be a while before everything was truly settled.

When Barrett came home later that night, the quiet, easy routine slipped back into place. He had eaten dinner in the city, and she hadn't felt like eating at all, so he joined her in the living room, hip-to-hip on the couch, one arm draped around her. The TV was off and they sat in comfortable silence, the only noise faint sounds of the old refrigerator drifting from the kitchen.

"You ready for tomorrow?" Barrett asked eventually, his voice low, as if they were sharing a secret.

Skylar hesitated before saying, "I don't know what I could do to *be* ready, but I'm going so I guess, yeah, I am."

Barrett kissed the top of her head and held her a

little tighter. "I've got a new melodic death metal playlist for the drive up. You and Levi'll love it."

She laughed despite the knot in her stomach and leaned into his warmth.

When Skylar finally went to bed that night, she stared at the ceiling for a long time, her thoughts refusing to leave her alone, even long enough to fall asleep. The week had been a strange sort of blessing, a gift of safety and happiness from a normally uncaring universe. But no matter how much she wanted to hold onto the last few days, the weekend was coming.

She hoped she would find the answers she so desperately needed, but she was afraid she would only find new questions.

Chapter 25.

Skylar – Saturday

The morning sun was barely climbing above the skyline when Skylar, Levi, and Barrett piled into Barrett's SUV, the leather seats still cold from the early April air. Barrett hadn't been kidding the night before and his newly curated death metal playlist was queued up and ready to blast the second the engine turned over. Skylar, still bleary-eyed and trying to settle into the passenger seat, winced at the first few guttural growls that bled through the speakers, shooting him a sideways look that didn't need words.

Levi, climbing into the back seat with his travel mug clutched in one hand, immediately groaned. "No way are we doing this for four hours, man," he said, leaning forward between the seats to poke at the volume knob.

Barrett grinned. "It's only a three-hour drive."

"Skyyyy," Levi whined. "We need a ruling."

Barrett, his fingers poised dramatically above the play button, said, "Okay, okay. It's a democracy, boys and girls, so let's settle this the adult way: rock, paper, scissors. Losers surrender their eardrums to greatness."

Skylar couldn't help smirking at his enthusiasm, even with the gnawing feeling in her belly. She agreed to the game, and after a few rounds of mock-serious battles, the compromise was struck: Barrett could play his music until they crossed out of New York, Levi would take over in Connecticut, and Skylar would have control once they hit Massachusetts.

They set off and the morning stretched out. Interstate 95 unrolled before them in a gray ribbon as Barrett's music pulsed and howled through the speakers, while the SUV rumbled steadily along. Levi kept up a running commentary of sarcastic critiques on the music, from the singer's unintelligible screams to the machine-gun drumming.

Barrett argued about the music's technical skill. "These guys are pros, and a lot of them *still* take lessons from people they feel are superior to them. They're dedicated."

"Dedicated to making my ears bleed," Levi countered.

Skylar laughed, soaking up the warmth of their banter. It was a small but welcome buffer against the nervousness that steadily built in her chest, growing as the distance between themselves and the prison shrank.

It was a long drive, but it didn't feel that way. The boys kept up their patter, keeping themselves entertained, and as soon as they passed the Connecticut state line, Barrett swapped his playlist for Levi's pick, a mellow and eclectic mix of 70s and 80s rock. The conversation quieted a little after that, the mood shifting, as if all three of them were beginning to feel the gravity of their destination even through the jokes and the music.

As the Massachusetts border approached, Skylar grew almost completely silent, her thoughts spiraling inward. The distractions the boys offered no longer matched up against the dread she felt. Her stomach churned until it actually hurt. When the "Welcome to Massachusetts" sign appeared along Interstate 91, she leaned forward and reached for the stereo, gently turning the music off.

"Do you guys mind if we ditch the music for a bit?" she asked quietly.

Barrett simply nodded, eyes flicking toward her briefly, as Levi leaned forward and gave her shoulder a squeeze. "Whatever you need, Sky."

The silence that filled the car wasn't awkward. It was heavy, but it wasn't uncomfortable. Barrett and Levi understood and Skylar knew that she didn't have to explain herself.

The last leg of the trip felt longer than the rest. Except for summers at camp and some vacations, Skylar had spent her entire life in the city and the open roads of western Massachusetts, flanked by spring greenery, fascinated her despite everything else on her mind. When the low, sprawling brick buildings of the women's prison came into view at last, though, the brief calm the landscape had gifted her dissolved.

Barrett pulled into the lot, parked, and cut the engine. As the engine ticked and pinged, his hands rested on the wheel and he looked straight forward at the drab buildings. Levi unbuckled his seatbelt but didn't open the door.

"I know we can't go all the way in, but do you want us to wait in the lobby?" Levi asked after a moment.

Skylar swallowed and shifted in her seat until she could see both of them. Both of their faces showed the same quiet concern, the same unwillingness to leave her alone. This was hard and they wanted to be with her. She wanted their support, their love, the comfort of being with them, but she knew the rules. No visitors beyond the admin area without prior clearance. There was no point in them waiting inside—it would only make it harder for her to walk in, knowing they were right there, worried and helpless. Worse, if they came in with her, it would make it that much simpler for her to turn on her heel and run back to them, back to where she knew she was safe.

She forced a smile. "You guys can't go past the front anyway," she said, her voice steadier than she felt. "There's no point in you waiting inside. I'll be okay."

Levi looked like he wanted to argue, but Barrett only said, "You've got this, Sky."

She opened the car door and stood, her legs shaky and stiff from the long ride. It still wasn't quite ten yet and the morning air washing over her was cool and fresh-smelling, at odds with the grim, fortress-like buildings ahead. The prison looked like a place designed to hold not just people, but secrets.

The guys climbed out of the car too, walking with her toward the entrance. At the gate, Skylar glanced back at them. "You know, it's weird," she said softly. "I stood up to Chet." She grinned for an instant before it faded. "I *wrecked* Chet, actually, if I say so myself. I felt *so* powerful then, but this scares the hell out of me."

Levi gave her a half-smile. "Yeah, but you're doing it."

She made a small affirming noise in her throat, drawing strength from the simple truth in those words. She briefly looked from Levi to Barrett then turned back towards the gate. She felt a deep sense of gratitude to both of them, but this was the part she had to do alone. She squared her shoulders, and stepped inside.

Signs directed her down a short, yellow-painted hallway towards the administration desk, her sneakers squeaking slightly as she crossed the tile floor. At the end of the hallway, a woman sat behind a glass partition. She was middle-aged, with a kind but weary expression, wearing a khaki uniform and heavy glasses.

"Hi," Skylar said. "I'm here to—" She stumbled, her heart fluttering. "I'm here to visit a prisoner. Sophia Hunt?"

"Name?" the woman asked.

"Skylar Hunt."

The woman's fingers flew across her keyboard, then she said, "Sign in," and slid a tablet chained to the desk through the hole in the partition. Skylar picked up the tablet, signed with the stylus and pushed the tablet back.

"ID, please," the woman said, only briefly glancing at Skylar's signature before it faded from the tablet's screen.

Skylar fished in her purse, took out her wallet—her purse was nearly empty, as she knew they'd confiscate it for the visit—removed her state ID and passed it across the desk. The woman picked the ID up, slid it into a small scanner and made a copy, the mechanical whirring of the machine sounding absurdly loud in the stillness of the waiting area.

Skylar hadn't expected that part, the ID copy, and her nerves must've shown, because the woman met her eyes and said, her tone softer, "First time?"

Skylar managed a tight, awkward smile and a little laugh. "That obvious, huh?"

The woman returned the smile, one corner of her mouth tugging upward in quiet understanding. "It gets easier, honey," she said gently. "You'll be fine."

Skylar nodded, clutching those words, a stranger's kindness, like a lifeline, even if she wasn't sure she believed them. She had faced so much lately—finally breaking up with Chet; Natalie's disappearance; the tangled emotions she shared with Barrett and Levi; the disintegration of everything she thought she knew about her small family. But this? She was going to talk face-to-face with the woman whose name was on her birth certificate, the woman who had given her life and then disappeared from it entirely. What could prepare anyone for that?

The woman behind the glass gave Skylar her ID back and told her to take a chair. She sat in an uncomfortable plastic chair, bolted to the wall. She hadn't realized that a line had formed behind her but now she saw nearly a dozen people—mostly either elderly or small children—waiting their turn at the window.

A door opened and an officer called Skylar's name. She stood and the man—slim, blond, younger than she was, to her surprise—motioned her towards a small alcove, where she was asked to surrender her purse and empty her pockets. This part she was prepared for. She had read up on security protocols for visiting prisoners and she had dressed as simply as possible for the trip: well-worn jeans, a plain pink t-shirt, her hair tied back, no jewelry. She only brought the bare essentials in her purse: wallet, phone, keys, and a single tube of lipstick. At the officer's direction she placed all those things into a clear plastic bin. The officer searched through the items briskly and briefly, gave her a quick but thorough pat-down, then waved her toward a heavy, metal security door.

The officer made a gesture, signaling to someone unseen, and the door at the other side of the alcove slid open with a buzz. Skylar stepped through.

The visitors' area wasn't quite what Skylar had expected, though she wasn't sure what she had imagined. It was a large room with bare concrete walls and floor, bolted-down tables with attached benches arranged in rigid, evenly spaced rows. The room had the sterile, joyless feel of a high school cafeteria stripped of any personality. A couple of old vending machines hummed softly in one corner. The faded Coke logo on the drink machine provided the only color in the room. The rest of the space was muted grays and dull orange—the jumpsuits worn by the inmates scattered at tables, deep in conversation with their visitors. Some were quiet, some were tearful, some spoke quickly and urgently, but all of them shared an aura of eagerness that Skylar had never seen. In that instant, her heart went out to every woman in the room.

"Hunt?" a middle-aged officer, another woman, asked. Skylar said she was and the officer led her to one of the small tables near the center of the room. The officer gestured for her to sit and said simply, "Wait here." Skylar lowered herself onto the hard bench, her heart pounding against her ribcage, hands clenched tightly in her lap. All around her, the sound of low conversations blended with the mechanical clink of coins being fed into the vending machines, punctuated by the occasional laugh from a child visiting their mother at a nearby table. Over all of that was the echo of boots on concrete as officers circulated around the room, keeping watch.

Skylar wasn't sure how long she waited, but the minutes felt like hours as her stomach twisted itself into even tighter knots. Sitting there, she noticed a faint tang of disinfectant in the air and its scent made her realize that sweat was gathering beneath her arms and dampening her palms. She wiped them discreetly against her jeans, trying to keep her breathing steady and almost succeeding. The night before, lying sleeplessly in bed, she had run through a thousand different ways this could go, but none of them had prepared her for the actual, agonizing wait.

And then, finally, the sound of heavy boots against the floor, moving purposefully closer, snapped her to attention.

A burly corrections officer stopped midway across the room, glancing towards where Skylar sat. He looked back towards the hallway he had come from, pointed towards Skylar and said, "Come on, Hunt. Your visitor's waiting."

The officer moved aside, and there, stepping into the visitor's room, was Sophia Hunt.

Skylar's breath caught in her throat.

Chapter 26.

Skylar and Sophia

Sophia was a little taller than Skylar expected, her frame slender and worn almost to the point of gauntness, as if life had pressed its thumb down hard on her and kept it there for years. Her face looked older than the forty-two years she must have been if she was fifteen when Skylar was born, but it still carried echoes of Skylar's own features. She could see in Sophia the shape of her own eyes and the line of her jaw. Sophia's hair was a dull chestnut, threaded with strands of gray, pulled back into a practical ponytail. There were deep lines around her mouth, and her eyes were faintly sunken, but when her gaze settled on Skylar, there was something soft inside of them, something that was at the same time both achingly familiar and foreign.

Sophia approached the table slowly, her hands kept carefully visible at her sides as per the unspoken rules of the visitors' room. She slid onto the bench across from Skylar, her movements stiff, as if hesitant. Skylar had wondered, while she waited, if Sophia would be as uncomfortable, as nervous, as she was—now she knew.

For a long moment, neither of them spoke. The noise of the room seemed to fade away, replaced by the rushing sound of Skylar's own heartbeat in her ears.

Sophia was the first to break the silence. Her voice quiet, husky with emotion, and edged with something that might have been regret.

"You look just like him."

Skylar's mouth opened and her brow furrowed, thrown by the comment. "Him?"

Sophia said, "Aaron. Your father."

Skylar swallowed, her throat suddenly dry. She hadn't expected the conversation to start that way. She hadn't known what to expect at all, really. She spent years believing Natalie was her mother—beautiful, blonde Natalie, who didn't look like Skylar at all. Now she knew why as she sat staring at her birth mother, a woman who upended Skylar's entire world with nothing more than a name on a birth certificate.

Sophia's hands rested lightly on the tabletop, her fingers curled inward. Her knuckles were strangely pale, Skylar thought. Sophia was pale all over—prison pallor, they called it—but her knuckles seemed chalk-white. Watching Sophia's hands, Skylar felt an urge to reach across the table, to lean in and bridge the gap between them—but she didn't. She didn't know if that's what she really wanted or if it was just something she thought she was *supposed* to feel.

"I didn't think you'd ever come," Sophia added softly, as if admitting it to herself more than anything.

Skylar's voice, when it came, felt like it belonged to someone else. "I didn't know you existed until last week. I was—surprised when they told me I was already on your visitors list."

Sophia winced slightly, her shoulders drawing inward. "Maybe that's my fault," she murmured. "But I thought—I thought Natalie would, I don't know. Prepare you. Somehow. At least tell you I *existed*." She made a low sound in her throat that might have been a sour chuckle.

Skylar sat back, her mind racing, questions piling on top of one another. But for the first time, it wasn't anger or fear that sat with her at the table. It was curiosity burning her up from the inside. And beneath that, there was a deep ache that she couldn't quite name, as if she'd been carrying around a wound her entire life and only just realized she was bleeding.

The woman across from her was both a stranger and her mother.

"I sent letters," Sophia said. "I guess you never got them if you didn't know about me." There was a note of hope in her voice, as if Skylar not getting the letters at all was better than receiving them without replying.

Skylar shook her head. "I never got them," she confirmed for the other woman. "Natalie…"

Sophia sighed. "My sister hates me. She has every right to." She met Skylar's gaze. "She still comes to visit every couple months though."

A tingle went through Skylar. "She does?"

"Uh huh," Sophia said. "She brings me candy, magazines, we chat."

"About what?" Skylar blurted, surprising both of them. If Natalie was visiting Sophia regularly, that would explain her disappearances that Brian was afraid to even ask about.

Sophia seemed suddenly embarrassed. "You." She looked away. "Used to be anyway. Last few months, all she talks about is Aaron." She met Skylar's gaze again. "Truth is, I'm worried about her. When she came last week—"

"She was here last weekend?" Skylar said, too loudly, shooting to her feet. A corrections officer's head whipped towards them and Skylar remembered where she was.

"Shhh!" Sophia hissed. "Keep it down!"

Flushing, Skylar sank back to her seat on the bench. "I'm sorry. It's just—Natalie's husband told me she's been disappearing regularly for years. He had no idea where she was or what she was doing."

"Figures. She's embarrassed of me. I can't blame her. But, yes, she was here last weekend. She wasn't much like herself though. She was just going on and on about Aaron, what a piece of shit he is and how he ruined all of us. Honestly, it worried me."

Skylar's mind raced, only half-hearing what Sophia had said. There was so much she wanted to ask this woman—*her mother*, that still felt so bizarre—and there wasn't that much time. They only had forty-five minutes. What should she ask? How best to use the time? Should she ask about Natalie or should she talk about Sophia? Maybe even about Aaron Needham? It was impossible to think of him as her father, despite what the birth certificate said. What little she knew about him was enough to make up her mind on that front.

"Skylar. Listen."

Skylar's eyes focused on Sophia as she realized she had drifted away, lost in her stormy thoughts for a moment. "I'm sorry."

"Don't be. It's heavy, isn't it?" Sophia smiled, looking tired and worn, but oddly happy at the same time. "I'm so glad to finally meet you."

Tears welled up in Skylar's eyes and she felt her face growing hot. Sophia's eyes began to look moist as well, but she didn't cry—prison had probably trained her to keep most of her emotions hidden. Skylar hated the thought of that, but it was just another aspect of a reality that was entirely new to her.

"Me, too," Skylar finally said. "What should I call you?"

"'Mom' would be weird, wouldn't it?" Sophia chuckled. "Just call me Sophia—or Sophie. It's what Natalie has always called me."

"Sophie…" Skylar said softly, as if rolling the name across her tongue. "I think I like Sophia better. It's pretty and kind of—dignified?"

Sophia laughed out loud. "Dignified I ain't, but call me whatever you want." She laughed again then placed both hands flat on the table and let out a sigh. "We don't have much time, but it's yours. I know you have questions. What do you want to know?"

Skylar wanted to say "everything," but it wouldn't

have been a useful answer. Sophia might even think she was being flippant, though humor was the last thing on her mind.

"Can you…" she began, the thought forming as the words slowly came to her. "Can you tell me about how you ended up here?" She had heard the story from Barrett, but she knew there had to be more to it.

Sophia breathed deeply through her nose and let it out slowly through her mouth. She leaned back slightly, hands flat against the surface of the table again, her eyes focused on some spot in the distance, as if staring into the past itself. When she spoke, her voice was dry, steady, any sharp edges it might have once had dulled by time and exhaustion.

"I was a wild kid. You wouldn't believe how wild, not even for a second. You think you've seen bad? Baby, I was bad before I could even drive. When mom and daddy—you know what happened to your grandparents?"

Skylar nodded and Sophia went on.

"After mom and daddy died, it was just me and Natalie and she really stepped up. I have to give her that. I was already a little shit, making trouble in school—kind of a bully I guess—and grief or trauma or whatever you want to call it just made me worse. Natalie had her own life to life, but she gave it up for me and I repaid her by being the absolute worst piece of shit kid I could be. I really don't know what was wrong with me. I've thought a lot about it, but…" She raised her hands in a shrug before placing them back on the table as her mouth quirked, not quite a smile; it was something more bitter than that.

"I met Aaron Needham when I was thirteen. God, I thought he was the coolest, hottest thing I'd ever seen. He was eighteen, had a leather jacket, a Camaro, and this sort of dirtbag charm. The minute he looked at me, I was gone. Hooked. I would've done anything for him. Anything."

She paused, her gaze flicking away to a crack in

the concrete wall as if the rest of the story was hiding there.

"From the moment I met him, it was like we were trying to live fast enough to outrun life itself. Parties, drugs, drinking, sex, all of it. Nothing mattered except whatever would get us high, whatever felt good. It was like the world was gonna end any second anyway, so why not live like it?"

Skylar felt her stomach twist. She couldn't wrap her head around what she was hearing. She couldn't even picture it, this woman with her worn-out face and prison-orange jumpsuit, young and reckless, burning through life without a second thought. The world Sophia described was so far from her own experience, and the way she said it, with a fierce, aching nostalgia that didn't quite hide the regret beneath it—it made Skylar ache too.

"Then I got pregnant. With you."

Sophia's eyes met hers, searching, soft but unflinching.

"And right around the same time, I got picked up. Cops caught me holding enough meth to make intent-to-distribute stick hard. It wasn't mine. It was Aaron's. But I wasn't gonna rat on him. I was fifteen, stupid and so much in love. I would have died for him if I thought it would do him any good."

Skylar nodded, though her throat had gone tight.

"Because I was underage, pregnant, and it was my first offense, the judge didn't send me straight in. They waited until after you were born. When you came, I left you with Natalie." Her voice cracked for the first time, just slightly, and she exhaled through her nose, steadying herself. "She was the only family I had in the world, and God knows she wasn't exactly excited about it, but she agreed to it—at least while I was in the reform school. It was only supposed to be temporary."

"I was in the reform school for two and a half years. They call it a school, but it's basically prison with classrooms. Uniforms, mandatory therapy, teachers who were basically only a step or two above us on the social ladder or they would have had other options. I didn't do much better in there than I did out on the street, but I got by. Didn't get a diploma or anything, but I did my time."

Skylar sat still, pinned in place by the weight of Sophia's story. The thought of her mother, barely more than a child, trapped in that place while she herself was a baby left, with an aunt who only took her in out of—what? A sense of duty? It sent a strange ache through her chest, somewhere between pity and sadness. She had to remind herself that Natalie hadn't always been cold or distant with her, that her early childhood had been good. "The Hunt girls," Natalie used to call the two of them and Skylar knew she had meant it, at least back then.

"When I turned eighteen, they cut me loose. I thought Natalie was gonna be there to pick me up. I waited. But it was Aaron who showed up first."

Sophia gave a hollow little laugh, shaking her head.

"I hadn't seen him in years, he hadn't come to visit me once, hadn't sent a letter or anything. But there he was, leaning up against that shitty little chain-link fence surrounding the school, another Camaro—a different one—parked nearby. I don't know how he knew I was getting out, and I never even questioned it I was so stupidly happy to see him. Just like that, it was like no time had passed at all. I forgot everything I learned, if I learned anything at all. I was his, all over again."

She folded her hands loosely on the table, her gaze distant.

"We took off. No plan, no future. Just bouncing from one place to the next. New York, Philly, Boston, Providence, back down the coast. Selling dope, living like we did before, always staying one step ahead of the law." She laughed bitterly. "Well, we thought so anyway."

Skylar was holding her breath without realizing it.

"We got away with it for a long time. A real long time, longer than we deserved, as stupid as we both were. Cops raided the house we were renting in Philly. Found over two hundred grand worth of heroin stashed around the place. It's funny—the thing I remember most about the place is how it smelled, like old fast food. If it's still there, it probably still does."

The corner of her mouth twitched again in another almost-smile.

"Somehow, we got lucky again. Some slick court-appointed lawyer trying to make a name for himself worked the angles, got us bail. I should've known better. I should've faced it then and there. But I was so God-damned stupid and even after all those years, I loved Aaron more than I can ever really tell you. And when he said we were gonna skip town, start over somewhere new and everything would be fine, I went along with it. He had always made all of our decisions so it was nothing new."

Skylar lowered her eyes, her hands clenched on the table in front of her.

Sophia leaned forward, her voice quieter now. "And you probably know the rest, since you're here."

Skylar nodded, her voice small. "The... the murder."

Sophia's eyes flicked up to Skylar's, steady, clear, like she had been waiting for that word.

"It was Aaron. But I was there. I was carrying a gun. I knew what could happen. I didn't really think about it until it did, and I don't know if I'd have cared if I *did* think about it, but when the moment came... there just wasn't any undoing it. That clerk ended up dead. Aaron pulled the trigger, but I was right there. I made my choices. And here I am."

The words settled heavily between them, lingering like smoke in the air, clinging to both of them, weighing them down. Skylar didn't know what to say. She imagined this conversation in so many forms: her birth mother was a mystery, someone who was stolen from her, or hidden, or lost. But the truth was messier than that. Sophia hadn't been taken from her. She'd left. And not for some noble reason, but because her own life had been a train wreck from the start.

And yet... there was no malice in Sophia when she spoke, and she made no excuses. There were no more places for her to run, so she didn't. She accepted what she had done and she accepted her punishment.

They sat in silence for a long time, the hum of others' conversations all around them. Skylar wasn't sure what she felt. Maybe her emotions hadn't even properly formed yet because her mind was still processing everything. But for the first time in her life, she understood where she'd come from. It wasn't pretty, but it was the truth and if Sophia could accept it, she would have to work towards that goal as well, because the woman across from her, for all her wreckage, was still her mother.

"Barr—" Skylar began, but corrected herself, realizing Sophia had no idea who Barrett was. "My friend who told me about you—he's a kind of private investigator. Well, he's in training, I guess, but he's working on it." She flushed slightly, realizing she was saying too much, that it didn't matter to what she really wanted to say. "He told me that Aaron—"

"Your father," Sophia put in.

Skylar ignored it. "That Aaron's conviction was overturned. That—that he's free?"

"I don't know about free, but I know he isn't serving for pulling the trigger. Long story short, one of the jurors who convicted him was the ex-husband of a cousin to the clerk who was killed. It wasn't disclosed until after the trial ended, and Aaron's lawyer got the whole thing thrown out based on 'juror misconduct.'" Sophia made a disgusted noise.

"They didn't—I don't know—do it again?" Skylar couldn't understand how a court system could let a man walk free after being convicted of murder, not on some technicality like that.

Sophia shook her head. "I don't know. I try not to think about Aaron. My trial was separate from his, something about making it easier to secure a lighter sentence." She waved a hand dismissively. "I don't know, but during my trial, when Aaron refused to testify that I was basically just along for the ride, like my lawyer wanted him to, I finally woke up a little and realized what he really was. Maybe he did care about me in his own way, but it wasn't the way I wanted—and it sure as hell wasn't the way I cared about him. I'd have done anything for him, but he wouldn't even man up and tell the truth when I needed him to.

"So no, I don't think about Aaron if I can help it—not that Natalie makes it easy lately, the way she goes on and on about how he ruined both of our lives and should be rotting in hell by now."

"Ruined…"

"'Ruined our lives,' that's how she put it." Sophia shrugged. "I guess you could look at it that way, but honestly, I'm kind of worried about her, she was—ranting, is the only way I can put it. She said she found out he was living up in Vermont, and she was finally going to do what she should have all those years ago."

Chills shot through Skylar. Natalie had been gone for close to two weeks. She had apparently been at the prison a week ago, but now, if she was looking for Aaron Needham…

She had a sudden premonition, as if the hand of something evil had touched her and given her a vision of the worst possible future: Natalie in a prison jumpsuit just like Sophia's, sitting across the table from her. Two mothers, two murders.

"Where does Aaron live?" Skylar asked, urgency in her voice.

Sophia looked surprised. "I don't know. Natalie

didn't say, just up in Vermont somewhere. Why? You're not thinking of going to see him? Don't do it—trust me on this. Just think of him as a sperm donor and forget about him."

Skylar's thoughts ping-ponged off one another, moving so rapidly she could barely grasp any single one. "This is important." She reached across the table for Sophia's hand, but a male voice barked, "No touching! Hands in sight at all times!" making her jump and then shrink back.

Sophia threw a dirty look at the corrections officer's back as he turned away, then said to Skylar. "What's up?"

Skylar shook her head. "I don't know for sure, but I have to go. I'm sorry." She stood, without taking her eyes from Sophia's. "I have to go, but I'll be back. I promise."

Sophia didn't reply, only gestured for one of the officers to escort Skylar out.

The officer approached and Skylar said to Sophia, "I really mean it, I'll be back. And it was… nice meeting you." It sounded weak and awkward, but it was sincere and she hoped Sophia knew that.

The other woman, older and worn down by a life misled, but still looking so much like Skylar that it was impossible to ignore, smiled. For the first time, Skylar could see some of the beauty she must have once possessed. "Sure. It was nice meeting you too."

Chapter 27.

Skylar, Barrett, and Levi – Late Morning

Skylar stepped through the prison's outer gate and into the bright, chill Massachusetts afternoon, barely letting the heavy metal door click shut behind her before she was hurrying, almost running, towards the SUV, where Barrett and Levi waited like sentries, their expressions tense. Before either man could say a word, Skylar blurted, "I know where Natalie is," her voice rushed and urgent.

Barrett had been leaning on the hood, and he straightened, eyebrows knitting together. "What? How?"

There was no time to waste, but Skylar had to explain or they'd think she was crazy. The words spilled out of her: "Sophia told me. Natalie's been visiting her more or less regularly, at least a few visits a year. Those times she'd disappear for a few days? The ones Brian always thought were her cheating on him or something, but was too afraid to ask about? She was here. Visiting Sophia. That's where she's been sneaking off to."

She paused for breath, her heart hammering in time with the pulsing excitement growing in her. She went on, "But that's not all. Sophia said that lately, Natalie's been, like, hyper-focused, obsessed even, with Aaron Needham. She blames Aaron—"

"That's your dad?" Levi asked.

Skylar's gaze flicked towards the tall blond man, then away. *Think of him as a sperm donor*, Sophia had said. "He's—yeah, he's my father. Anyway, Sophia said Natalie blames Aaron for everything. She said he ruined her life, and Sophia's, and mine too. I guess Sophia thought Natalie was just bitter at first, but it became like—like she can't let it go."

"Well… I, uh," Barrett said, exchanging a look with Levi. Both men immediately sensed what Skylar was driving towards. She didn't need to wait for them to say it out loud.

"My life's great now, by the way," Skylar said quickly, resting a hand on each of their arms, needing them to understand, needing to anchor herself. "But maybe Natalie really does believe it. In her head, I think she's convinced Aaron ruined all of us. She's been fixated."

"It would explain some things," Barrett mused. "I mean.. if she began to see you as a connection to Aaron rather than to Sophia."

"Right," Skylar said, matter-of-factly. "I guess it would, but either way, if Sophia's right and Natalie's—I don't know, gone off the deep end—it means she's out there looking for him."

Barrett's jaw tightened, but his voice stayed level. "You think she's trying to find Aaron Needham?"

"I'm sure of it," Skylar answered without hesitation. "Sophia said Aaron's living somewhere in Vermont now and Natalie's out for—I guess you'd call it revenge or whatever."

Levi let out a low whistle.

"Would she do something like that, though?" Barrett asked. It wasn't an unreasonable question.

Skylar hesitated before saying, "I don't want to believe it, but you know what else she's been doing lately. Something's *wrong* with her, and I'm worried. She wouldn't have hurt me like she did unless something was *seriously* wrong inside her head and now we know what it is."

"Look, Sky," Levi said. "Vermont's not far, but it's an entire state. Where would we even start looking?"

Skylar's nerves, already strung tightly, snapped. "I know all that! But that's probably why she's been gone so long. She's looking for him. She might even have found him by now. We're wasting time standing here. We have to get in the car and go!"

Barrett lifted his hand, steady and calm as ever. "Hold on, Sky. Levi's right. It won't do us or Natalie any good to drive around blind, hoping we just happen to bump into her or Aaron. Vermont's bigger than it looks on a map. Besides, we don't even know what Aaron looks like."

Skylar blinked, her voice softening with a strange, distant ache. "Sophia said... I look just like him."

For a second, the three of them stood in silence. The guys exchanged another look, heavy with things they didn't say out loud, but both understood. Skylar, feeling their hesitation, opened her mouth to say something, to push again, to try to browbeat them into just going along, but Levi beat her to it.

"We need a plan."

Barrett was already pulling his phone from his jacket, his mind moving quickly even as his voice remained measured and steady. "Yeah, we do. Give me a second."

He stepped a few paces away, hit a familiar contact icon on his phone, and waited for the click on the other end. "Tamika? Hey, it's Barrett. Sorry, but I need a favor."

Levi and Skylar stood close together. The wind seemed colder up here than it did back in the city, and it gnawed at them. Skylar's hand found Levi's, and he pulled it into his pocket to warm up, giving her a little nudge with his shoulder.

Barrett turned towards them, phone half-covered, and called, "What's Natalie's cell number?" Skylar rattled it off. Barrett relayed it then asked, "Tamika, can you run a trace on that number? A specific location would be ideal, but even a general area—state, city, anything—would help. Just note the charges as Hunt. Mr. Whittington will know what it's about. Thanks, Tamika. I owe you."

He hung up and slid his phone into his pocket as he moved back towards his friends. "Tamika at my office is gonna run Natalie's cell records. If her phone is on and pinging a tower, Tamika will find it. Shouldn't take more than an hour."

Skylar pulled back her hand from Levi and crossed her arms tightly. Her entire body felt wound up like a spring. "So we just... wait?"

"For now, yeah," Barrett said gently. "Look, for all we know, she could be in California or Canada or anywhere in between by now. Let Tamika work, and then we'll know where we should be headed."

Levi chimed in, playing peacemaker. "And besides, we've been on the road all morning. It's a little early, but we should find some place for lunch. Can't think straight on an empty stomach." He tilted his head, offering her a soft smile. "And we wanna hear how it went with Sophia."

Skylar opened her mouth to argue again. Her instincts were screaming at her: *get moving, do something— anything*. The calm, grounded way both Barrett and Levi were looking at her made her pause. Logic was winning, no matter how badly her heart wanted her to throw herself into action. She exhaled, her shoulders sagging.

"Okay," she said finally. "Lunch. We'll get some lunch while we wait for Tamika to call back."

Levi gave her shoulder a squeeze, and Barrett nudged her gently toward the car. "We passed a diner a few minutes down the road on our way in—one of those old-timey, chrome ones. Let's eat and you can tell us about Sophia over something greasy."

They climbed back into the SUV, Barrett and Skylar up front again, Levi in back, and the engine rumbled to life. As Barrett turned the car around in the parking lot, then eased them back onto the road, Skylar let her head fall against the window and closed her eyes.

She was already mentally replaying the

conversation with Sophia, remembering her birth mother's tired, hardened voice describing a life Skylar could barely comprehend. Sophia had no excuses, no sob stories, and there was no tidy ending to wrap it all up in a bow—unless you counted a prison cell. But she didn't hide anything: she gave Skylar the raw, unvarnished truth without trying to downplay any of her mistakes. Skylar respected that and while hearing it all left her reeling, it also made her feel somewhat clearer too.

She had some answers, but it wasn't over yet. Now they had to find Natalie, her aunt, the woman who'd raised her, apparently lost in an obsession with a man Skylar had never met. A man she apparently looked just like. *"A sperm donor."*

Skylar opened her eyes again, glancing at her friends. Levi was leaning forward between the seats and he and Barrett were talking softly, pointing out items of interest as they drove. They were trying to act natural, trying to hold the tension at bay, but she could see it on both of their faces. They were as worried as she was in their own way.

Skylar felt the fear bubbling inside of her, but she did her best to push it down. They would find Natalie and they would bring her home safely.

Chapter 28.

Skylar, Barrett, and Levi

Barrett was halfway to pulling his wallet out when Skylar reached across the table and laid her hand over his, stopping him.

"No," she said, her voice quiet but firm. "I've got it. Lunch is the least I can do for you guys." She gave him a look that left no room for argument, a mix of gratitude and determination and stubbornness.

Barrett opened his mouth, ready to protest just out of habit, but before he could get a word out, his phone buzzed to life, its high-pitched trill cutting through the laidback hum of the diner. All three of them froze for a split second, any argument over the bill forgotten. It was as if the universe itself had decided for them: Skylar would pay.

Barrett glanced at the screen, his face shifting into that calm, all-business look he always wore when something important came up. Without a word, he slid out of the booth, phone already to his ear as he headed toward the diner's glass door.

"That must be Tamika," Levi said, watching Barrett weave through the tables and disappear outside.

Skylar nodded, her stomach tightening. She didn't speak—couldn't, really—as she clutched her half-empty water glass with both hands, silently willing the call to bring good news. Her heart thudded so hard she was sure Levi could hear it, but he didn't press her. He just sat there, the same tense hope flickering across his face as

205

Skylar finally pushed her glass away, took her wallet from her purse, and began laying bills on the table.

Skylar and Levi were just barely through the diner's door when they heard Barrett's voice, low but clear, saying, "Yeah, thanks, Tamika. I appreciate it. I'll see you Monday, hopefully."

He hung up, pocketed his phone, and crunched across the gravel parking lot towards his friends.

"Natalie's phone has been pinging towers in a place called Saint Johnsbury for the last two days," he said, cutting straight to the point.

Levi's brow furrowed. "Saint Johnsbury? Where the hell is that?"

Barrett rubbed a hand along his jaw, an uncharacteristic edge of worry creeping into his voice. "According to Tamika, it's the biggest town in the county with the biggest drug problem in Vermont."

The information was more than trivia and it settled over all three of them like a cold fog. None of them spoke for a few moments, the weight of it saying more than words could. Saint Johnsbury, Vermont. Drugs. Natalie. Aaron Needham, with his long history of drug-use and drug-dealing. It didn't take much imagination to fill in the blanks, and what it suggested made Skylar's stomach twist.

"Let's go," she said, cutting through the silence, the urgency in her voice already rising.

Levi glanced at her, then at Barrett. "How far is it?"

Barrett gave a small, grim smile and a half-chuckle. "Only a little closer to here than we are to home."

Skylar didn't hesitate. "Let's go," she repeated, firmer this time, the decision already made in her mind.

The two men shared a look that said everything. They had come this far and they were with her all the way.

Barrett nodded, fishing out his keys as they headed for the SUV. "We'll have to get gas first."

"And snacks," Levi put in. "Drinks too, if it's another three hours."

Skylar climbed into the passenger seat, her mind already racing ahead to Saint Johnsbury and whatever was waiting for them.

It was almost five o'clock as they rolled into Saint Johnsbury and the reality of how small and isolated the town was finally hit Skylar. She lived her whole life in New York and knew that places like this existed, but seeing them felt like something out of a movie.

The wind kicked up, sending tiny bursts of gravel skittering across the cracked pavement as Barrett slowed the SUV to a crawl at the edge of the town center. The sun hung low in the sky, painting the mountains in shades of violet and gray, but Skylar barely noticed. She kept her focus locked on her phone, reviewing her short-list of motels for the hundredth time.

Skylar spent the last hour of the drive north staring at her phone, her eyes flicking back and forth over Google Maps, hotel listings, and local directories like she could will Natalie into existence if she just searched hard enough. She scrolled past the same names over and over, cross-referencing addresses, comparing them to what she knew of Natalie's habits and comparing them to what Natalie would likely be thinking as she searched for Aaron Needham. Skylar decided that Natalie would choose something low-key and out of the way, somewhere she could slip in and out unnoticed. And she would probably pay cash, realizing Brian could find her if she used a credit or debit card. That narrowed the options considerably.

When they first set out for Vermont, Skylar had a realization: Barrett had been able to find the exact location of Chet's cellphone that night in New Jersey, so why couldn't Tamika do the same with Natalie's? And Barrett had explained the limitations of cellphone tower pings in rural states like Vermont, where the towers were fewer and distance was farther between them. He spoke with the patience of someone used to handling tense situations, but Skylar could hear the undercurrent in his voice: technology was only going to get them so close. The rest would be instinct and luck.

"I've got a few places in mind," she announced, her voice sharp and clear, the tension wrapped tight behind each word. "Places Natalie would pick."

Barrett nodded, his hands steady on the wheel as he pulled off onto the side of the street. "Sooner we start checking, the better," he said, trying to offer a sliver of reassurance.

Levi, from the back seat, leaned forward, his elbow braced on the center console. "We hit them one by one?" he asked. "Or split up? A small town like this can't have too many options."

Skylar pointed to the top name on her list. "The King's Rest Inn. It's got the right vibe—quiet, cheap, the kind of place no one asks questions if you pay in cash."

Barrett nodded, shifting the SUV back into gear. "Alright. I'd rather not split up since none of us know the area, so The King's Rest it is."

The drive to the motel only took a few minutes. Saint Johnsbury was tiny compared to even the smallest areas of New York, and the King's Rest Inn sat on its outskirts, a place with sun-bleached siding and a neon vacancy sign that flickered against the fading evening light. The parking lot was only half full, and as they drove its length, Levi said, "None of the cars have New York plates."

Skylar stared at the lot through the window, her stomach contorting itself into knots. Natalie's car wasn't here. But that didn't necessarily mean *she* wasn't. She might have rented a car, or borrowed one, or—something. Skylar's instincts were telling her this was a good bet and if luck agreed...

Barrett pulled the SUV into a space near the office

and shut off the engine, already reaching for his wallet as he stepped out.

"Stay here," he told Skylar and Levi. "Let me do the talking."

Skylar pressed her forehead against the window, watching Barrett stride into the motel's office. As she watched, his demeanor changed from her quiet, steady friend to a professional investigator's, wrapping around him like a cloak. Did he stand a little taller? Walk a little more aggressively? She couldn't put her finger on it, but it was there and she had seen firsthand how Barrett was able to get information out of complete strangers. If there was anything to learn about Natalie here, Barrett would find it.

The wait felt endless, minutes dragging by in silence except for the wind rattling the SUV. Levi glanced at Skylar, but didn't speak, leaving her to her thoughts. He didn't know what he could say now anyway.

Finally, Barrett returned, sliding into the driver's seat and shutting the door with a soft, deliberate click. The second Skylar looked at him, she knew.

"She's here," he confirmed. "Not *here* here, but she checked in last night. Paid in cash. Hasn't checked out. The clerk saw her drive out about an hour an ago."

Skylar let out a shaky breath, waves of both relief and dread washing over her. Natalie was here, she was alive—the possibility that something had happened to Natalie in the last twelve days was very real, she could now admit—but the fact that Natalie hadn't contacted either her husband or her adopted daughter only confirmed Skylar's worst fears. Natalie was on a mission.

"She's out looking for Aaron," Skylar said flatly, staring straight ahead at the dark windows of the motel.

"Or she's already found him," Levi said, his voice low.

The words stung and Skylar turned to him, her expression tight, but before she could snap something back at him, the moment passed. Levi wasn't trying to be cruel. He was just being realistic.

"What now?" Skylar said to Barrett instead.

Barrett drummed his fingers on the steering wheel, weighing their options. "I think I could get into the room, but I don't see what good it would do, and sitting around waiting for Natalie to come back isn't going to be much better."

Skylar leaned against the headrest, her mind racing. It felt like even a second wasted was too long. Natalie wasn't a fool, but she could be impulsive, especially when it came to slights against her, and lashing out at those who inflicted them. Skylar knew now what kind of wounds her mother—it was still impossible to think of Natalie as her aunt—carried with her, and as far as Natalie was concerned, Aaron Needham was the deepest wound of all.

Barrett pulled out his phone, scrolling through contacts until he paused on one, his jaw tightening. "I was hoping not to have to do this," he muttered, more to himself than to them, "but we have to find Needham."

Skylar watched, puzzled and anxious, as he made a call. The call was answered quickly, and Barrett's voice was low as he said, "Mr. Whittington? It's Barrett Teller." He briefly explained their situation in clipped, professional tones.

When he hung up, he looked at Skylar and Levi. "Mr. Whittington's gonna make a call, see what favors he can wrangle. It might take some time."

Skylar shook her head, frustration boiling over. "We don't *have* time," she said, her voice tight with panic. "What if she's found him already? What if something's happened—"

Levi reached for her shoulder, but she brushed him off, not wanting to be calmed or placated. She was on the edge, her mind looping through scenarios faster than she could process them.

But before she could spiral any further, Barrett's

phone rang again.

He answered immediately, and the tension in his body visibly eased as he listened. "Thank you, sir. Thank you very, very much."

He hung up, turning back to them. "Whittington pulled the right string on his first try," he said, his voice excited but serious. "Mount Pleasant Mobile Park, lot fourteen."

Skylar felt her heart stop for a moment, then kick back into gear, higher than before. An address. A real place. Maybe the end of this long chase.

"Let's go," she said, no trace of hesitation in her voice.

Barrett shifted the SUV back into gear, and as they pulled out of the motel lot, the last traces of sunlight faded from the sky.

Chapter 29.

Skylar, Barrett, Levi—And Natalie

The Mount Pleasant Mobile Park was a few miles out of town. They drove the winding stretch of rural Route 5, the SUV's headlights racing ahead of them, carving a tunnel out of the night. Before long, the park came into view, its existence announced by a battered sign whose paint had long since faded, the metal poles that supported it streaked with rust and fragments of peeling paint. The name was barely legible, little more than a memory of some long ago grand opening.

The place stretched out beyond the sign like something the rest of the world had gladly forgotten. Rows of sagging trailers sat crooked on patchy lots, some of them with broken steps or windows covered in plastic. Weeds grew tall around rusted bicycles and dented lawn chairs, and trash bins overflowed. The whole place radiated neglect, as though hope had long since packed up and moved away, leaving everyone who once knew it behind.

Barrett guided the SUV slowly through the narrow, rutted drive. None of them spoke, eyes alert for the number 14 marker, and the silence inside the car matched the quiet desperation of the park. A few porch lights flickered against the growing dusk, and a handful of people lingered on worn stoops, watching the vehicle crawl past with the dull, wary eyes of those too used to bad news arriving in strange vehicles.

"There!" Skylar shouted, finger pointing. Barrett's

eyes followed and saw Natalie's Lexus, parked off to one side of the dirt pathway. Its gold color caught even the smallest fragments of the headlights' sheen, reflecting it back brilliantly, looking as out of place in the park as an elephant in a suburban pet shop.

"That's Natalie's car," Skylar said. She whirled to look at first Barrett, then Levi. "She's got to be close."

"It does have New York plates," Levi said, a trace of doubt in his voice.

Barrett didn't answer right away. His eyes were fixed on the Lexus, his brows drawn together in careful calculation. His instincts were firing, and he wanted to believe they had finally found Natalie, but he didn't want to jump to conclusions. The car sitting there, dark and lifeless, seemed ominous in the stillness of this place.

"Maybe," he finally said, voice low and cautious. "But her car being here doesn't mean she is."

Skylar's heart hammered so hard she could feel it in her throat. She stared at the Lexus, every part of her screaming that Natalie was close, that her mother—her aunt, an irritating voice in her head reminded her—had to be nearby. She had followed the trail this far, and the car was just evidence they were on the right path. She *knew* they were on the edge of something, and that the truth, the end of all of this, was only a few steps away, out there somewhere in the darkness.

Levi shifted in his seat, glancing around at the dimly lit trailers, the scattered glow of porch lights and the flicker of televisions in a few windows. "If her car's here, she probably left it for a reason," he said carefully. "If she found what she was looking for, maybe she didn't think she'd be coming back."

Skylar looked at him sharply, reading the unspoken meaning behind his words: *Or maybe she couldn't come back.*

"Or maybe she just wanted to arrive unannounced," Barrett said, pulling the SUV off to the side of the road, killing the headlights, but leaving the engine idling. "Lot 14 can't be far," he said, unclipping his seatbelt. "Let's keep moving. Slowly."

They drove on, creeping through the winding lane of the trailer park. The atmosphere grew heavier, as if gravity itself was increasing the deeper they went. And the deeper into the park they traveled, the more the place seemed to bleed hopelessness: sagging porches, junk-strewn yards, trailers that looked like they were one bad storm away from collapsing. Skylar barely noticed any of it. Her eyes scanned the shadows, looking for any hint of Natalie.

The road curved to the left and they saw it: a trailer with a small metal post, painted with number "14" stuck in the dirt at the end its tiny driveway. Beyond the sign was a pea-green-colored trailer. It was even older than most of the others, but aside from one cracked window facing the narrow road, it seemed in better shape than most of the others in the park. As Skylar watched, there was a dull flicker of movement behind that window. It was just a shadow, there for only a second and then gone.

"There." Skylar's voice was almost a whisper. "Someone's in there."

Barrett shifted into park, the pace of his heart picking up. Ghosts of possibilities flitted through his thoughts and for the first time in his short career as a private investigator, he wished he had a weapon.

"Both of you stay behind me," he said, opening his door.

Before he stepped out, a sharp, unmistakable sound split the night—the crack of a gunshot.

Skylar froze, her blood turning to ice. The sound was close. Too close.

"It's her," she breathed, her voice shaking. "It's Natalie. It's got to be."

Levi grabbed her arm before she could jump out of the car. "Sky, wait. We don't know that."

Somehow, she did know. She could feel it in the deepest part of herself, something terrible and unshakable. "It's Natalie."

Barrett was already out of the SUV, moving fast but low, using the shadows for cover as he closed the distance to the trailer. Skylar followed before Levi could stop her, her heart pounding, every nerve tight as a drum. Levi swore under his breath and moved too, unwilling to let either of them go into this alone.

They reached the side of the trailer, crouched low against the thin aluminum siding. The front door stood ajar, the faint smell of burnt gunpowder lingering in the night air. The wind had finally died and everything hung still and quiet. No more gunshots, no movement—no Natalie.

Barrett looked through the open door, seeing a dim and empty living room, the furnishings sparse and battered. A coffee table was piled high with objects that seemed familiar but unrecognizable from this angle, at this distance. A lamp lay shattered on the floor, its bulb still working despite the broken base. On the threadbare gray carpet, near the center of the room, there was something darker than the worn fabric—fresh, wet, and unmistakable.

Blood.

Skylar pushed past Barrett before he could stop her, moving into the trailer to stare down at the dark stain. Her knees went weak. The sight made it real in a way no sound could. Her stomach clenched painfully, but she forced herself to look away, scanning the room, the floor, the open door that led deeper into the trailer.

"She's not here," Levi said quietly, stepping past the broken lamp and into the narrow hallway beyond. "But somebody was hurt."

Skylar's mind raced, replaying every second of the last few moments—the Lexus, the shot, the blood—trying to piece it all together into something she could understand. Natalie had been looking for Aaron. She had found him. And something had either gone very wrong—or Natalie had done what she came to do.

Barrett's voice pulled her back. "The blood trail's fresh. Somebody was dragged."

He gestured toward the back door, which hung open just enough for a gust of cold air to slip inside, stirring the thin curtains, as the wind picked back up. Skylar moved toward it, following the faint streaks on the worn linoleum, out onto the small, splintered wooden stoop.

There, in the weak moonlight, she could see drag marks in the dirt, leading away from the trailer and into the darkness between the rows of rundown homes.

Levi came to stand beside her, his face grim. "Whoever it was, they didn't go far. We're close."

Skylar swallowed the lump in her throat, her voice flat and steady despite the fear coiling in her chest. "We need to follow them—Natalie's out there! She needs our help!"

Barrett and Levi shared a glance, both of them knowing that wasn't necessarily the case, but then Barrett turned back to her and nodded. "Stay sharp," he said and stalked forward, scanning the darkness.

Barrett led, with Skylar behind him and Levi bringing up the rear. Skylar's pulse thudded in her ears, the fear and determination warring inside her, driving her forward. Their footsteps crunched over gravel and dead leaves, the cold night closing in around them like a vice. She shivered inside of her thin jacket, wishing she was back in Bay Ridge, back in the comfortable little house that already felt like home. A sudden surge of emotion momentarily pushed aside the fear and doubt and all the tension, and deep feelings of love and gratitude towards both Barrett and Levi engulfed her. These two men, her best friends for so long, had already done so much for her and now they might literally be risking their lives to help her find her mother. She loved them. She loved them both *so much* and she knew they felt the same towards her.

The sharp, brutal sound of flesh striking flesh echoed through the night like the crack of a whip, followed instantly by a scream—high, raw, and so full of agony that it stopped Skylar, Barrett, and Levi dead in their tracks. The sound hung in the air, stretching the moment into something surreal and weightless, as if the world itself had forgotten how to move.

"Natalie!" Skylar screamed, the name ripping from her throat before she could even think. Panic overtook her, flooding every cell of her body as she shoved past Barrett with both hands, stumbling forward as fast as her legs would carry her, blood roaring in her ears.

"Sky, wait!" Barrett shouted after her, but his voice was a distant thing, nearly drowned by the pounding of her own pulse, too insignificant to overcome the urgency she felt. Levi, the only one of them breathing easily, was already following Skylar. Barrett tore after them and the three of them raced into the darkness.

They pushed through the tangled fringe of undergrowth that ringed the mobile park to find that the uneven ground sloped sharply downward toward the low glint of water. The scent of the river hit them first: sharp and cold, with an earthy, wet dirt undertone. The trees parted at the bottom of the incline, opening up to a wide clearing along the riverbank, lit perfectly by the bright moon rising overhead. The clouds, which had overcast the night sky all evening, had scudded away at just the right time, as though the moon itself had decided to spotlight the scene for a better view.

Skylar halted, coming to a skidding stop. Natalie was on her knees in the dirt, her head bent at an awkward angle, her hair tangled tight in the skeletal fingers of a man who barely looked human. He was tall, but wiry and gaunt, little more than skin stretched tight over bone, with long, greasy hair that hung in lank clumps around his face. His clothes were in better shape than his ragged body, but the blue jeans and flannel shirt hung on him like wash of a line, reflecting either drastic weight loss or an inability to properly dress himself. A hole high up on his left thigh was still bleeding, soaking the fabric around it, but the wound didn't seem to hamper him or make him any less dangerous.

As Skylar watched, his hollowed-out face twisted into something hateful and he jerked Natalie's head back sharply, the gun in his free hand glinting like cold death in the moonlight.

Skylar stood at the edge of the clearing, gasping, barely able to comprehend what she was seeing.

This man had to be Aaron Needham. Her father.

"Shut up, bitch," the man snarled at Natalie, shaking her like a ragdoll. "I'll do worse than that before we're done."

His voice was like sandpaper on metal, a voice that belonged to a lifetime of hard living and bad choices. Natalie gasped for air, her face already red and wet with tears. She managed to turn her head slightly, as if she knew Skylar was there but couldn't look at her.

First Levi then Barrett crashed noisily into the clearing and the man's attention snapped toward them, the weight of their presence finally registering. His eyes were dark, sunken pits in the moonlight, but there was a sharpness to them that Skylar felt as they focused on her. Just for a moment, a fraction of a second, she thought he looked startled, as if her face held something shocking.

And then his gun-hand twitched, and the barrel came up, trained right on Skylar.

Time seemed to buckle and slow. Skylar felt every heartbeat like a hammer-blow inside of her chest, as if it was trying to shatter her sternum. Her breath stuck in her throat and her limbs went stiff as the reality of what was happening took hold of her. She saw the faint tremor in the man's gun-hand, the way his lips pressed together like he had already made his decision and was steeling himself to carry through.

She heard Barrett hiss a sharp, low curse under his breath and Levi made a noise in his throat as both men processed the threat at the same time.

No one moved.

Skylar's world had narrowed down to the black, hollow tunnel of the gun's barrel, a small circle somehow wide enough to swallow her whole.

The man held her in his sights for a long moment, tension crackling in the air between them as his expression flickered between something like recognition and something much darker.

It was Levi who broke the silence, his voice low, calm, and cautious, like he was speaking to a rabid animal. "Hey. Easy," he said, his hands slowly raising, palms open. "You don't want to do this. That's your daughter, man."

Aaron Needham didn't answer, but his eyes briefly shifted towards Levi, then back to Skylar. He didn't move from the edge of the riverbank, but seemed to look at her more closely. He wasn't distracted from his original purpose though; his grip on Natalie didn't loosen, and he didn't move the gun an inch. Skylar stood frozen, the cold air flowing off of the river seeping into her skin. Her body refused to obey her instinct to move or even breathe.

Barrett shifted his weight and moved to flank Skylar, his own hand hovering near the inside of his jacket. Skylar caught the movement and wondered if he had a plan. He didn't carry a gun, but maybe Aaron wouldn't realize that. Could Barrett be trying to bluff the other man? And would it work?

Aaron's gaze flicked back to Barrett and the gun shifted in his direction for a moment before settling back on Skylar.

"Let's all stay calm, okay?" Barrett said, his voice as low and steady as if he was suggesting they all have another cup of coffee. "Levi's right. Nobody wants to do anything they'll regret."

Still, the tension hung in the air like the moment before a lightning strike.

Skylar's mind spun as she watched the way Aaron's his eyes lingered on her face, the way his jaw tightened and slackened in quick succession. Levi had told him who she was, but it wasn't necessary, she realized. Something in how he looked at her said that he knew exactly who she was. The question was whether or not it mattered to him.

"Let Natalie go."

Skylar said those words softly, barely louder than the whisper of the river, but it was enough to cut through the brittle, suffocating atmosphere. She could have shouted or screamed, or begged and cried, but instead she made a simple plea for an end to the violence.

For a single, breathless second, the night seemed to freeze. The wind stilled again and the water's churning felt quieter, as if the whole world had paused, teetering on the edge of this moment. Skylar could hear her own pulse thudding in her ears again. Her hands curled into tight fists at her sides, but she didn't flinch. She met the eyes of the man holding Natalie captive, the man whose blood she shared, and she didn't back down. She wouldn't.

Aaron stared back at the daughter he had never met for a moment before barking a laugh like hailstones on a rusted tin roof—a sound less of amusement and more of a reflexive defense mechanism.

"This bitch?" he spat, jerking Natalie's head with a rough tug of his fist, forcing another choked, helpless sound from her throat. Natalie didn't fight him; her hands braced against the cold ground, too spent and too afraid to resist, but her eyes flicked briefly toward Skylar, wide, pleading, wet with tears. As miserable as Natalie looked, Skylar thought something had changed in her. She couldn't have said why, but she felt as if the old Natalie—the Natalie who laughed and played with her when she was little—was looking out at her from behind the mask of this tortured woman.

Aaron sneered, his voice rising, cracking under the strain of his own anger and something deeper and desperate.

"You know what this bitch did? She walks into my house flapping her mouth about how I ruined her life. Ruined her life!" He repeated the words with a mocking sharpness, as if the idea was absurd, as if he were the victim.

"Anything happened to her whore sister was something Sophia wanted. I did everything I could for that girl until I couldn't do no more. It ain't my fault I had a better lawyer than her. *She* was the one testified against *me*. I didn't testify against *her*, did I? She's got no right to complain, that fucking *bitch*." He literally spat the last word, his sunken eyes glinting darkly in the moonlight, wild and hollow. He shifted just slightly and Skylar saw his pupils for the first time—they were huge, either from adrenaline or some chemical churning through his system.

"And this one," he said, shaking Natalie again, making Skylar wince as her aunt whimpered. "When I tell her to get the hell out, she pulls a gun on me and *shoots me*! Like I'm just supposed to stand there and take that?" He gave a sharp snort, shaking his head, the grip on the gun tightening. "I got every right to do whatever the hell I want to her. The love-taps I give her so far ain't nothin'."

His gaze slid back to Skylar, locking onto her like a snake coiled to strike, and his voice dropped to a cold, almost conversational threat. "And I'll take care of you too, if you're dumb enough to try and stop me. That goes for any of you!" he finished with a roar.

The words sent shivers of absolute terror down Skylar's spine, but before she could even think to reply, another voice cut in.

"That's not exactly true." Barrett's voice wasn't raised, but it carried a quiet, iron-clad authority.

Aaron's head snapped toward him, sharp as a

whip crack, the gun shifting from Skylar to swing towards Barrett.

"You have a right to defend your home," Barrett continued, slowly and deliberately, as if were laying stepping stones across a river of burning gasoline. His hands were relaxed now, spread slightly and held at his sides, well away from where a holster would be if he were armed. "But this isn't defense. You dragged her out of your home and you've got her on her knees with a gun pointed at her head. You pull that trigger, it's murder—and you won't get away with it twice."

Aaron's lip peeled back into a snarl. His fingers twitched, his hold on Natalie tightening, making her wince.

"Shut the hell up," he growled. "You talk like a lawyer. Shifty bastards, all of you. Think you can talk your way out of anything."

But the veneer of his bravado was thinning, like paint peeling off rotted wood. He shifted his weight from one foot to another, as if the old survival instincts of a man used to running, used to being cornered, were starting to bubble up. As if something inside of him was screaming for him to run.

And in Aaron's moment of distraction, Levi took a silent step sideways, edging out of Aaron's direct line of fire. He moved slowly enough not to raise suspicion, but maybe enough to shift the odds. Aaron didn't notice. His attention was on Skylar again, caught in the gravitational pull of her gaze as she spoke again.

"Listen to me," she said.

Aaron's eyes locked onto hers, and for the first time there wasn't just anger in them—there was confusion, a tiny flickering shadow of doubt.

"My name's Skylar." She hesitated, her throat tightening, but she pressed on. "Maybe you already know. Maybe you already know this too, but I'm your daughter."

Her heart pounded so hard it hurt, but the words kept coming.

"I met Sophia today," she said, her voice cracking against the name. "I met my mother. And for the first time in my life, I know where I came from. About her and about you."

She saw Aaron's eyes blink, slow and heavy, as if he was trying to process a lifetime's worth of buried truth in a handful of seconds. His mouth opened, but no words came before snapping closed again.

"And I want to know you," Skylar said, her voice dipping lower, threaded with sincerity. "Both of you. I want the chance to know my parents, to *really* know you. But Natalie... she raised me. She loved me and kept me safe when there was nobody else to do it."

Her eyes flicked to Natalie, who, despite the pain, met her gaze, something fragile and wounded behind her eyes.

"Natalie gave everything she had for me for so many years," Skylar half-whispered. "Until a week ago, I thought she was my mother. I didn't know you or Sophia even existed. But now that I do, and now that I know what Natalie did for all three of us... don't you owe her something? For raising your daughter when you couldn't?" She looked at Natalie again, but the older woman's head was lowered. "I know I do, no matter what else there's been between us."

The silence that followed pressed down on all five of them with the weight of a falling jetliner. No one moved. The wind whispered through the trees all around them, and the river's voice rose up to fill the silent vacuum. Skylar stood, barely breathing, waiting, suspended in the moment, balanced on the sharpest of edges, wondering if Aaron—if her father—had heard her, had understood her, if he cared.

It felt like time itself was holding its breath—and then Levi moved.

His body surged forward, muscles driving him like a spring uncoiled, his sneakers pounding the cold, packed dirt, the sharp thud of his footsteps pattering against the night air like gunfire. And Aaron, caught off guard by the sudden explosion of motion, barely had time to twist his head before Levi was on him.

Levi's shoulder slammed into Aaron's chest with brutal force, knocking the thin, wiry man backward with the power of a wrecking ball. The air whooshed out of Aaron's lungs in a strangled, broken sound, and his grip on both the gun and Natalie broke. The pistol flew from his hand, spinning end over end under the pale wash of moonlight before it clattered against the hard-packed earth and skidded towards the edge of the water and disappeared, swallowed by the night.

The tackle sent Aaron sprawling to the ground; the back of his head struck the dirt with a dull thud, sending up a small puff of dust that glowed silver in the moonlight before fading back into the dark.

Natalie, wrenched free from his grip, hit the ground on her side. She lay still for a moment, stunned, before scrambling away towards the nearest clump of trees and the safety they offered, putting as much space as she could between herself and the man who had held her captive.

Aaron groaned and rolled over, his hand groping blindly for the weapon, not realizing that it was no longer within reach and not getting the chance before Levi was on him again, straddling his chest. All the emotions new and old, all the fear for Skylar when he saw Aaron's gun pointed at her, the horror of Natalie helplessly held captive—all of it combined into a white-hot anger that fueled Levi's fist as it cut a short, hard arc through the air, and his knuckles crashed squarely into Aaron's jaw with a sound like cracking stone.

The snap of bone on bone echoed across the clearing, sharp and final. Aaron's head jerked violently, slammed into the ground again by the force of the blow, and his body sagged immediately, collapsing against the cold earth like a string-cut marionette. His limbs twitched once, then he was still except for the slow rise and fall of his chest as he fell into deep unconsciousness.

Silence fell again except for the sound of the river whispering past them and the sharp, wheezing gasps of Natalie's broken breathing as she hugged herself tightly, rocking back and forth in the underbrush.

Skylar was already moving before the last echo of Levi's punch faded into the night. She stumbled toward Natalie, her knees giving out as she dropped down beside the older woman. Her hands trembled as they reached for her mother's, gripping them tightly, grounding both of them, trying to send a message through the contact: *everything's okay now.*

Natalie's face was pale, almost gray in the moonlight, streaked with tears and dirt, her lips trembling too hard to form words at first. When she finally found her voice, it was a paper-thin whisper, rough and hoarse from crying and the chokehold of fear. "Skylar…"

Skylar's throat seized, as if just hearing her own name from Natalie's lips broke something inside of her, something that had been bracing against this moment, this reunion. She squeezed Natalie's hands tighter, fighting against the tears threatening to overtake her.

"I was going," Natalie choked. "I was going to kill him—but he—he—I must have been out of my mind… I—"

"Shh, it's okay," Skylar whispered, her voice catching. "I've got you. You're safe now. He's not going to hurt you anymore. I promise."

A few feet away, Levi slowly lifted himself from Aaron's motionless body, his chest rising and falling, taking deep breaths. His fists were still clenched and the adrenaline still surged through him, but now that it was over, the aftershock of violence began to creep in and his limbs started trembling. He stared down at Aaron, dazed by the sudden, brutal end to the standoff, awed that it was his fist that brought it about. The reality of it all caught up to him and he had to sit down before he fell down.

Barrett's voice broke through the quiet, steady and controlled the way it always was, though his relief was plain. He was already at Skylar's side, one hand on her shoulder to steady her, the other fishing his phone from his pocket.

"Stay with her," he told Skylar quietly, glancing back towards Levi, and then to the shadowed edge of the river where the gun had vanished. "I'm calling for help."

The night had held its breath, but finally, it seemed to slowly release it. The thick, suffocating atmosphere thinned and then disappeared, drifting away on the cool breeze whispering through the trees. The danger was over now, but the ache of it would linger like gun-smoke.

Skylar held Natalie's hands, then shifted and wrapped her arms around her mother, clinging to her protectively. For the first time in years, Natalie clung back.

Chapter 30.

Skylar, Barrett, and Levi

The spring sun hung low behind the rooftops, painting the sky in soft streaks of lavender and fading gold, as Skylar walked up the house in Bay Ridge's short driveway. The spring evening felt like it belonged to winter, the air crisp and sharp at the edges. She took a deep breath before digging in her purse for her keys. Work had dragged in a way that only normal life can feel after something extraordinary has shaken you, but coming home was a relief. It felt... good in a way she hadn't felt in a very long time.

She fitted her key into the door, noticing for the first time the warm glow of the living room lights through the curtained front window. She hadn't expected anyone else to be here yet. Barrett's hours were often irregular, and Levi usually had a client on Wednesday nights. When she stepped inside, the soft murmur of voices and the comforting scent of coffee reached her first. She rounded the corner into the living room and found both Barrett and Levi already there.

Levi was stretched out sideways on the couch, socked feet propped on its arm, flipping lazily through a sports magazine. Barrett had his laptop open on his knees, frowning slightly at whatever he was typing.

Both of them looked up as she came through the door, and a pair of smiles met her like porch lights clicking on. It wasn't anything special, just a simple acknowledgment, but it warmed her in a way she hadn't quite expected.

"Hey," Levi called, lifting his hand in a lazy half-wave. "You're home early."

Skylar slipped off her coat and stepped out of her shoes, the tension of the day already releasing her from its grip. "Not really," she replied, setting her bag down. "You guys are though. What happened to your Wednesday night guy?"

"Cancelled," Levi said, nonchalantly, shrugging.

Barrett leaned back slightly in his chair, stretching his stiff body with a faint groan. "Paperwork beat me to half to death." He grinned. "Remember that favor Mr. Whittington called in for me? I'm paying it back, plus the favor from Tamika, but I bailed as soon as Mr. Whittington went home." His voice was calm, but she knew he was watching her, the same way he had been the last couple of days, always trying to reassure himself that she was really okay.

Levi's voice chimed in, light and easy. "Beer in the fridge. You look like you could use one."

Skylar stood there for a beat, letting the comfort of the moment sink in. It was all so normal—and so *safe*. Unlike her life of the last few years, walking through the front door didn't feel like stepping into loneliness or frustration. This was a world away from the chaos of the past couple weeks. Had it really *only* been two weeks since Barrett drove her to that motel in New Jersey?

But that was over. Barrett and Levi were here, the people she cared about most, and they were glad to see her. To *see* her, not just waiting to be fed.

For a split second, though, another name curled at the edges of her mind.

Chet.

The thought crept into her mind like an old splinter that hadn't worked itself free, jagged and uninvited. The ghost of his voice, his smirk, the weight of all the bad choices she let herself make hovered over her.

But she shook her head, brushing the thought aside like dust off a shelf. That part of her life was over. She left it behind and it was going to stay in the past where it belonged. Whatever pieces Chet had taken from her, they didn't belong to him anymore. She had taken them back once and for all.

Skylar headed into the kitchen, the sound of Barrett and Levi's conversation drifting behind her— something about what they should do with the evening. She opened the fridge, grabbed a beer, and popped the cap off. When she returned to the living room, Levi had sat up and she flopped onto the couch next to him, tucking her legs beneath her and leaning back into the worn cushions. The warmth of the room and the rhythm of their conversation wrapped around her like a blanket.

Skylar let the hum of the conversation between Barrett and Levi envelop her as she nursed her beer. Just being near them, hearing them act so normally, made her weariness fade away. She waited for a natural lull in the discussion before speaking.

"I talked to Brian this afternoon."

The effect was instant. Both Levi and Barrett looked toward her, expressions open but expectant.

"How's Natalie?" Barrett asked.

Skylar set her bottle down gently on the coffee table, steadying the swirl of emotions the conversation left her with. She'd been too busy most of the afternoon to think about them, but the train ride home gave her time to sort it all out. "Better. Or... on her way there, at least."

She paused, her fingers idly twisting the bottle's label, then lifted her gaze back to them.

"Brian took a leave of absence from his company," she said. "He's the boss and it's running pretty smoothly, I guess, so he's stepping away, for however long it takes, so he can help my mom—Natalie, I mean."

"Still not used to that, huh?" Levi asked, softly, his eyes flicking towards Barrett for an instant, as if waiting to see he had any comment. He didn't, only settled himself back in his chair and waited for Skylar to go on.

"They talked, Brian told me. I mean really talked, all day Sunday and most of the night. He said... that he finally understands what she was going through. Not just the surface stuff, but the bitterness and the anger and the guilt those things made her feel. She's kept it bottled up all these years until she started lashing out.

"He wishes she'd told him sooner." She swallowed, the memory of Brian's voice on the phone still fresh in her memory, raw with regret but filled with determination. "About how she resented Sophia and Aaron, how much she sacrificed for them, gave up her career, her freedom, her future—all of it, for me. And how she felt like she was just... a placeholder, while they ran off and self-destructed."

She paused, took a deep breath and added, "And she told him about how she came to see me as a symbol of everything she'd lost and how it twisted her feelings towards me. She didn't even realize it until they talked, I guess."

Levi shifted slightly on the couch, as if uncomfortable, and Barrett's eyes darkened with quiet understanding.

"Brian told me that if she'd said something, he would've helped her carry it. He really does love her and he's going to make sure she gets the best help, no matter what it costs and no matter how long it takes," Skylar finished quietly.

Levi's his voice low and sincere when he said, "That's great, Sky. Brian is a good guy."

Barrett's gaze roamed the room, like he was measuring the shape of the news. Finally he said, "She deserves another chance. And so do you."

Skylar gave a small smile, though her throat tightened as she did. "It won't fix everything. But... it's a start."

Barrett leaned forward, setting his laptop aside, then resting his forearms on his knees. "It's more than most people get. Sometimes all it takes is one person deciding to stay, instead of walking away."

"Yeah." Skylar sat back, letting the truth of that sink in. After everything, after all the lies and losses, there was still room for healing. It wouldn't be the clean kind, where the wound disappears without a trace. There would be scars, but eventually even those would fade.

"What about Sophia?" Levi asked.

Skylar came back to the moment, turned towards Levi and said, "I told him about Sophia. He wants to meet her."

"I'd like to as well," Barrett said.

"Hey, me too!" Levi put in.

"Speaking of Sophia…" Barrett began. "Well, more Aaron Needham really. I heard from the Vermont State Police today," he said.

It was like a stone dropped into still water, sending out ripples that first froze Skylar then pulled her back to that night, as vivid and sharp as if it had been moments earlier instead of days.

She felt again the chill of the night air, she could taste the tang of adrenaline in the back of her throat. The sound of flesh meeting flesh, that sharp crack, and Natalie's scream rang through her all over again. Aaron's voice, sneering and bitter, snarled threats with a gun in his hand, holding Natalie hostage. It was a memory she might never be able to wash away, even if the wounds healed.

But alongside the terror were better memories too. The way Barrett stood firm even as Aaron's gun swung between them, refusing to let fear tear away his calm as he tried to talk Aaron down, buying seconds at a time, giving them that much more chance with every word.

And Levi, brave and reckless, charging like a freight train across the clearing without a second thought, throwing himself into Aaron, maybe saving all of their lives. She heard the scrape of the gun skittering away across the dirt, and the sharp crack of Levi's fist landing squarely on Aaron's jaw, leaving him unconscious and finally harmless.

If not for them, both of these men—so different, but each so incredible in his own way—she didn't know if any of them would have made it out of that clearing.

She blinked hard, forcing the thoughts back down, trying to will the tears away before they formed.

"What did they say?" she asked quietly, her hands curling into the fabric of her skirt, heedless of wrinkles.

Barrett noted the sudden paleness in Skylar's face and kept his voice deliberate and calm to steady his closest friend.

"I think we can safely say he's never getting out of prison. The charges against him are stacking up: unlawful restraint, aggravated assault, kidnapping. Not to mention tens of thousands of dollars of heroin in his trailer. The prosectors up there won't be playing around, and he still has charges to face in Pennsylvania too."

"Oh, yeah," Levi said. "I totally forgot about that."

Barrett chuckled. "So did everyone else." He sobered and went on. "With the killing of that clerk in Mass, it took a backseat and I guess it just slipped through the cracks." He placed his palms on his thighs. "Now, though, with our testimony and Natalie's, he's never getting out of prison. They'll try him in Vermont, then send him back to Pennsylvania to face trial there, then figure out where he serves first."

Skylar nodded slowly. The weight of it was both relieving and strange. It should have felt final, like a door slamming shut on something dark, knowing that neither she nor Natalie nor Sophia would ever have to worry about Aaron Needham again.

Barrett's voice softened. "He can't hurt you or anyone else ever again," he said, as if reading her thoughts.

"I know he's your father, but…"

"No," Skylar said, remembering what Sophia had told her. *Think of him as a sperm donor.* "No, he's not. Brian is the only father I've ever had. I don't care what happens to Aaron as long as he's behind bars."

Barrett and Levi shared a look before Barrett turned a small smile back on her. "Fair enough."

"I guess that wraps everything up, then, huh?" Levi said.

Skylar looked at him, her throat tightening again, but this time for another reason entirely. There was an unspoken truth in the room that hung over all of their heads: they had all gotten each other through that night. No single act, no single person, but all of them together, choosing to stand their ground for each other.

Together.

The way it had been since that long-ago summer at camp when two boys who'd known each other most of their lives stepped in to rescue a lonely girl from a pack of bullies and changed her entire world. She knew it went both ways—she had changed them as they had changed her and each other until it was the three of them. *The three amigos*, Brian called them when she was younger. It was more than that now. Maybe it always had been, and it was time to put things out in the open.

"Not quite," Skylar said quietly. "There's one more thing."

She let out a long breath, as if all the emotions that had been building up inside of her were finally too big to keep sealed up. She shifted on the couch, the weight of the moment building between the three of them. Barrett and Levi had gone silent, their earlier ease replaced by something cautious, almost wary. She could feel the nervous energy coming off of each of them.

She looked at both of them, at Levi's open, boyish face that so often tried to hide his true depth with humor and goofiness, and at Barrett's steady, quietly protective gaze, the look of a man who always has his feet on the ground no matter how wild or confusing the world becomes.

"We've all had so much going on lately," Skylar started softly, her voice catching just slightly. "It's like... one minute I was caught up in the worst days of my life and the next, some of the best things I've ever experienced started happening too. It's been a mixed up, messy—I don't know what to call it."

"Chaos," Barrett quietly put in.

Skylar nodded without otherwise responding. "But somewhere in the middle of all it, I realized something really important."

Both men were watching her now, holding their breath like her next words might tilt the whole world on its side, rearrange everything they knew and everything they'd built together. Skylar focused on her hands, her fingers fidgeting, searching for the courage to say it. Somehow, this was more nerve-wracking than facing Aaron Needham's gun.

"I realized that I love you both."

The words settled over all of them. Their meaning couldn't be any clearer, but still...

Skylar's heart thudded painfully in her chest, waiting for their response, their reaction.

Levi's back straightened slightly, his easy posture stiffening as if bracing for a blow. Barrett's jaw tensed. His expression remained calm, neutral, but his shoulders subtly drew in, his body language becoming more guarded.

Neither of them spoke for a long, uncomfortable moment, and Skylar saw it—the flash of worry in their eyes. They were both thinking the same thing: that she couldn't choose either of them so she was about to tell them she wouldn't choose either. That was the most common thing in this scenario, wasn't it?

Both men opened their mouths at the same time, the same name tumbling from their lips: "Sky..."

It was said almost perfectly in sync, and it caught both of them off-guard. They glanced at one another, faces flushing with sudden embarrassment, and then both looked away. That tiny moment of shared vulnerability struck Skylar right in the heart.

"Guys," she said gently, her voice trembling with feeling. She shifted positions, moving from the couch until she could reach out and take both of their hands, one in each of hers. Levi's fingers were warm and a little calloused from work, the sensation familiar and warm. Barrett's were steady, firm, and strong, like holding onto an anchor in choppy waters, knowing that he would never let her drift away.

"I love you both," she said again, the tears finally coming, slowly running down her cheeks. "And what I'm saying is... I don't want to choose. I don't see why I have to. I want all of us to be together."

Her throat felt tight, but the words kept coming. She couldn't have stopped now if she wanted to. With realization of the truth inside of her came the anxiety and indecisiveness of what to do with it. Now that she'd made a decision, there was no turning back—there was only forward.

"I love both of you and I love what we are together, and I never, *ever* want that to change. I know it's not, like, the usual thing, and I know it might not be easy, but... I've never been more sure of anything in my entire life."

There was complete stillness in the room. Neither man moved, and none of the three even seemed to breathe. The only motion was Skylar's tears rolling freely down her cheeks. Her heart was laid bare and it was up to them to pick it up or cast it aside.

After a small eternity, Levi's mouth curved into a smile, slow and genuine, a kind of quiet relief breaking across his face like dawn pushing through clouds after a stormy night. He glanced at Barrett, his voice low but clear, full of feeling.

"I love you too, Sky. I think maybe I always have."

His eyes drifted towards Barrett, soft with a different kind affection that had been there long before either of them realized it. "And I love you too, bro. You've always been my wingman, even when I didn't know I needed one. You're the best buddy a guy could ask for, man."

Barrett's face relaxed, the tension draining from his shoulders as a wide grin spread across his face. He let out a quiet laugh, shaking his head, the worry finally melting away. "I love you guys too," he said, his voice a little roughened by the emotions he felt. "Looks like we were all worried over nothing, huh?"

Skylar couldn't hold it in anymore. Tearful, feeling overwhelmed, but smiling so hard her cheeks hurt, she tugged them both toward her, pulling them into a tight three-way hug. Their arms wrapped around her and around each other, solid and warm and real and safe and all three of them sank down onto the couch as one. For the first time in a long, long time, Skylar felt like she was exactly where she was supposed to be—surrounded by the two people who had become her entire world.

She tilted her face up, pressing a soft kiss to Levi's lips, full of all of her love and all of her gratitude, and then turned, brushing another kiss against Barrett's, sealing the truth between the three of them.

Skylar let out a small, happy sigh, running her palms over each man's thighs. Levi leaned in and kissed her ear, while Barrett's lips found her throat. She made a noise of surprise, turning first to Levi, kissing his chin, then lifted Barrett's face to kiss his lips. She was still stroking the boys' thighs, but now Barrett's hand found hers, moving over the fabric of her skirt and then under, his fingertips sending electricity sparking up her inner thigh. Levi's hand roamed over her back as his lips explored the spaces behind her ears and in the hollow of her throat.

"Guys…" Skylar murmured, making small sounds of pleasure in her throat. "I love you both so much."

And then some of the pressure disappeared as Levi moved back, then reached around her to unbutton her blouse, slip it off her shoulders and then over her head, tossing it towards the back hallway where the bedrooms were. Barrett's probing fingers found the zipper of her skirt and pulled it down, then pulled the skirt off entirely, leaving her wearing only her bra and panties.

"You're so beautiful," Barrett whispered, his hand moving up her thigh, fingers lightly brushing her mound through the thin fabric of her panties. At his touch, she realized how wet she already was.

Levi undid the clasp of her bra, and she leaned forward to remove it, then lifted her hips. Barrett understood and without needing to be told, slipped her panties over her hips, down her thighs and then off. He pulled his own shirt over his head, exposing his chest, before moving in again and pressing his face to her pussy, making her gasp and shiver.

She opened her eyes and found Levi standing over her, unbuckling his belt, then letting his jeans falls to the floor. His cock was so hard the head and part of the shaft poked through the opening in his boxers. She looked higher and her eyes met Levi's. He grinned down at her and slid the boxers off, leaving him naked below the waist. Skylar gasped as Barrett's tongue found a particularly sensitive spot, then gripped the base of Levi's cock and took the head into her mouth.

Levi's hips swayed back and forth in a slow, steady motion, pushing the tip of his cock against the softness inside her cheek as she stroked the shaft. He threw back his head and let out a low moan of pleasure that matched her own as Barrett's fingers slipped inside of her for an instant, tickling her before pulling back out. From the corner of her eye, she saw Barrett stand and strip his pants and shorts off, leaving him fully naked, his thick cock standing at full mast, the head glistening with precum.

Barrett said something to Levi that she didn't catch and then she was being lifted between them, gently, and set down on the couch on her back. Levi knelt by her head, his cock and balls hanging over her face, while Barrett positioned himself between her thighs. She reached out, cupping Levi's balls in one hand then looked towards Barrett and said, "Please, Barr. I want it."

Barrett swallowed, making his Adam's apple bob, then rubbed his palm over her pussy before spreading her lips with his thumb and forefinger and pushing himself inside of her. She gasped, louder and sharper than when Barrett had fingered her before letting out a husky sound of absolute pleasure.

"Sky…" Levi said. She looked up at his grinning face, upside down from her perspective, and grinned back, then used her hand to tilt his penis down as her head went back. Levi's cock pushed gently into her mouth, but she wanted more than that—she shifted herself slightly closer to him, feeling Barrett moving inside of her to take up the slack, then rammed her mouth against Levi's cock as hard as she dared, until he was fucking her throat. The position was slightly awkward, but she didn't even notice—she only felt the throbbing length of his stiff cock in her mouth, against her face, tasting the faint saltiness of it, as Barrett's thick dick pushed into her again and again, fast for a few strokes, then slowly, gently, the varying rhythm and pace making her shudder with delicious sensation each time he shifted between them.

Suddenly, Barrett began thrusting more quickly, faster than he had before any other time they had made love. She thought he was going to cum and was about to tell him to pull out when he did on his own, grabbed her around the waist and lifted her, spinning her around and turning her over until she was on her belly. Levi's hands we were on her hips and he lifted her up until her butt was in the air and then he was inside of her, his long, hard cock pushing so deeply it made her cry out.

Then Barrett's penis was in her mouth and her head was bobbing back and forth, matching the timing and rhythm of Levi's thrusting inside of her pussy. Barrett's head went back and he let out soft sounds of pleasure as his fingers tangled in her hair, stroking her head gently, lovingly.

Levi's penis slid in and out of her quickly, sending waves of pleasure through her. She felt the fires building inside of her belly and her pussy tighten around Levi's cock. He felt it too and, encouraged, picked up the pace even more, his hips working, his balls slapping against her ass. One finger found her asshole and he rubbed it gently in a circular motion, making her shiver with delight as she remembered what it felt like to have his cock up there.

And then she exploded, her pussy spasming as she orgasmed, a gush of pussy juice welling up, spilling out of her. She felt it running down her thighs as she felt Levi change his rhythm, still moving quickly, but now pulling all the way out of her before plunging back inside of her as hard as he could, making her cry out each time, the sound muffled by Barrett's cock in her mouth.

Her body was hot all over and she felt limp, as if she were a balloon that most of the air had escaped from. The boys weren't done though, and she had her pleasure—she wanted to give them the same, show them just how much she loved them.

With one hand, she took Barrett's penis by the shaft, squeezing as hard as she could, and bobbed her head back and forth over his rock-hard penis while her hand quickly stroked.

It was only a moment or two before Barrett put his palm on top of her head and said, "I'm gonna cum, Sky! I'm gonna cum!" and tried to pull back. She kept her hold on his cock, gripping as tightly as she could, no longer bobbing her head now but swirling her tongue around the tip. She felt his penis begin twitching, both in her hand and inside of her mouth, and then Barrett let out a guttural groan and his cum erupted, filling up her mouth in one hot sticky spurt, then another and another. At the same time, she felt Levi's grip on her hips grow tighter and his penis plunged into her even harder.

She pulled back, swallowed once, letting the remaining cum dribble out of the sides of her mouth. She grinned up at Barrett, then looked over her shoulder at Levi. Their eyes met before his flicked away, looking over her head to Barrett, then he suddenly pulled out of her pussy, laid his cock in the furrow between her butt-cheeks and started pumped against them as quickly as he had her pussy—once, twice, three times and then his cock erupted, spewing thick, ropey streams of cum all over her back, so forcefully one splattered between her shoulder blades.

All three of them were breathing heavily, tired and spent and happy.

Slowly, Skylar shifted until she was half-sprawled on the couch. Levi whipped off his shirt, wiping his cum from Skylar's back while Barrett eased himself down onto the couch next to her. His cock still stood tall between his thighs, a little bead of cum clinging to the tip. Levi tossed his shirt towards the bedrooms and collapsed heavily on her other side. Skylar put a hand on each of her boys' thighs, gently stroking them once before kissing Barrett, long and lovingly, then turning to Levi and giving him a kiss that expressed her love just as openly and deeply and genuinely.

She let out a sigh of absolute contentment and pulled Barrett and Levi to her until all three were cuddled up.

No one said anything right away. Nothing needed to be said. Finally, they were together, they were happy. It might not always be easy, but they would make it work. These were her best friends, and now her lovers—the people she cared about more than anything else in the entire universe. She couldn't imagine any other way of life now. Skylar and Barrett and Levi forever.

And for the first time in a very, very long time, the future didn't feel uncertain—it felt wide open.

End

ABOUT THE AUTHOR

"Beth Anderson" is the joint penname of a veteran author of numerous novels of several different genres and a developing author who loves romance novels.

This is their second work together.